THE LAST LIBERATOR

THE LAST LIBERATOR

JERRY YULSMAN

A DUTTON BOOK

HOUSTON PUBLIC LIBRARY

DUTTON
Published by the Penguin Group
Penguin Books USA Inc., 375 Hudson Street,
New York, New York 10014, U.S.A.
Penguin Books Ltd, 27 Wrights Lane,
London W8 5TZ, England
Penguin Books Australia Ltd, Ringwood,
Victoria, Australia
Penguin Books Canada Ltd, 10 Alcorn Avenue, Suite 300,
Toronto, Ontario, Canada M4V 3B2
Penguin Books (N.Z.) Ltd. 182-190 Wairau Road,
Auckland 10, New Zealand

Penguin Books Ltd, Registered Offices:
Harmondsworth, Middlesex, England

First published by Dutton, an imprint of New American Library,
a division of Penguin Books USA Inc.
Distributed in Canada by McClelland & Stewart Inc.

First Printing, December, 1991
10 9 8 7 6 5 4 3 2 1

 REGISTERED TRADEMARK—MARCA REGISTRADA

LIBRARY OF CONGRESS CATALOGING-IN-PUBLICATION DATA
Yulsman, Jerry.
    The last liberator / Jerry Yulsman.
      p.   cm.
    ISBN 0-525-93382-4
    1. World War, 1939–1945—Fiction. I. Title.
PS3575.U4L37   1991
813'.54—dc20   91-12414
                                                     CIP

Printed in the United States of America
Set in Garamond #3 and Stencil

PUBLISHER'S NOTE
This is a work of fiction. Names, characters, places, and incidents either are the products of the author's imagination or are used fictitiously, and any resemblance to actual
persons, living or dead, events, or locales is entirely coincidental.

To Sam
From his grandfather

Special thanks to Parker H. Harlow for his valuable assistance in checking the manuscript for technical errors. During World War II, Mr. Harlow flew thirty-four combat missions as a B-24 pilot with the 740th Squadron of the 455th Bomb Group, Fifteenth Air Force.

CONSOLIDATED B-24D LIBERATOR

MANUFACTURER	Consolidated Aircraft Corporation, San Diego, California
TYPE	Heavy bomber
ENGINES	Four Pratt & Whitney R-1830-43, Twin-Wasp, 14-cylinder, radial, air-cooled, turbo-supercharged 1200 hp. each
WINGSPAN	110 ft. (33.52 m.)
LENGTH	66 ft. 4 in. (20.22 m.)
HEIGHT	17 ft. 10 in. (5.44 m.)
WEIGHT	60,000 lbs. (27.216 kg.) (loaded)
MAXIMUM SPEED	306 mph (490 km/h) at 25,000 ft. (17,620 m.)
CEILING	32,000 ft. (9.750 m.)
RANGE	2,850+ miles (4,585 km.)
CREW	9–10
ARMAMENT	6 50-cal. machine guns mounted in 3 power-operated gun turrets; 2 flexible 50-cal. machine guns in waist windows; 2–3 flexible 50-cal. machine guns in nose ball-socket mounts
BOMB LOAD	8,800 lbs. (4,000+ kg.) on 4 bomb racks. Provisions for wing-mounted bomb racks and 2 4,000-lb. bombs.

UNITED STATES ARMY AIR FORCE

Ninth Air Force (M.E.)
Lt. Gen. Louis Brereton, Commanding

287th Bombardment Group (H)
Col. Edward Tecumsuh Greeves, Commanding

415th Bombardment Squadron
Berka One
Benghazi, Libya
1943

B-24D-160-CO, serial # 42-72843.
Consolidated Aircraft Co.,
San Diego, Cal.

#82 (Sally's Wagon)

Original Crew

Pilot	Capt. M. F. (Mickey) Maguire
Copilot	2nd. Lt. Jordan P. Deutsch
Navigator	1st Lt. Clyde Taylor
Bombardier	2nd. Lt. Russell Beel
Flight Engineer & Top Turret Gunner	T/Sgt. Abraham Cohen
Radio Operator & Spare Gunner	S/Sgt. Charlie Crenshaw
Tail Turret Gunner	S/Sgt. P. B. (Yardbird) Smith
Ball Turret Gunner	S/Sgt. Alexander Darling, Jr.
Waist Gunner	S/Sgt. Earl Woike
Waist Gunner	S/Sgt. Frank D'Amato

Crew Chief—M/Sgt. Samuel Fibich

THE UNSUNG HERO'S LAMENT
or
An Ode to the B-24

For there's a sort of manic madness in the supercharger's whine,
As you hear the ice cubes tinkling in the Turbo-Balance line,
The runway strips are narrow, but the snowbanks they are wide,
While the crash trucks say, in a mournful way, you're on your
  final ride.

The nose gear rocks and trembles, for it's held with bailing wire,
And the wings are filled with thermite, to make a hotter fire,
The camouflage is peeling off, it lends an added luster,
While pilot heads are filled with lead, to help the Load-Adjuster.

The bomb bay doors are rusted, they close with a ghastly shriek,
And the Plexiglas is smeared with some forgotten oil leak,
The oleo struts are twisted and the wheels are not quite round,
The bulkheads are thin (Ford builds with tin) to admit the
  slightest sound.

You taxi out on the runway, 'mid groans of tortured gear,
While you feel the check-rider's teeth, gnawing your tender rear,
The copilot sitting on the right, in a liquor-laden coma,
Mixes his breath, the kiss of death, with the put-put's foul aroma.

So it's off to the overcast yonder, though number one is missing,
While the hydraulic fluid escaping, sets up a gentle hissing,
The compass dial is spinning in a way that brooks no stopping,
And row by row, the fuses blow, with an intermittent popping.

It was named the "Liberator" by a low and twisted mind. . . .

Anonymous airman: 484th Bomb Group,
Foggia, Italy, 1944

CHAPTER 1

OCTOBER 1980

She sat in a champagne glass, naked, blonde, peach-colored, sporting oversized breasts out of proportion to a slender torso comprising an intricate combination of artistic S curves. Champagne bubbled about her flaring hips and plump buttocks. Her legs, though shapely, were anatomically flawed, idealized; longer than those provided by nature to women of flesh and blood. Like a flagstaff, one of them was thrust upward, a high-heeled pump dangling from its chubby toes. The other was hooked gracefully over the edge of the glass. A silver bracelet bearing the name "Danny" decorated its slim ankle.

She exhibited none of the elegance, the sultry sophistication common to the European ideal—the femme fatale. There was no mystery, no hidden depths in her eyes, no exotic promise on her parted lips. She was a uniquely New World idealization from another time: open, joyful, unliberated; apple-pie- and corn-fed; her yellow hair flowing in the slipstream, her Bo Peep mouth frozen in an eternal smile. Extinct.

Her colors now were faded. The desert sun and a hundred khamsin-propelled sandstorms had weathered them to the pastels of an aging fresco.

Her name was Sally, as attested to by nine-inch-high faded-blue letters painted under the navigator's window beneath the spiked heel of her left shoe: "Sally's Wagon."

Sally's Wagon was a four-engined Liberator bomber, a homely, desert-pink B-24D, her body scarred and dented, her paint chipped, marred by mud splatters, oil stains, and the black effluvium of engine exhaust. Her official designation was *SB-24D-160-CO, U.S. Army Air Force serial number #42-72843*, one of 18,482 Liberators built by Consolidated Aircraft and Ford; a little heavy bomber from an old war.

The upper swell of Sally's right breast was embellished with the Purple Heart. She had been wounded. A four-inch aluminum patch on her thigh served as a surgical dressing. There were fifty others scattered about: patches covering equally ancient punctures in the aircraft's skin. Some had been inflicted by German or Italian flak gunners, others by cannon shells or machine gun bullets fired from Focke-Wulfs, Messerschmitts, Folgores, and IAR-80s. It had been, in the words of her crew chief, a terrible way to treat a lady.

Lost and forgotten for almost forty years, she lay on her belly on the edge of the Great Libyan Sand Sea. One wing was canted up; the other had its tip buried in the sand. The blades of all four propellers were curled back. Like a beached whale, her aluminum carcass was the target of a swarm of flies, the only indigenous life within ten thousand square miles.

An oil exploration team discovered her. They were surprised to find that one of the radio receivers, when powered with a line from their generator, still functioned perfectly. There was water aboard, still potable; the oxygen bottles were half-filled. The magnetic compasses, radio compass, flare pistols, fire extinguishers, and auxiliary generator were functional.

The team's Italian geologist found a navigator's map on the flight deck. A red-penciled line traced a course between Benghazi, two hundred miles to the north on the Libyan coast, and a point in central Rumania.

He wondered why the bomber was so far south. War was inconceivable in this place. It was the wrong place for the paraphernalia of combat. There were no features with which to punctuate a battle map; no infrastructure; no towns, no roads, rivers, factories, railroads, air bases, ports, oil refineries. There was nothing to attack, nothing to defend, no strategic terrain to deny an enemy, no targets on which to drop bombs. It was on the way to nowhere. The nearest enemy, the strategic targets for which the long-range high-altitude Liberator bomber had been designed, lay across the Mediterranean, to the north—Europe.

On the flight deck he noted that the main switches were still in the on position, the throttles still advanced. Standing alone behind the empty pilot's seat, he conjectured on the possibility that the crew had bailed out and that the aircraft had eventually run out of gas to glide in for a landing on the flat desert floor all by itself. He could arrive at no other explanation for the switch and throttle settings.

They found a zippered canvas bag on the radio desk. It contained a shrunken, mummified head. The eyes, like tiny blue marbles, made contact with any that looked their way. An officer's cap, sporting a brass replica of the Great Seal of the United States, was secured to the head by a pair of earphones. It was three sizes too large. A pair of dog tags read, "COHEN-ABRAHAM-13027217 H." There were no other signs of the crew. He dropped the tags in his pocket.

The oil exploration team boarded their trucks. The puzzled geologist patted Sally on her rump and joined them. The pat was a gesture that had been practiced by the bomber's crew before each takeoff, forty years earlier. Like the geologist, they had possessed little knowledge of art but had known what they liked.

THE MISSION

August 1, 1943

Leutnant Hermann Stumacher poked his head out the tiny makeshift tent. It was still dark. One of the camels snorted, arose laboriously, its left hind leg tethered to a stake.

Stumacher crawled out into the night, stood upright, brushed the sand off his striped kaftan, stretched. He upended the water bottle, rolling the alkaline liquid around in his mouth in an attempt to conjure the flavor of coffee. As was the case every morning, it was a futile effort. Stumacher sighed, gargled briefly, then swallowed, leaving his mouth with an even more appalling taste.

He removed the kaftan. For the next ten minutes, naked to the cool desert night, he exercised; running in place, doing sit-ups and push-ups on the hard-packed sand. Finally, he grabbed his kaftan and his headdress and ran the hundred yards to the sea. It was a daily ritual.

In the light of a half-moon, he could see that the water's edge was once again mottled with oil slicks; patches of black, tarlike sludge. A ship, or perhaps more than one, had been sunk during the last few days; merchant vessels sent to the bottom by torpedoes, or with luck, maybe warships sunk as the results of a sea battle won by the Axis—victory in the Mediterranean that would bring the Afrika Korps and Rommel back to this hellhole to liberate him. Stumacher dwelled on the idea for a few moments. He knew it to be unlikely, but if a little predawn exercise was good for the body, then a little early-morning optimism was probably equally good for the soul.

Naked, he walked along the beach, looking for a relatively clean area. He knew nothing about the progress of the war other than what he could see, and it had been made clear from the evidence of his own eyes that ships were being sunk and that the British and the Americans were conducting massive air raids. Months earlier, he had noted that enemy aircraft had ceased flying toward the west. Now, the Allied formations flew only to the north. That surely meant that there were no longer Axis targets in Africa— no German or Italian troops. *Defeat.* But aside from that, he knew nothing. What was happening in Russia? Was there fighting anywhere else? Where did the big American bombers go after disappearing beyond the Mediterranean horizon? His radio told him nothing, it was merely a portable transceiver, pretuned to a single frequency. All he ever received were brief, enigmatic acknowledgments of his transmissions. And there were no newspapers to read, no magazines, no newsreels; no one to spread rumors, nor even to disseminate propaganda. A kind of silent purgatory.

He shook himself, breathed deeply, clearing his mind of futile speculation. Pessimism was *not* good for the soul. He strode purposefully, humming "Lili Marlene" in march tempo.

Finally, he came on an area that seemed free of tar. Grasping the kaftan and headpiece in one hand he walked into the surf. Shoulder deep, he reached down, grabbed a handful of sand, and rubbed it into the crevice between his buttocks. He repeated the procedure under his arms and around his neck and shoulders. He rinsed his mouth out, taking a measure of satisfaction from the astringent quality of the saltwater. He splashed around for a few minutes. Then, floating on his back, staring up at the moon, he masturbated, quickly and efficiently. Finally, standing with his toes dug into the soft sand, he swished the kaftan about.

Bath and laundry completed, he made his way back to the tent. He wrung out the kaftan and headdress, wetting his face in the process. Opening a small leather shaving case, he removed a straight razor, honed it on the built-in whetting stone, then proceeded to shave. As he did so, a series of raucous snorts from an aircraft engine shattered the silence. In a few moments it was joined by others. Stumacher listened carefully. The engines were being tested individually. There were now, he determined, about seven or eight of them running discordantly up and down the scale; clattering, sputtering, roaring. Transmitted through the still desert air, their decibel level, despite the three-mile distance, seemed hardly diminished.

From inside the tent, Lance Corporal Strink coughed, said, "What do you think?"

"I think they'll fly today."

"More practice," said Strink, between coughs. "We might as well stay in bed."

Strink, as usual, showed a greater interest in his own comfort than in his duty. Leutnant Stumacher had no doubt that if the aging lance corporal had anywhere to go, he would desert. It was, he conceded, a perfectly understandable attitude, certainly not what one would call militarily correct, yet not irrational. In fact, during moments of depression, he himself had toyed with the idea. It was a wonder they both weren't mad. He said, "We have work to do."

The lance corporal emerged on his hands and knees from their makeshift tent, a sour look on his wan, beard-stubbled face, a cigarette butt dangling from his cracked lips. He wore a striped kaftan that he rarely removed.

Leutnant Stumacher said, "Up you go, Strink."

Without a word, Strink grabbed their big Zeiss binoculars, put the cord around his neck, and started up the palm tree they used for an observation post. He was in much better physical condition than he looked to be. In less than a minute, making use of the notches carved into the trunk, he was within a few feet of the top. He hooked a leg over a convenient branch, then twisted to the left. The American air base had its work lights on. He raised the glasses to his eyes, focusing carefully. There were a half-dozen tugs making their way across the tarmac, each towing a string of small trailers loaded with what he took to be five-hundred- and thousand-pound demolition bombs.

Through the binoculars, he toured the revetments. Ground crews, bathed in the yellow glow of work lights, some of them standing atop spindly work stands, were inspecting engines, loading bombs, cleaning guns, checking engines and gun turrets. But, even more important, they were fitting big black Tokyo tanks into the forward bomb bays.

After a few minutes of observation, he came down from the tree. He said. "It's not practice today. They're slinging bombs and loading auxiliary fuel tanks." He poured some water from the leather water bottle into a cupped hand, splashed it on his face. "It's going to be a long trip."

The two men unlimbered the transceiver, setting it on the ground beneath a palm tree. They rigged the antenna to another tree about twenty feet away.

With Strink cranking the small portable generator, Stumacher established contact on the third try. He tapped out Strink's weather report, then transmitted the information concerning fuel and bomb loading. After receiving acknowledgment, he sent the stand-by code.

Strink stopped cranking, looked up at the naked Stumacher, then sighed. "In the best of all possible worlds, you would be a beautiful woman."

Stumacher said, "It wouldn't matter if I were. You're beginning to stink. You should bathe."

Strink looked away, struggled to his feet. He slapped a red tarboosh onto his head and, with a mock show of military courtesy, saluted smartly. He said, "Thank you, sir, but I would rather be convincing." With a flamboyant show of grace, he salaamed. "When the British catch us, they'll take one whiff of you and know you're Bavarian. That will be that. But I'll smell exactly like an Arab—authentic."

"On the contrary," said Stumacher. "They will probably shoot you out of hand because they can't stand the stench."

Strink was quiet for a moment, staring south into the desert. "I think that maybe we're crazy. I mean truly mad . . ."

"I was just thinking about that and decided it's unlikely," Despite the damp kaftan, Stumacher started dressing, donning the bedouin headdress to conceal his blond hair. "Crazy people never question their sanity." Reaching into the provision sack he handed Strink a hard-boiled egg, a few figs, and a handful of grapes, then helped himself to the same. "I mean, if you think you're crazy then you're probably not."

Lance Corporal Strink tapped his egg on a tent peg. He had the gray, debilitated look of a man recovering from major surgery. "Well, you convinced me. I no longer think I'm crazy." He laughed maniacally.

"Actually, it's the Americans who are crazy," said Stumacher.

"Suicidal. Big airplanes were not meant to fly so low." In the Luftwaffe he had been a bomb aimer on a Heinkel 111.

Strink, looking glum, said, "I'm glad I'm not an American airman."

"So am I," Leutnant Stumacher grinned. The western sky was glowing from the predawn sun.

They had been there for eight months, left behind by Rommel's retreating army to spy on enemy activity. Picked specially for the assignment, both men spoke Arabic. Stumacher had studied the language at university, Strink had learned it while a steward on a Greek passenger-freighter sailing the Mediterranean. He was a quick study. In the Luftwaffe, Strink had been assistant to a weather officer.

The day before the defeated Afrika Korps moved west, the field marshal himself had wished them luck. They were supplied with three months' rations, a pair of field glasses, a pair of Lugers, a portable radio transceiver, and a few thousand Egyptian pounds. Their food, mostly canned, had been cached in the cellar of a bombed-out building just outside Benghazi.

Disguised as Arabs, they had stayed in the ruined building, transmitting weather reports and what they could see from the roof of British military endeavor. Except for some harbor activity, it hadn't been much.

They moved west to headquarter themselves in a wadi, about a half-mile from the Coast Road. The badly rutted two-lane highway was the main artery of the Middle East war, stretching in a straight line for over eight hundred miles across Libya, from the Egyptian to the Tunisian border, near where Mussolini had marked it with a triumphal arch. The road was lined with burned-out tanks and the gutted paraphernalia of the three armies that had been fighting up and down its length for four years.

From their new location, Stumacher and Strink reported daily on enemy troop and supply movement. Every five days or so they would return to their ration cache in Benghazi to survey the port activity and stock up on food. Finally, they returned for the last time to find their stores gone.

Their only hope for survival was to find an Arab with whom it was safe to do business. They chose carefully. He was an elderly Senussi named Fahdi, who for an exorbitant fee procured a pair of decrepit camels for them. Stumacher then set up an arrangement where they would meet the toothless old Arab at a prearranged location every fifth night. Fahdi supplied them with eggs, grapes, figs, dates, goat meat, tins of Argentine corned beef, an occasional chicken, and, on rare occasions, Egyptian rum and British army-issue V cigarettes. They paid him liberally for his efforts and for what they hoped would be his unquestioning loyalty. This, despite the fact that on a few occasions he supplied them with some of their own late, lamented rations.

After a few months, most of the activity along the Coast Road had faded to a trickle. Libya, fought over for four years, had become a backwater. For a while the two men had little else but the weather to report. Then the Americans arrived: two groups of heavy bombers that they recognized as B-24 Liberators. The two men saddled up and moved their operation to a grove of palms just off the beach, between the two bases. From atop one of the trees, it was possible to observe ground activities on both bases: bomb loadings, fueling operations, battle damage, aircraft losses and replacements, and seemingly unimportant activities such as mail call and chow lines.

Whoever it was that received their daily radio communiqués seemed pleased with their initiative. They were informed that even the most inconsequential surveillance produced invaluable intelligence.

Every few days, the big airplanes, loaded with bombs, would take off in a cloud of dust. They formed up over the sea, coalescing into a tight mass formation of fifty or sixty that gained height as it disappeared toward the west or the north. After a while the westward flights had ceased. The targets seemed now to be to the north—Europe.

The German officer and the lance corporal began to identify with their enemy, particularly the 287th, on their left. They became familiar with the nose art on individual aircraft, identifying them by name: Sassy Suzy, High Falootin, Raspberry Bitch, Watermelon Man, Sally's Wagon, Pride of Dubuque. Strink observed that for a year the only women they had seen were those painted on the sides of some of the enemy aircraft. They developed an affection for them and were saddened on those occasions when a favorite did not return.

Recently, three more B-24 groups had joined the original two. From the tail markings observed by Stumacher and Strink, Luftwaffe intelligence had ascertained that the new groups were on detached service from the American Eighth Air Force in England. There were now five air bases along a thirty-mile stretch of Libyan coastline.

Two weeks earlier, a combined mission of the five groups had taken off, then wheeled south at low level. The two Germans had been mystified. There were no possible targets to the south. There was nothing but a thousand miles of barren desert.

The unusual aerial activity was repeated a half-dozen times over the next three days. On the fourth day, Fahdi mentioned that according to a nephew the crazed Americans were bombing empty desert about twenty-five miles to the south.

Strink and Stumacher reacted immediately, spending the night on their camels. Finally, the rising sun found them slumped in their wooden saddles, barely awake, in the center of a large area crisscrossed with shallow trenches filled with white lime. Clusters of thirty-foot metal poles topped with shredded petrol tins thrust upward from the desert floor. Barrels, arranged in geometric groupings, punctuated the area, which stretched for four or five miles in each direction. It seemed, thought Stumacher, like some monstrous gaming board on which he and Strink had become markers.

Suddenly, with no warning, five huge bombers, preceding the shattering thunder of their own engines, materialized forty feet above their heads. It was an instantaneous phenomenon akin to an unexpected explosion. The two men recoiled as if from a physical blow. Strink howled like a frightened dog and clapped his hands over his ears as the camels bolted, launching the pair on a frenzied ride.

An instant later, the first wave of aircraft was followed by a second. As they roared overhead at two hundred miles an hour, Stumacher glanced up fleetingly into the dark maw of an open bomb bay. Their camels, in a state of headlong panic, raced through a forest of exploding hundred-pound black-powder practice bombs.

Stumacher turned his head to see Strink thrown from his

mount. A few seconds later, he too was dislodged, to land, breathless but intact, on the hard-packed sand.

Hugging the ground like an infantryman under fire, he made his way through the acrid black smoke to his compatriot. Over the next seven or eight minutes, what Stumacher took to be about two hundred aircraft roared overhead in groups of four to six. They banked left and right, dropping their small blue bombs on different areas.

The sound of explosions was continuous thunder. Leutnant Stumacher estimated that the American bombers had dropped well over a thousand bombs.

Then, as quickly as they had materialized, the airplanes were gone. It took hours to round up the camels.

For the next week, from their vantage point near the beach, Stumacher and Strink observed and reported the Americans' daily training flights to the south. Then, for a few days, all flight activity ceased.

Strink once again climbed the palm to within a few feet of the top. Less than four miles away, barely visible in a cloud of dust of its own making, the 287th Bombardment Group was lined up at the head of its mile-long metallic-mesh runway.

Now, once again, the engines were being run up. This time, unlike the unharmonious ruckus of an hour earlier, they were more an orchestrated chorus than individual discordant solos. The sound was coming from the left. The 287th was on the move. Moments later, the roar was echoed from his right—the 98th. He assumed the other three groups, farther down the coast, were also moving.

Over the symphony of engines, a soloist came to the fore, growing from a deep growl into a sustained roar. Strink, from his forty-foot perch, observed a single aircraft emerge from the dust to lumber down the runway. Raising binoculars to his eyes he tracked it as it gained speed. It was airborne by the time a second B-24 was halfway down the strip. He observed two more, then called down to Stumacher, "They're fully loaded . . . using every inch of runway."

Pretty Polly was next in line. He locked his glasses on a pulchritudinous redhead in a diaphanous gown. A colorful parrot was perched on her bare shoulder. He tracked her as she released

her brakes to lumber down the runway, picking up speed as she went. She was one of Strink's favorites; he had adopted her as his own, sweating out her takeoffs and landings as if he were a member of her ground crew.

He sensed something wrong, then a second later realized that, with three quarters of the strip behind her, she still hadn't lifted her nose wheel off the ground. Strink tensed his muscles, stretching his body upward in an effort to urge her off the ground.

At 140 miles an hour, Pretty Polly ran out of runway. She plowed ahead for another hundred yards stirring up sand, then exploded silently into a great ball of fire. The sound of her death was submerged beneath the takeoff roar of the airplane behind her.

Strink looked away quickly, then descended. Silently he began cranking the generator. Stumacher reestablished contact, then tapped out the information that the Americans were airborne.

Ten minutes later, Stumacher was counting airplanes as the Americans formed up over the Mediterranean. All five heavy bombardment groups were up and headed north. He counted over 170 aircraft. The practice missions to the south had ended. He glanced up to find that the still-silent Strink was weeping. It was true, thought Leutnant Hermann Stumacher, they really were mad, both of them.

On the second floor of a small but well-guarded brick building just outside Athens, Ober-Leutnant Christian Ochsenschlager put his pencil down and lit a cigarette. It had taken him less than five minutes to decipher an enemy radio transmission in which the Americans were alerting all Allied ground and naval forces to a mass flight of their own aircraft. The enciphered message was by way of a warning: a new American procedure to prevent the repetition of a recent blunder when the U.S. Navy, off Sicily, had downed some U.S. Army C-47 troop transports, mistaking them for German bombers. The Luftwaffe could not have done better.

Ober-Leutnant Ochsenschlager handed the plaintext of the intercept to Major Prager, the section's chief intelligence officer. Prager grinned. "The Americans insist on making it easy for us. My guess is that it's the American heavies from Benghazi." The major, using a compass with its point centered on the North African city of Benghazi, drew a radius on his map of two thousand scale kilometers. The penciled half-circle represented the approximate range of the four-engined Liberator bomber.

The enclosed area included Crete, Greece, Bulgaria, Rumania, Hungary, Austria, Yugoslavia, Albania, Italy, and southern France—half of Europe. The area was covered by six Luftwaffe defense zones, each comprising roughly 190,000 square kilometers. He sent the same message to each of them: "Large Formation of American aircraft expected over Mediterranean."

CHAPTER 2

DECEMBER 1941

The corporal held his flashlight steady, bathing the area in brilliance. The captain perched on a stool, bent forward, peering through a magnifying glass into a tangled red forest. "Crabs," he said. "Unfit for duty." First Sergeant Nabbie made the appropriate marks on his chart.

The victim was a small, quiet PFC named Alexander Darling, Jr., who occupied the bunk above Cohen's. In a state bordering on shock, he buttoned his raincoat and shuffled out of the way.

Now it was Cohen's turn. He crossed himself, stepping forward to call out loud and clear, "Cohen, Abraham, PFC, one-three-oh two-seven-two-one-seven."

"Skin it back and milk it down."

Cohen opened his raincoat, grasped his penis between thumb and forefinger. He pulled back the foreskin, squeezed forward.

The medical officer leaned closer to look for a telltale, pearl-like gleam of aberrant discharge. He nodded, cuing the corporal to click on his flashlight. Then, with the magnifying glass to his eye, the captain completed the examination with a hunt for tiny quarry in the tall, brilliantly lit grass of Cohen's pubic hair. "Fit for duty."

First Sergeant Nabbie made the appropriate entries on his chart. The captain, for the first time that morning, rose to his feet. "Cohen, right?"

"Yes, sir."

The captain reached for Cohen's dog tags. *"H for Hebrew."*

"Yes, sir." Private First Class Cohen locked eyes with the captain, a ploy that always seemed to work. As a child he had learned to open his eyes wide, throw his vision just slightly out of focus, then refrain from blinking while locking eyes with his opponent. The result was an intense stare, innocent and forthright; an effective tactic to convince others of his truthfulness, sincerity, and strength of character. A little later in life he found it a deadly weapon to dominate the enemy in personality confrontations. His mother had been certain she had borne a child possessing the evil eye.

The captain said, "I've never seen an uncircumcised Hebrew."

"Yes, sir," said Cohen, slowing his breathing.

"How is that?"

"I missed out on it, sir. My mother died in childbirth, my father was killed in an automobile accident the next day." He held eye contact, mouthing the well-rehearsed words in an emphatic, rhythmic cadence. "I was in an orphanage until I was five and my aunt adopted me." He inhaled deeply, expanded his chest, increasing his stature.

The captain's turned away abruptly. "Next man, please."

Cohen released his pent-up breath. The rain slicker was clammy against his skin. He had been waiting in line for an hour. Stepping aside, he buttoned up and walked slowly down the length of the barrack. There were only about ten men left in the short-arm inspection line, all wearing GI raincoats and shoes. Most of the others had already gone into town. The few left in the barrack were putting on their civvies. It was Saturday.

He stood by the head of his bed, stared out the window. A group of three Negro men, accompanied by a white MP, made their way slowly up the company street, emptying trash cans into a truck. The backs of their fatigues sported large white *P*'s. They seemed to be functioning in slow motion in a contrasty, black-and-white landscape whose soft, gray middle tones had been blanched out by the Florida sun. They were prisoners from the MacDill stockade. The sight of them set Cohen on edge.

He opened his footlocker. He laid out a pair of olive-drab boxer shorts, a pair of socks, and a set of suntans. The base laundry insisted on starching and ironing everything. The socks were rigid, capable of standing to attention without him.

He grabbed a towel and went to the latrine at the end of the barrack to shower and shave. He slapped his face with a few drops of Aqua Velva.

Most of the other GIs wore civvies off the base. The only civvies he owned consisted of a pair of buckled brown Thom McAn loafers. Unlike the others, who felt a uniform drew attention from the MPs, Cohen felt safer in uniform.

When he returned to his bunk, Junior Darling, who occupied the upper, was stripping it of bedclothes.

Junior looked down at him. "I don't know how it happened, Abe." He seemed about to weep. "Unfit for duty . . . wow." Standing on his footlocker, he rolled up the mattress, stuffed the sheets, pillowcase, and blanket into the mattress cover. He said, "I mean, I ain't done nothing bad to get them, or anything like that." He had a voice that seemed pitched close to basso profundo, a peculiar incongruity for someone only five foot five.

Cohen said, "It's not the worst thing in the world." He sat on the edge of his bunk to tie his shoes. He liked Junior Darling. He was a kid, only eighteen; a practicing, teetotaling Baptist whose ambition was to be a preacher—man's highest calling. Managing a weak smile, Cohen looked up at him through the bedsprings. "Everybody gets crabs once in his life. Make a man of you."

"You ever had them?"

"Not yet." Cohen turned to see Yardbird Smith, a distorted beach ball of a man, leaning against the next bunk.

"I've had the little sonsabitches," said Yardbird. "Two, three times."

"You've had everything." said Cohen.

"Fucking-A, good buddy."

Junior said, "What do they do at the infirmary?"

Yardbird's features softened for a moment in bogus sympathy. "They shave your hair off, all of it; your crotch, your head, your legs, under your arms, even your fucking eyebrows. Then they pour kerosene over the bleeding stubble. It smarts real bad, like some bastard's got a blowtorch on your balls. Those sonsabitch medics really like their work."

Junior was quiet for a moment. In a small voice, he said, "What they going to do with my mattress cover—all my goods?"

"They burn the whole fucking shebang . . . everything."

Cohen said, "They did that with you, Yardbird, it would be an improvement."

Junior said, "Civvies too?"

"Even neckties," said Yardbird. "It's like they don't fuck around with those little buggers. I mean, you give them half a chance, they'd be gnawing away on the whole squadron, even the officers."

"It ain't fair . . ."

"My daddy—he was in the artillery in the World War. They used to pack crabs into the one-oh-five shells and let fly at the Krauts." Yardbird scratched his belly, a plump triangle of hair-matted gut protruding through a gap in his shirt. "They shot off millions of them. It's how we won the war."

Cohen, knotting his tie, turned to the small mirror on the barrack wall. He brushed his crewcut briskly, working up the nap. A few feet behind him he could see Yardbird Smith lowering himself to a seated position. In a quiet, matter-of-fact voice, Cohen said, "Off my bunk."

I'm just being friendly, hot buddy—neighborly." Yardbird's moonface blossomed into a smile totally lacking in amiability. "Like, how about you and me go into Ybor City and get us some eaten pussy?"

"Get off my bunk,"

"Nigger kooze, a buck a throw. My daddy used to tell me how you Jews liked to save money."

"Off my bunk, Yardbird."

"Like I said, I'm just being friendly."

Cohen tucked the khaki tie into his shirt between the second and third button. He turned, reached down, and with a delicate gesture, removed Yardbird Smith's wire-rimmed GI glasses. He grasped the seated man by the throat, raising him to a standing position until his toes barely touched the floor. As Yardbird struggeled for breath, his smile curdled into a fearful grimace. Cohen shook him from side to side, then replaced his glasses and released him. Red-faced, Yardbird collapsed onto his knees, puffing heavily.

Cohen spoke in placid tones totally lacking the menace of his words. "Beat it. I catch you on my bunk again, I'll break both your arms."

Yardbird, about to say something, changed his mind. Rubbing his neck, he stood. He turned, with what seemed to be a parody of a military about-face, to make his way haltingly down the length of the barracks.

Cohen looked up at Junior. "Don't worry, you'll be out of the hospital in a couple days, like a new man."

"What about my service record?"

"I don't think they put crabs on service records."

"Thanks, Abe."

Abe Cohen grabbed the bus into town. As he did every Saturday, he checked the post office, to find the wanted poster still on display. It pictured a young man with a mustache and slicked-down pompadoured hair wearing a pin-striped, wide-shouldered jacket and striped necktie. He repeated the words to himself: *"Escaped from custody. Armed and dangerous . . . "*

The bastards had it all wrong. Danny Esposito was neither armed nor dangerous—at the moment—not even to the enemy, and he was certainly still in federal custody. It was a thin joke.

He spent a profitable afternoon at the racetrack, then took his winnings to the Tremont, one of Tampa's better steak houses. Though the place was half-empty, the headwaiter insisted he wait for a table at the bar. It was the way in which many such establishments treated uniformed enlisted men. Despite this, soldiers considered themselves lucky to be stationed near big cities. The small ones were worse. The rural South was the worst of all. There one was liable to see signs reading:

NIGGERS, JEWS, SOLDIERS, AND DOGS
—KEEP OUT—

Peacetime army enlisted personnel were for the most part escapees from the Depression. Largely southern, many were the sons and nephews of those same civilians who put up the signs. Negroes were at the bottom of the list. Jews, though unsegregated, were just a few notches up the scale.

* * *

Nine months earlier, sweating and gritty under his pin-striped suit, Cohen was part of a contingent of twenty-three newly arrived recruits from the Northeast—Boston, New York, Philadelphia. Toting their cheap suitcases they had been met at MacDill Field's rail siding by a fat, taciturn sergeant who assembled them in a ragged formation and marched them off. The one-mile trek through the small city of company streets was orchestrated by a chorus of derisive taunts. *"Here come the New York kikes!"* The jeering soldiers stood about in groups or hung out the second-story windows of the white clapboard barracks like victorious soldiers watching prisoners of war being escorted through their camp. *"New York fairies!"* *"Yankee, nigger-loving, Jewboy cocksuckers!"*

A few recruits attempted rejoinders but were silenced by the sergeant. Some, outraged by unjust accusations, glanced about, checking their companions for signs of Jewishness or homosexuality, suspicious that somehow they themselves had been contaminated by an alien presence in their midst.

Finally, with the sound of aircraft engines in their ears, the taunts ceased. They reached their barracks. It was in the area assigned to the Nineteenth Bombardment Group, Ninth Squadron. The Nineteenth was an old outfit that had its prestigious roots in the Air Service of 1917. Currently, at least half its officers were West Pointers and most of its noncoms were veterans of the World War, gone to fat.

The next morning, the new recruits were welcomed into the Nineteenth by its commanding officer. They were informed that since they were all high-school graduates and obviously of high caliber, they were vital to the future of the new and greater Air Corps mandated by the Congress and their Commander-in-Chief. Instead of basic training they would all be sent off to technical schools, more or less of their own choosing. This would determine their Air Corps MOS, or military occupation specialty. Currently there were openings for radio operators, gunners, armament specialists, engine mechanics, photographers, flight engineers, aircraft instrument mechanics, and bombsight maintenance specialists. The courses lasted from two to four months.

Upon completion, they would return to their outfit, the Nineteenth Bomb Group.

Three days later, MacDill Field erupted in a race riot. It was set off when two Negro GIs attempted to seat themselves at the lunch counter in the white PX. The Nineteenth and the three other operational units at MacDill were restricted to barracks. They played no part in the disturbance, which lasted for two days and resulted in the death of two men, both Negro.

Given his choice of specialized training, Abe Cohen opted for radio operator's school. The following week, in a typical SNAFU, he was shipped off to Wright Patterson Field in Ohio to earn his wings as a flight engineer.

He was on his second scotch and soda when the management gave up and seated him at an isolated table in the rear, a few feet from the swinging doors leading into the kitchen. He started with a shrimp cocktail, then ordered a half-bottle of Burgundy with his medium-rare filet mignon. He had a baked potato with sour cream and chives and a house salad with vinaigrette dressing, followed by a slice of pecan pie and a cup of coffee. Including drinks and tip, it cost him five dollars, half his track winnings.

The next morning he slept till eight. Breakfast consisted of chipped beef on toast and fried eggs. By nine-fifteen he was out on the flight line in an attempt to bum a ride. He needed only forty minutes more flying time to qualify for flight pay. A total of four hours would raise his monthly salary fifty percent, from thirty to forty-five dollars.

Flight activity, as was usually the case on Sundays, was at a minimum. He gave up before eleven and strolled to the infirmary in a futile attempt to visit Junior Darling. He was told that all patients in the venereal ward were quarantined.

Lunch at the mess hall consisted of pork chops fried to the consistency of case-hardened steel. He had three, with apple sauce, black-eyed peas, boiled potatoes, and a glass of milk. Desert was peach cobbler and vanilla ice cream.

At noon he went to the post theater where he sat through a newsreel, *The March of Time*, a Popeye cartoon, coming attractions, and the feature: *Citizen Kane.* He exited, blinking in the sunlight. *Rosebud* . . .

"Hey Cohen." It was Tech Sergeant Blanchard, their barracks chief. He seemed breathless with suppressed excitement. "Don't send out any laundry."

"Why the hell not?"

"The Japs just bombed Pearl Harbor."

THE MISSION

AUGUST 1, 1943

The headquarters for Luftwaffe Defense Zone 24-East was housed in a windowless concrete bunker at Otopenii, about halfway between Bucharest and Ploesti. Within its cavernous war room, Biggy Fiedler sat at a long table with seven other young women. They were dressed in the natty blue uniforms of the Luftnachrichtenhelferinnen—Luftwaffe Airwomen. Each wore headphones hooked into a circuit of radar installations, visual observers, and radio detectors. Directly in front of them, a massive glass map climbed almost to the ceiling. It was crisscrossed with grid markings, defining the defense zones and their sectors covering southern Europe and the Mediterranean area. At the moment four airmen sat on the lower rungs of their ladders on the other side of the glass map.

The main part of the amphitheater was occupied by radar and communications personnel and by liaison officers responsible for German and Rumanian day and night fighters, flak installations, and civil defense in the hundred sectors of Zone 24-East. Close to the wall, on the left, stood the Wurzburg table—the main radar monitor for the Ploesti-Bucharest area. A balcony stretched half the length of the amphitheater. At the moment it was unoccupied.

Biggy Fiedler was pleased to be in Rumania. The country seemed untouched by the war. Bucharest, though lacking in some of the cultural amenities, was a decided improvement over wartime Berlin. It was rarely bombed by the Russians, and there were even a few shops still selling silk stockings.

Unlike Berlin, there was no shortage of handsome men or good champagne. As a German airwoman she was much sought after by those gallant young Luftwaffe flying officers who craved a touch of home. She accepted the popularity graciously, but it was, for the moment, academic. Biggy Fiedler was in love. He was a Rumanian army major. As chief liaison officer of the Rumanian antiaircraft forces he was attached to the German staff of Defense Zone 24. She found him to be extremely handsome, sporting, as he did, a few interesting character lines and just a touch of gray at the temples. He was married, but sophisticated Rumanians, both men and women, were romantic beyond reason and made a national sport of discreet infidelity. Biggy herself played the game well, taking pride in her amorous success. She had become a self-styled expert on the complex subject of Rumanian men and therefore a source of sage advice for the other aspiring Luftnachrichtenhelferinnen of Headquarters, Defense Zone 24-East.

Biggy Fiedler's lover, Major Anton Brayer, was a second cousin to Rumania's queen and the highest ranking of the three consecutive Rumanian paramours she had cultivated during her six months in exotic Rumania. Love was everything.

Her headphones were buzzing. The Athens radio intercept station was reporting possible enemy activity. She made a note on her pad, switched on her flashlight to project its beam onto the big map. She blinked it rapidly. One of the airmen reached to chalk a yellow question mark within the circle of light on the Libyan coast just west of Benghazi. A loud buzzer sounded as yellow alert lights began blinking on the upper corners of the map.

She glanced up at the balcony. There were now two men standing there leaning on the railing. One of them was Anton. She tilted her head and signaled with a quick smile, but his eyes had gone to the map.

Major Anton Brayer had seen her, but had turned away with a stab of annoyance. Had she expected him to blow her a kiss? She rarely seemed to know the proper time and place for such gestures. He had lately grown disenchanted with Fräulein Fiedler. She was a pretty enough thing, but in the midst of orgasm, she had a tendency to flail about like an uncoordinated punch-drunk fighter. She had knocked out one of his teeth. As if that were not enough, her hands were ugly, and worse, she had big feet. Most German women had big feet—a racial characteristic. It all went to reinforce his secret conviction that Rumania was on the wrong side of the war.

Major Brayer was joined on the balcony by Captain Pitcairn, a tall blond Prussian who seemed always to be standing at attention. On this day, because of the indisposition of Colonel Bernhard Woldenga, Pitcairn, his deputy, was for the first time acting as fighter command senior controller. His legal name included the family seat. He had been christened Douglas Pitcairn of Perthshire. The Scottish identity dated back to 1830 when some members of a Protestant clan, at odds with its Catholic neighbors, emigrated from Scotland to East Prussia.

As a fighter pilot Captain Pitcairn had flown a Heinkel 51 for Franco in Spain and later a Messerschmitt Bf109 during the Battle of Britain. Finally, with a dozen kills and an Iron Cross First Class to his credit, he was shot up, but managed to make it back across the Channel. Major Brayer took pleasure in speculating that the Spitfire pilot who had accomplished this feat had been one of Pitcairn's clansmen.

Brayer, pointing at the map, said, "It looks as if the Benghazi B-24s might be up."

"It could also be the B-25 mediums from Pantelleria," said Pitcairn.

Major Brayer stared at the yellow question mark near the bottom of the huge glass map. He had a strong feeling that it was the B-24 heavies and that a major effort was afoot. It was, he felt, a reasonable apprehension. They had been receiving intelligence that the two groups of American heavy bombers in Libya, along with the three groups who had recently joined them from the U.S. Eighth Air Force in England, had been flying low-level practice missions over the desert for almost two weeks. During that time the Yanks' augmented Ninth Air Force heavies had suspended all offensive operations. It was logical to assume that soon they would fly the mission for which they had been training.

"What do you think, Major?" said Pitcairn.

"I think it's the Benghazi crowd on a real bombing mission . . . low-level."

"Why?"

"It's time." Once again, the Rumanian stared at the large map. "We're sitting on the target . . . Ploesti."

"I doubt it, Major Brayer."

"I'm certain of it."

"Just what makes you so?"

"There's not a juicier target in all of Europe," said Brayer. "A successful attack on these refineries and your Luftwaffe would run out of petrol in less than a week."

The German captain's grin was deprecatory. "Indeed, Major. But what makes you think it will be today?"

The Rumanian thought about it for a moment. He smiled. "Like many Rumanians, I've got Gypsy blood."

Pitcairn laughed. "One can't fight wars on precognition."

"Your Führer does."

Captain Pitcairn's smile grew stiff. With his eyes on Brayer's, he lit a long, slim cigar.

The major wondered how the man could smoke the damned things so early in the morning. He said, "And those poles."

"What poles?"

"The ones planted in the desert floor at the American practice site. I think they represent smokestacks, Ploesti smokestacks."

"With all due respect, sir," said Captain Pitcairn, "that's foolish. Even the Americans would not be insane enough to use heavy, lumbering, four-engined bombers en masse at smokestack level."

"I don't think it would be insane."

"Listen, Major, I'm a fighter pilot with a good deal of experience, and I tell you it's suicide. I would consider myself a dead man if I were ordered to bomb such a target at low level, even in an FW-190 that's well over a hundred miles per hour faster than a B-24. And what you're suggesting is a round trip of twenty-five hundred miles, mostly over enemy territory, in big, lumbering, unmanueverable aircraft, to bomb the most heavily defended target in Europe from under a hundred feet!"

"Perhaps they're not aware of the extent of the defense," said Brayer. "We've hidden the guns from their reconnaissance aircraft."

"I don't think you have to worry about it," said Pitcairn. "I'm sure that their practice has been for low-level tactical missions; infantry and armor support—Sicily. It's also possible that those poles you speak of might be standing in for the smokestacks of Italian battleships."

"Then why did we bother to make Ploesti, as you say, the most heavily defended target in Europe?"

"To insure it against high-altitude conventional daylight bombing. You know that. That's what the Americans specialize in and it's said that they're the only ones who can reach Ploesti in force, though I personally doubt that they can."

"They've brought three groups down from England to reinforce the two they have. Why?"

"I don't know why . . . perhaps for tactical purposes in Sicily." said Captain Pitcairn. "But five groups are not enough to stage a successful high-level attack on these oil fields."

"And that's what you expect?"

"Yes, I do, but only when they have adequate forces available and air bases closer to the target. It would require many more aircraft than they've managed to get airborne today."

"Then I'm even more convinced that I'm right," said Major Brayer. "In fact, if today I were in command of the American bomber forces, a heavy, low-level raid is just exactly what I would order."

Pitcairn looked at him with disdain. "Why?"

"Because you, and others with the same fixed ideas, least expect it, or think it impossible."

Pitcairn came erect, exhaling a cloud of blue smoke. "Nonsense. It *is* impossible!"

"I would suggest two things, Captain," said the Rumanian major. "The first is to consider your army's own use of surprise in the Ardennes, which was also considered to be impossible, and the second is to ingest a good dose of Clausewitz."

The two men moved wordlessly down onto the floor. Captain Pitcairn made his rounds. Major Brayer took a seat at the flak desk, checked with his deputy to make sure that all the Rumanian antiaircraft units in Zone 24-East were on low-grade alert.

A few minutes later, a sharply focused flashlight beam highlighted the map. The question marks were erased, to be replaced by red circles. The flashlight blinked four times, and four more circles appeared, interlocked with the first. The red markings were about six inches above the Libyan coast. An enemy force consisting of five heavy bombardment groups was headed north across the Mediterranean.

Major Brayer was handed a typewritten note: a smudged carbon typed in German:

BENGHAZI LIBERATORS—5 Groups—aprox. 170
BOMBS—500 & 1000-pound general-purpose demolition
FUEL—Maximum, including auxiliary tanks

He lifted the phone and dialed 6. "What's the source of that last intelligence?"

"L-18, sir."

Brayer hung up the phone, his curiosity satisfied. L-18 represented two Luftwaffe men planted on the Libyan coast. They had the reputation of being a reliable source. He glanced over his shoulder at Captain Pitcairn, who was deep in conversation with one of the Wurzburg radar technicians. Brayer had been hoping for eye contact—a small victory. No matter. He turned to his deputy and ordered him to alert all Rumanian antiaircraft commanders in the Bucharest-Ploesti area to the probability of a low-level attack and to move in two special Q trains, armed with agile 37mm guns, from east of Bucharest.

He hoped his German counterpart was doing likewise.

CHAPTER 3

FEBRUARY 1942

The coffee was lousy, not much better than the tasteless dishwater they served in the mess hall. He made a mental note to mention it to Vinnie when he showed up in the afternoon—ask him to bring a strong dark Italian roast from Ferraro's on Grand Street instead of the canned Chase and Sanborn crap he had brought last time.

Nevertheless, adding three more spoonfuls of sugar, he freshened his cup from the electric percolator. He was worthless without plenty of coffee in the morning, even lousy coffee. He helped himself to another prune Danish.

As they had been every morning for the past three and a half years, the *News* and *Mirror* were rolled up, wedged between the bars of his cell door. They featured identical pictures on their front pages: the French liner *Normandie*, surrounded by fire boats, burning at its dock at Fiftieth Street. The *Daily Mirror* headline read, "SABOTAGE!"

Page two of the *Mirror* featured a story about the battle for Bataan. He was tired of reading about Americans getting the hell kicked out of them by lousy little buck-toothed Japs wearing thick eyeglasses. Only in the comics was his side winning the war. Little Orphan Annie, with Sandy's help, had foiled a German plot to steal Daddy Warbucks' secret death ray, Tailspin Tommy had just shot down his seventeenth Jap Zero, and Dick Tracy was hot on the trail of an evil Nazi saboteur.

With the coffee mug and Danish pastry in hand and *The New York Daily News* tucked under his arm, he stepped behind the lacquered Chinese screen, lowered his silk pajama bottoms, and sat down. Despite prison regulations, he had insisted on retaining the screen, a thoughtful going-away gift from his close friend and associate Meyer Lansky. He would have preferred the death penalty to spending thirty years on the crapper in full view of anyone who happened to be passing. It had cost him a fifteen-thousand-dollar contribution to the prison library for that privilege and a few other amenities. The library even got a few new books.

He read Winchell, who seemed to be having a love affair with J. Edgar Hoover. A hard knot formed in his belly. He turned to the sports section. Only the fights interested him, but there was nothing except a short piece about one-time contender Two-Ton-Tony Galento training on beer and pasta for a comeback, a possible second shot at Louis and the title. The man Galento was a pig. It would be no contest. It was, he realized, unusual to favor a nigger over an Italian. To hell with it, class was what was important, and Joe Louis had it.

At eleven o'clock one of the screws unlocked his cell, stating he was there to escort him to the warden's office. With the guard behind him he paced the length of the cell block accepting the greetings and accolades of its inhabitants. It was his due. He was Don Salvatore Luciano—*capo di tutti capi*—boss of bosses. Though it might be heresy to admit it aloud, the Pope himself was no more deserving of respect.

The warden's inner office was comfortably furnished with a large rolltop desk, a few wooden filing cabinets, a leather couch, and two leather wing chairs. The green walls, highlighted by the morning sun from three large windows, were decorated with a few fly-specked hunting prints, an aerial photograph of the prison, framed portraits of Washington and FDR, and a photograph of the warden accepting a plaque from Governor Thomas E. Dewey.

The warden, in his best formal manner, introduced Luciano to two naval officers: a portly, balding, somewhat disheveled Commander Louis Stark, and a tall, mustached Ensign Dabbit, whose uniform fitted him as if it had been hand-tailored.

These were the first military uniforms Luciano had seen since war had been declared two months earlier. Lucky Luciano visualized the outside world crawling with soldiers and sailors. And just like the last time, the world would change. Things were never going to be the same again. The thought depressed him. It would all happen without him.

"These gentlemen," said the warden, "are from naval intelligence. They want to speak to you . . . privately." Blinking rapidly through wire-framed bifocals, he turned to Commander Stark and stared for a long moment as if expecting an invitation to remain in his own office. Finally, he turned back to Luciano, his tone soured with a note of petulance. "I'll lock the door behind me. When you're finished, knock, and the guard will return you to your cell." Then, with his face lengthened in disappointment, he turned on his heel and was gone.

Luciano took one of the wing chairs, the sun behind him. He tapped a cigarette on the back of his hand and wondered what it was all about.

Ensign Dabbit offered a light from a Zippo decorated with the U.S. Navy insignia. He seated himself on the couch. Commander Stark balanced himself casually on its arm.

Luciano noted that Commander Stark's blouse sported three rows of ribbons. They seemed a little premature for this war. The man was probably a retread from the last one.

The commander said, "Mr. Luciano, have you ever heard of Black Tom?"

"It's a small island in the harbor, near Jersey City. Couple of warehouses."

"No, I mean the explosion."

"Something blew up there . . . the last war . . ."

"Correct." Commander Stark took his time inserting a cigarette in a holder as long as Roosevelt's.

Luciano watched him closely. Despite the uniform, he had the look, the smell of a lawyer.

"It was an act of sabotage." The commander waved his cigarette holder in the air. "July thirtieth, 1916—we weren't in the war yet. Munitions. Some freight cars carrying artillery shells and other stuff went sky high. The explosion was heard in Hartford and Baltimore. That's a few hundred miles. It was like the war had come to America. Live seventy-five-millimeter shells fell on Jersey City. People in Manhattan were killed by shattered window glass—two million dollars' worth."

"I was out of town," said Luciano.

Commander Stark laughed, giving the cue to Ensign Dabbit to do likewise. Luciano rewarded them with a tight grin. He said, "I'm a patriotic American."

"We assumed that," said the commander. "That's why we're here."

Luciano nodded. It was getting interesting, but he was wary.

"The Krauts did it," said Louis Stark. "It was the worst act of sabotage ever committed in this country . . . that is, until yesterday. Do you know what happened to the *Normandie?*"

"Yes. It was in the papers this morning."

"The biggest ship in the world, burned out, capsized at its dock, finished—dead. Even worse, it's lost to the war effort. It had the capacity to transport twenty thousand troops across the Atlantic in five days." His voice was deeply pitched, resonant, like that of a network radio announcer heard through a big Stromberg-Carlson. "The investigation is barely off the ground, so we're not certain it was sabotage. The point is, if it wasn't, it could have been. There is hardly anything in place to prevent that sort of thing." He paused, locking eyes with Luciano. "We don't want another Black Tom or another *Normandie,* or worse. New York Harbor is the country's most vital shipping area, an absolute necessity to the war effort, and it's a sitting duck, totally vulnerable. And there've been lots of little accidents that should not have happened. The little ones can be just as bad if there are enough of them. We need your help, Mr. Luciano."

Luciano nodded. His enigmatic stare concealed a curiosity tempered with apprehension.

"In wartime," continued Commander Stark, "all bets are off and this is a hell of a big war, even bigger than last time. We need all the talent we can lay our hands on. You, with all your management skills and strategic ability, would make an excellent general."

The guy was good, thought Luciano, real good. He said, "You get me out of here?"

"In all honesty, no, at least not right away."

"Then I can't help you." He glanced at Ensign Dabbit, seated on the other end of the couch. The ensign was staring down at his shoes. Guys who stare at their shoes were a bad sign. It went a long way toward confirming his apprehension. The two men could easily be state crime commission types in disguise, or even feds. The bastards would try anything to nail him with another rap in order to clean up their books. Or, worse: they could be setting him up for something entirely new.

"I'm here to appeal to your patriotism."

Luciano spoke quietly, "Come back in thirty-nine years, Commander Stark, maybe twenty-two if I'm lucky. I might be a little more patriotic then."

The commander stood, paced to the desk. "We thought you might be reluctant—suspicious. I don't blame you. Call your lawyer. At least give me that break."

Polakoff answered his private number on the first ring. Luciano said, "Mo, there's a guy in a sailor suit, name of Stark."

"Lou Stark, I've known him for years. He was an assistant D.A. in Queens. He's straight."

"So what?"

"I checked out the whole megillah with certain impeccable parties. It's true, the navy's worried that the entire waterfront will blow and go sliding into the Hudson." A sudden solemnity caused Moses Polakoff's voice to go hoarse. "It's our country, Lucky."

"What's in it for me?"

"When the time comes you'll get good press and there'll be a new administration in Albany. You'll be a real patriot, a man who gave his all for his country from a jail cell. We can bring a lot of pressure on certain parties. You'll get a pardon when it's over—a year or two—at worst maybe a deportation. Of course if we lose the war, all bets are off."

Luciano hung up the phone. Still seated, he handed it back to Commander Stark, nodded, then leaned back, tapping another cigarette. "Tell me more about this."

"Our interest is to prevent enemy activity, sabotage and spying in the Third Naval District," said Commander Stark. "The unions—teamsters, longshoremen, seamen, fishing boat skippers—even the cab drivers and hookers, they know the territory. They can do more for security than a regiment of marines." The commander perched on the edge of the desk, leaned forward, using his cigarette holder like a baton. "And there are ships—freighters, tankers—being sunk right here, a few miles off the coast. The oil slicks are washing up on the Long Island beaches. There's a cordon of Kraut submarines that practically control the approaches to New York Harbor. They know about the convoy sailings—time and place. The bastards are being fed information."

"Loose lips and traitors," said Ensign Dabbit, rising from the couch to light Commander Stark's cigarette.

"We got Socks Lanza on the East River, the Fulton Fish Market. Mr. Lanza's doing okay, but the West Side is even more important, and it's naked. We need you, Mr. Luciano."

"Socks Lanza's not sitting in a jail cell."

"Listen, Mr. Luciano," said the Commander. "There are also Italian-American seamen going down on those merchant ships, young men from Little Italy, Brooklyn . . ."

"Don't bullshit me." Luciano's eyes narrowed. "This isn't a war between Little Italy and Nazi Germany, so lay off the soft soap. We're men, we talk like men, or you and your lieutenant can leave and I'll go back to my cell."

The commander sighed. "I apologize."

"All I know about the war is what I see in the papers," said Luciano. "Is it that bad, or even worse?"

"Worse."

"We're losing?"

"Yes. Almost everywhere. The Nips hurt us badly at Pearl. We're going to lose the Philippines, and the Japs look as if they're getting ready to invade Australia. The British and Russians are fighting, but unless we can get stuff through to them, past the German Wolf Packs, it doesn't look good. In other words, we can lose this war."

Luciano was silent for a moment, staring at the ceiling. It was against his principles to make an honest commitment to authority. He required an act of faith in return. The government, too, must put itself on the line; commit to something it found unpalatable. Finally, his eyes zeroed on Stark's. "Okay, I do something for you, you do something for me."

"If it's within reason," said the commander.

"That's for you to decide."

"Shoot."

"There's a guy named Daniel Esposito. I heard he might have joined the army, maybe the navy. I'm looking for him."

"Why?"

"He went state's evidence at my trial."

"You're asking the United States military to be a party to your retribution?"

"I just want to talk to him."

A petulant frown warped the naval officer's face. "You mean, that's your price?"

Luciano, exhaling smoke through his nose, said nothing.

Commander Stark seemed suddenly hoarse, the melodic strains of amiability gone from his voice. "Was this guy Esposito granted immunity?"

"Yes."

"It will be extremely difficult."

"Lots of things are difficult," said the capo.

"I'll have to check on it."

Ensign Dabbit, notebook and Parker 51 at the ready, said, "Is that E-s-p-o-s-i-t-o?"

"Right," said Luciano. "But if he was smart, he changed his name."

"Terrific," said Stark, sourly.

"He's been printed by the FBI and the New York cops," said the capo.

Commander Stark said, "I'll be in touch."

A few days later, they were back, just as Luciano had expected they would be. He shook hands with Commander Stark and accepted a light from Lieutenant Dabbit's Zippo.

"We've got a deal," said the commander, his voice once again toned with amiability. "It took a little doing."

"You mean they found him?"

"Not yet, Mr. Luciano. They've found that he's not in any of the services under his own name. But they have his fingerprints and if he enlisted under a false name I can guarantee that he'll be located. And there's this." Stark passed a sheet of paper to Luciano. It was an FBI "Wanted" poster. "We got us a judge who found some difficulty with Daniel Esposito's immunity agreement."

"How long?"

"It's hard to say. The War Department is a little busy these days. But I'll keep you posted every step of the way. Believe me, there are important people who believe this project is too vital to sacrifice because of a little thing like this."

The wanted poster featured a photograph of a young man with a mustache and slicked-down, pompadoured hair wearing a pinstriped, wide-shouldered jacket and striped necktie. Luciano read aloud. "Escaped from custody—armed and dangerous . . ."

Stark said, "That'll be hanging in every post office from coast to coast as soon as you give the word."

"Okay."

"We want to get started on the West Side docks as soon as possible. Anything you need . . ."

Luciano said, "I have a free hand?"

"Exactly . . . whatever it takes."

Lieutenant Dabbit said, "You'll be in touch with the FBI."

"Are the cops involved in this thing?"

"Yes," said Stark, "a special squad."

"Then I'll deal with them and the Navy. No FBI."

"Okay."

"I don't want J. Edgar to have a heart attack."

Stark smiled. "Understood, Mr. Luciano."

"I'll need meetings with certain people."

"It can be arranged."

"A telephone in my cell, privacy."

"Done."

"A draft deferment for three of my lieutenants and a couple others."

"We'll look into it."

"And I think I should be moved to a joint closer to New York. This place is halfway to China."

"Makes sense," said the commander. He paused, then, "Anything else?"

Luciano thought for a moment. Finally he said, "Yes, a personal favor."

"Name it."

"There's an outfit that does shows for the service."

"The USO."

"Right. There's a friend of mine, a canary, nice kid, good voice. I've been helping her with her career—clubs—you know how it is. She just got an audition offer from the Harry James band, but she wants to sing for the troops. She's a very patriotic little broad."

"Show business is a little out of my line," said Stark. He turned to his assistant. "Dabbit?"

"I know a major in Army Special Services."

Luciano smiled sourly. "I'm sure you guys can take care of it."

"Right," said Stark.

Dabbit opened a small notebook. Luciano spelled out the names of his three lieutenants.

"We have a deal." Stark stood, extending his hand. "You'll have the phone tomorrow and everything else will be in place by the end of the week." With the capo still seated, they shook on it.

"And the lady?" said Dabbit.

"She goes under the stage name of Bonnie Astor. She's working at Leon and Eddie's on Fifty-second street." He drew deeply on his cigarette. "She's with MCA." He sat quietly as they got into their coats.

At the door, the commander said, "Anything else you need, just call me." He grinned, "As long as it's not too illegal."

Later, back in his cell, Luciano made a mental note to tell Vinnie, when he came up tomorrow, that he'd need someone new for the regular Wednesday visits, a classy young college broad just like the last one: Sally Shank or Bonnie Astor, or whatever the hell her real name was.

CHAPTER 4

MARCH 1942

Second Lieutenant Michael Maguire called out the altimeter setting, the actual altitude of the runway relative to sea level. It was the initial item on the copilot's checklist for what was to be the first of four touch-and-go landings and takeoffs. They had spent the earlier part of the afternoon flying a dry practice bomb run on Havana harbor.

Captain Hammond said, "Check the tower."

"I was just about to . . ."

"I want the barometer reading from them, Lieutenant, not altitude guesswork from you. Always. Understood?"

"Yes, sir." Maguire had set the altimeter before takeoff, but it was obvious that the son of a bitch was a stickler for tight-assed cockpit procedure. Maguire experienced a hot flush of anger. Captain Earl Hammond had transferred in from a B-17 outfit—prima donna Flying Fortresses. Maguire had more B-24 time: thirty-two hours to Hammond's seven. He deserved and had expected to get his own crew. He knew he was a better pilot than Hammond—as good as anyone in the outfit. But now he would probably spend his war as a second lieutenant sitting to the right of a chickenshit glamour boy. Taking a deep breath in an effort to keep his voice flat, he called the tower for landing clearance. The warm southern drawl of the tower operator soothed his nerves. The guy sounded as if he were yawning. The prevailing wind was practically nil. Maguire actually had to ask for the barometric pressure. Practically every strip in southern Florida was the same: just a few inches, give or take, above sea level. Hammond was making a chickenshit big deal about nothing.

They turned into the downwind leg of their first touchdown. Captain Hammond nodded, indicating that he too had heard the tower. Using the formal tones of an airline pilot on an approach to Pittsburgh, he said, "Landing instructions received."

Maguire fingered his throat mike. "Copilot to engineer . . ."

Staff Sergeant Cohen's voice was loud and clear in his headset. "Engineer to copilot . . ."

"Crew at stations?"

"Roger—crew in landing positions."

Maguire wondered if the Jew-boy had actually checked it out. He said, "You saw for yourself?"

"Yes, sir, nose and waist."

Maguire glanced down at his checklist. "Auxiliary hydraulic pump."

"Wilco," said Cohen. There was a pause while the flight engineer hit the hydraulic pump switch so that power could be applied to flaps and brakes if number-three engine conked out. Finally he said, "Auxiliary pump on."

Maguire had met Sergeant Abraham Cohen that morning when Hammond, their new pilot, assembled the crew for the first time. An hour later, over coffee, Maguire suggested to Captain Hammond that they get rid of the Yid. He should have known better. Along with everything else, the bastard was a Jew lover.

Hammond said, "Brake pressure checked. Parking brake off. Autopilot off. Airspeed?"

"One fifty."

"Gear down. . . ."

Maguire pulled the landing gear lever. "Gear handle down."

"Mixture?"

Maguire, using one hand, depressed all four levers. "Mixtures in auto-rich." Next, he increased RPMs, reporting, "Props at twenty-four hundred RPMs."

Maguire said, "Intercoolers?"

"Intercoolers open."

"Cowl flaps?"

"Cowl flaps closed."

"Booster pumps?"

"Booster pumps on."

"Wing deicers?"

"Deicers off." Maguire glanced to his left. They were flying parallel to the runway, which was about three miles to the right.

Hammond said, "Wheels?"

Maguire glanced over his shoulder noting that the gear was down. He said, "Wheel right."

The captain checked his side. "Wheel left."

From his position in the waist, Sergeant Cohen confirmed, "Main gear down and locked."

Once again Maguire consulted the check list on his lap. "Ball turret and trailing antenna?"

"Trailing antenna retracted," said Cohen. "But are you sure you're on the right airplane, Lieutenant?"

"What the hell you talking about, Sergeant?"

"This airplane ain't got a ball turret."

Maguire's pique climbed the scale. The Jew-bastard was trying to make a fool of him. He said, "Just answer the question, Sergeant." He was instantly disappointed with the unassertive quality of his own words. In frustration, he heard himself say, "There's no room for wise guys on this crew." It was even worse.

"Yes, sir," said Cohen. "But I looked again and we still don't have a belly turret, sir."

Somebody else said, "We also don't have a seventy-five-millimeter howitzer, sir."

"Okay, who said that?" Maguire's words were tightly spaced, the tone louder but somehow pitched too high. He searched in vain for a more virulent rejoinder, a verbal equivalent to the physical violence he longed to commit. "I want to know who said that . . . now!"

Somebody laughed.

"Knock it off!" Captain Hammond's voice boomed over the interphone. "This is an airplane, not a kindergarten!"

Maguire felt flushed—he was sweating. He was sure it was Cohen who had laughed. It was their initial flight as a nine-man crew, and already the flight engineer was a disruptive influence.

Hammond said, "I want airspeed every ten seconds."

"Roger . . . one fifty." Maguire watched as the pilot, with a show of delicacy, lowered the nose slightly. He wondered why.

They had all the airspeed they needed. But why should he give a damn? Their Jew-loving pilot had put him in the kindergarten with the rest of the crew. Fuck him. He slowed his breathing to get hold of himself. He called out, "One fifty-five."

"Flaps, ten degrees."

Maguire lowered them, saying, "Roger, ten degrees flaps." As they grabbed hold, he reported, "Airspeed, one fifty." A few seconds later, he said, "Copilot to engineer—nose wheel?"

Cohen, now up front, reported, "Nose gear down and locked."

Maguire had to admit that the Yid engineer was on the ball. But nevertheless, he'd watch him like a hawk, have his ass at the first opportunity. Sooner or later the sergeant would fuck up—everybody did—it was only a matter of time. The thought cheered him. He said, "Airspeed, one forty-five."

Captain Hammond turned onto the base leg. He straightened out about three miles beyond the end of the runway, flying a gyro-compass course at a precise right angle to it. Finally, at a mile from the runway axis, he called for half-flaps and began the turn into a final approach.

With his eye on the indicator dial, Maguire lowered the flaps, saying, "Flaps at twenty degrees." He watched as Hammond reduced power to twenty-five inches of manifold pressure. A few seconds later, he called out, "Airspeed, one forty."

"Props at high RPM," said Hammond. "Superchargers at six."

"Airspeed, one forty."

They rolled out of the turn slightly to the left of the runway center line. Hammond applied light pressure on the right rudder pedal, lining up the airplane. He maintained airspeed by raising and lowering the nose slightly while holding a gentle glide slope with delicate throttle adjustments. He said, "Full flaps."

"Roger, full flaps down."

With eighteen inches of manifold pressure Hammond maintained a rate of descent of 650 feet a minute. They were flying a little hot, but it looked to Copilot Maguire like it was going to be a good landing—their first as a crew. He said, "Airspeed, one thirty."

When they were down to 150 feet, he glanced over at Hammond, anticipating that the pilot would raise the nose and further reduce power. A big, heavy airplane required an early flare-out to get it onto the runway in the nose-high attitude that would bleed off speed and lift—a kind of controlled stall. The pilot seemed to have other ideas. Feeling a twinge of anxiety, Maguire called out the airspeed. They had picked up another five miles an hour. He clutched the armrest and tightened all his muscles. It was obvious that Hammond was going to hit the concrete in a dead run in order to give him a short takeoff roll. It was a hell of a way to practice landings in a relatively unfamiliar airplane.

Hammond greased it in, touching down on all three wheels at 137 miles an hour. A hot-shot, three-point landing, smooth as silk, thought Maguire. Except the third point was not the tail wheel of a B-17 but the delicate nose wheel of a B-24. Cohen sensed a downward pitch as the oleo strut compressed to its maximum. Unlike a conventional airplane using a tail wheel, in which a three-point landing resulted in a nose-high attitude, a three-point landing with a tricycle landing gear put the airplane on the runway in a slight nose-down attitude that induced speed, rather than killed it. Proper procedure was to stay nose high by holding the nose wheel off the ground until it came down naturally. Hammond refrained from hitting the brakes as this was a transition landing that would roll into a takeoff.

Maguire braced himself. Rolling, at speed, with full flaps, the B-24's efficient Davis wing did its duty, lifting them twenty feet off the ground before stalling. The second time they touched the runway was more a crash than a landing. There were two more "bounces," each less severe than the one before it. On the last of these, just as Hammond hit the throttles for the takeoff run, the nose gear gave way.

Maguire was thrown forward as sixty thousand pounds of airplane, at full throttle, slammed down nose first onto the concrete. With a sound like ripping paper, monstrously amplified, the B-24 skidded headlong down the runway, shedding sparks and pieces of her forward section. Three of her propellers were curled back like wilted flowers. The fourth, a giant boomerang, was hurled into the air. Its runaway engine roared, then climbed the scale, adding its high-pitched whine to a screeching cacophony of tortured metal.

Three seconds after they hit, the left tire blew, turning the aircraft sharply off the runway onto a verge made muddy from recent rains. The deflated tire dug in, sinking the gear to its main strut into the mud. Twisting sharply now on the fulcrum of a locked landing gear, the B-24 completed a half-circle, snapping the gear's side-bracing strut. Under enormous strain, the landing gear folded, dropping a wingtip onto the ground. Maguire felt a blow on his forehead. With a final jolt, the airplane came to a stop, causing him to bite into his tongue.

Seconds later, he emerged from a darkness filled with flashing stars. The flight deck was tilted to the left. There was dust in the air. He realized he was groaning. Sergeant Cohen was kneeling between the seats. Maguire, feeling as if his skull was filled with dry cotton, said, "What the hell is going on?"

"I'm cutting the main-line switch."

The number-two engine sputtered to a stop.

Maguire's head hurt. He reached up to touch his forehead, winced, withdrew bloody fingers. It took a moment to reorient himself. It occurred to him that it had been his, not Cohen's, responsibility to cut the switches. He should have done it earlier, on impact. It was the second time he'd had to take crap from Cohen.

Over his shoulder he could see a pair of legs disappear out the upper escape hatch. It was, he figured, radio operator Sergeant Crenshaw. Through the left window a lick of flame danced around the cowling of number-two engine. A dozen vehicles were speeding toward them; fire engines, jeeps, ambulances, weapon carriers, tugs. He heard Captain Hammond say, "I think my leg is broken . . . the left one . . ."

Cohen put his hand on Maguire's shoulder, saying, "You okay, Lieutenant?"

Maguire shook it off. "I'm okay."

"You better get out."

"When I'm damned good and ready, Cohen." Maguire's tongue was swollen, making it painful to form words. It was all a big fat pain in the ass, none of it his doing, and now he was being ordered around by a sergeant.

Tasting blood, he glanced to the left. Clyde Taylor, the navigator, was trying to help Captain Hammond out of his seat. Hammond said, "It's stuck, jammed in . . . my leg . . . Christ, it hurts. Don't pull me."

"It's okay, Captain." Lieutenant Taylor ceased his efforts. "Just take it easy."

Cohen squirmed in between the seats, worked his head and one arm beneath the pilot's control column. Captain Hammond said, "What's it look like, Cohen?"

"Lot of crumpled sheet metal. Your foot's caught under the rudder pedal."

Maguire, irritated by the sound of their voices, got out of his seat. He was weak in the knees. The effort of standing made him dizzy. He should be taking charge—something.

He said, "Stop bullshitting about it, Sergeant, just get him loose."

Outside, they were dousing the burning engine with prodigious amounts of CO_2. A head and shoulders appeared in the escape hatch. It said, "Let's go. Everybody out." It reached down. Maguire grabbed a hand, allowed himself to be helped up and out. Through a veil of red he saw a few dozen men milling about on the ground. Using his sleeve, he wiped the blood from his eyes and saw one of the gunners—Sergeant D'Amato—emerge from the waist window.

There was a lot of shouting. Everyone seemed to be yelling orders. They had a ladder rigged to the right side of the fuselage. On the left, the number-two engine, despite the firefighting efforts, was still burning. Maguire smelled gasoline. Shaky, he started down as Lieutenant Taylor's head popped out of the escape hatch.

"We got a man in here . . . trapped!" The navigator was waving his arms, shouting. "We need cutters . . . a crowbar."

Two medics helped Maguire to the ambulance, where Captain Colfax, the squadron MO, seated him on the rear step. Maguire said, "Anybody else hurt?"

"You're the only one so far." The captain patted a liberal application of sulfa powder onto the cut in his forehead. He taped a large surgical pad over it. "We get you to the infirmary, this is going to need a few stitches."

A medic began wrapping his head in two-inch gauze as Maguire stared straight ahead at the B-24, about thirty yards away. It seemed to shudder. There was a whooshing sound, like escaping air, and then as he watched, the left wing, with its tip buried in the mud, sprouted flame. A second later he felt the heat on his face.

He stood up, unaware of the bandage unwinding from around his head. A figure emerged from the flight deck escape hatch. It was Lieutenant Beel, the bombardier. There were groups of men running from the burning aircraft, others running toward it. A tongue of flame climbed to a hundred feet. He watched as Major Caesar, the group engineering officer, scurried up the ladder. He was carrying a pair of sheet metal cutters and a crowbar.

A trail of burning gasoline had spread fire to the bomb bay and a few seconds later to the rear of the aircraft. Flames were licking around the tail turret; long red feathers reached out of one of the waist windows. Hydraulic fluid, thought Maguire, highly volatile stuff. Just about everything burned on an airplane.

The fire wagons were pumping CO_2. A cloud of black smoke boiled up to a thousand feet. The flames were spreading. Using acetylene torches, a half-dozen men were attempting to cut loose the nose section. As he watched, a flicker of red made itself visible through what was left of the shattered Plexiglas.

A tremor of keen apprehension coursed through Maguire's body, localizing itself in a pair of tightening gonads. The B-24 was a primed bomb on a short fuse. When the fire reached the still-intact gas tanks in the right wing, it would be all over. Another thousand gallons of hundred-octane gasoline would ignite, instantaneously this time, spectacularly. Maguire lit a cigarette and thought about the Jew-boy, playing hero on the flight deck with Hammond. He attempted to conjure up some feeling for the two of them. But though he knew he should, he felt nothing. Tough, too bad, but Captain Earl Hammond had brought it on himself with flying that was lousy enough to have washed out a cadet in a primary trainer. If it hadn't happened the way it had, then chances were that sooner or later he would have killed the entire crew. As for Sergeant Cohen, if it had to be anyone, it might as well be him. It was nature's way of cleaning the slate. With a sharp twinge of envy, he thought of Hammond's car, a bright red 1941 convertible Oldsmobile with leather upholstery and Hydromatic transmission, parked just inside the main gate.

Sergeant D'Amato stood with six members of the crew, about twenty feet forward of number-four engine. They stood, sweating in silence in their heavy flying clothes and parachute harnesses, staring up at the flight deck windows. They were too close for safety. Each of them felt the fear, but with two of their number still on the flight deck, none would either voice it or act on it. They were, thought D'Amato, playing hostage against the inevitable.

D'Amato looked up to see Major Caesar atop the fuselage. Silhouetted against the flames from the left wing, he was kneeling over the cockpit escape hatch. D'Amato stared dumbly, noting the unbleached area on Ceaser's khaki sleeve delineating the master-sergeant stripes that had been there until just a few months ago. The major, a frantic look on his face, turned, spotted D'Amato, and shouted incoherently.

The sergeant caught the word "ax." Coming alive, he grabbed one off a nearby fire truck. Wondering what Major Caesar intended to do with it, he scurried up the ladder. Before he got to the top, the engineering officer reached down, seized the ax, then disappeared down the hatch into the cockpit.

Atop the fuselage the heat was a palpable mass, a solid wall that brought D'Amato to his knees. Glancing over his shoulder, he inched back toward the ladder. Beyond the frantic activities of the firefighters, he could see Lieutenant Maguire seated on the rear bumper of one of the ambulances. The copilot was smoking a cigarette, watching the proceedings as if he were sitting in the stands at a ball game.

With his foot on the top rung of the ladder, Sergeant D'Amato hesitated, then wondered why. He was under no orders, and a smart GI never volunteered. Under such circumstances it was a soldier's duty to survive as best he could. He orchestrated his decision with a single four-letter word, then proceeded to struggle out of his heavy flying jacket. It was a mistake. The heat seemed even worse without its protective insulation. He draped himself over the top turret. Grasping the metal rim of the escape hatch for support, he leaned forward, peered downward.

Captain Hammond was seated almost directly below, his head thrown back, eyes closed tightly, his mouth frozen in a grimace. Sergeant Cohen's body rested on the control console, his head and shoulders hidden in the foot well. Major Caesar stood, the ax dangling from his left hand. He seemed unruffled, now, his tone conversational. "Sergeant, can you get him loose within the next minute?"

"I don't know." Cohen's words were tightly spaced, strained. "Maybe . . ."

"I figure, that's all you got—with luck, maybe two minutes."

Hammond's eyes opened. With his head tilted back on the seat, he stared up at D'Amato, whose head and shoulders filled the escape hatch. He said, "Oh, Jesus." Breathing heavily, he closed his eyes again. He was dripping sweat.

There was a sound of ripping metal. "I can see it now." Cohen's voice went hoarse, and he coughed. A thick curl of smoke was rising from the footwell. "The foot's twisted all the way around."

D'Amato got to his knees and turned to shout at some fireman involved with the nose section. "We need an extinguisher up here. Fast!"

He turned back to the hatch to find the cockpit filling with smoke. Hydraulic fluid was burning in the nose-wheel well just under the flight deck. Major Caesar had dropped the ax onto the deck and was leaning over the trapped pilot's shoulder, grasping his upper thigh. Cohen was kneeling with a firm grip on Hammond's calf. Cohen's right hand was bleeding. He counted aloud to three. Together the two men yanked sharply.

Captain Hammond's eyes shot open. His scream segued into an extended whimper.

They yanked again. This time Hammond merely grunted.

Because of the smoke, Sergeant D'Amato could see nothing now. A fireman kneeled next to him, shouting, "You guys get the hell out of there! She's going to blow any second!" There was a flickering orange glow, like a neon sign on a foggy night. The fireman leaned forward, squirting halon into the cockpit.

D'Amato's heart was pounding. He called out, "You dumb sons of bitches, get the fuck out of there . . . Cohen!"

Captain Hammond's voice was high-pitched, fighting for control. "It's hot . . . my foot. Oh, Christ, it's burning! My foot's on fire!" His scream, this time, was sustained.

"We're going to take his leg off." It was Major Caesar's voice. Cohen said, "Oh, shit."

"The ax, I left it . . . got it, okay . . ."

"There's no room down there to swing an ax," said Cohen, "I couldn't even use the metal cutters."

"Right, it'll have to be higher . . . here . . . the knee . . . just above the knee." Major Caesar coughed. "Hold him . . . his shoulders . . . We're going to have to chop at it."

"Got him."

"Oh God, I can't see!" Major Caesar broke out in a paroxysm of coughing.

The hatch was venting billows of caustic smoke. The halon was breaking down chemically into phosgene. Sergeant D'Amato had to turn away to breathe. The right wing was burning. Hammond was screaming. D'Amato reached down and grasped a handful of hair. A hand clasped his wrist. With the help of the fireman they pulled Major Caesar up onto the fuselage. He was drenched in sweat. His breathing was a series of deep wheezes. His eyes were closed tight, streaming tears. The fireman grasped the major under the arms, lowered him down the side into the arms of a couple of medics.

As D'Amato turned back to the hatch, there were two shots in quick succession. There was no mistaking the sound of a GI forty-five. Hammond's screams ended abruptly. With his eyes closed against the smoke, D'Amato reached down once again, grasped the collar of a flight jacket. Cohen emerged. They pulled him on top. His right leg was on fire. The streams of a half-dozen hoses converged, dousing the three men. Cohen was lowered to the ground. They were all running now, putting distance between themselves and the flaming wreck.

Less than a minute later, Cohen was in the ambulance. Face up on a stretcher, he was holding an oxygen mask to his face. The back door was still open. He felt a burst of heat as the right wing blew.

As they sped toward the infirmary, the MO slit open the right leg of Cohen's flight pants. One of the medics was dressing a mass of bloody cuts on the palm of his hand.

Breathing heavily, Cohen said, "How is it, Doc?"

The captain looked up at him. "These heavy pants, all this leather and sheepskin saved your ass, Sergeant—I mean literally."

"It sure hurts like hell."

"Yes, well, you'll be okay in a week or so." The captain loaded a morphine syringe "There are a few burns, mostly superficial. There'll be some scars, but nothing really disfiguring. You were lucky. Another few seconds . . ."

Maguire said, "I'm glad you made it, Cohen."

"Yeah."

"Just lie still, Sergeant," said Captain Colfax, injecting the morphine into Cohen's arm. "Easy does it."

Maguire said, "Tough about Captain Hammond."

"Thanks," said Cohen.

Maguire wondered what he was being thanked for. He said, "Poor bastard, but it was his own fault. I mean, there's a war on . . ."

Cohen was quiet for a few moments. Finally, he said, "Lieutenant?"

"Yeah?"

"Fuck you."

THE MISSION

August 1, 1943

A bout three and a half hours out from the Libyan coast, with the island of Corfu in view, the lead aircraft of the lead group of Operation Tidal Wave, Wingo Wango of the 513th Bomb Squadron, 376th Bombardment Group—the Liberandos—nosed up precipitously. In a matter of a few seconds, she stalled and fell off on her port wing. The airplanes in her immediate vicinity broke formation, spreading out to give her room as she proceeded into a series of descending gyrations like a roller coaster riding an invisible track.

Most of those observing the desperate phenomenon were at a loss as to the reason for it. A few thought the trouble might be due to a malfunctioning gyro in the C-1 autopilot. The C-1 had a reputation for unreliability. Many pilots refrained from using it.

For a moment it seemed as if Wingo Wango was under control, until, once more, her nose went up. The angle increased second by second till finally the airplane was literally standing motionless on her tail. Then, before the incredulous eyes of the 376th, she tumbled over onto her back and dove two thousand feet into the sea.

The entire phenomenon had lasted less than half a minute, and now Wingo Wango's memorial was a floating funeral pyre, punctuated with a black plume of smoke that billowed rapidly to over a thousand feet.

A wave of apprehension spread throughout the formation. Lost, along with Wingo Wango's entire crew, was the task force's lead navigator.

Despite standing orders against breaking ranks, a single B-24 turned and dropped down to check the area for survivors. There were none to be seen. It dropped a life raft, then attempted for fifteen minutes to climb back into the receding formation, only to find it an impossible task for an overloaded airplane. Finally, the would-be rescuer turned back, taking the force's deputy lead navigator back to Libya.

Leaderless and under orders to maintain radio silence, there was confusion in the ranks of A-Section. Then Brewery Wagon moved up to take over the lead. Route navigator for Operation Tidal Wave was now a nineteen-year old second lieutenant, talented, eager, but untested.

As the 376th crossed the coastline near the Greek-Albanian border, this incident, plus previous aborts and takeoff problems that had plagued the five groups, had reduced Operation Tidal Wave from the original 178 B-24s to 164.

The big map in the Otopenii war room showed the American force headed north, as reported by a ground spotter on the Island of Corfu. Captain Pitcairn chewed on the stub of an unlit cigar, visualizing the line extended on its current heading. It was a spear thrusting into central Austria. *Vienna.*

But Vienna was improbable. The Americans, unlike the British, had not as yet indulged themselves in terror attacks on cities. They preferred well-defined industrial objectives. Just to the south of Vienna was Weiner Neustadt, the Messerschmitt plant. If they didn't turn within the next hour, Pitcairn was certain that would be the target.

The large aircraft factory complex at Weiner Neustadt, with its large buildings concentrated in a small area, was ideal for the high-altitude daylight precision bombing on which the Americans prided themselves. Half of the Messerschmitt Bf 109 fighters were manufactured there. Its destruction could be a death blow to the Luftwaffe.

But then why the low-level practice missions in the desert? Weiner Neustadt hardly lent itself to such an approach.

For a moment, he considered Colonel Brayer's insistence on Ploesti. But the man was a music hall turn, a dedicated *schürzen-jäger* who used too much grease on his hair. Pitcairn shrugged it off. The Americans wouldn't dare. A low-level attack on the oil fields of Ploesti would be a death trap for them.

About halfway back in the 376th formation, in Teggie Ann, the mission commander, Brigadier General Ent, flying as a passenger, was wedged tightly into a makeshift seat behind the copilot, Captain Thompson, and the pilot, 376th Group Commander Colonel Compton.

Ent's field order, issued to all group and squadron commanders, had read, "The Ninth Air Force will attack and destroy the seven principal oil refineries in the Ploesti area on August 1, 1943, employing seven target forces in a minimum altitude attack, in order to deny the enemy use of the petroleum production processed in that area." Colonel "Killer" Kane, commander of the 98th in his group crew briefing, paraphrased it: "In other words, we're going to knock out Ploesti or die trying."

As the leading element of Tidal Wave neared the 8,000-foot mountain range in Albania, Teggie Ann moved forward to take over the lead position of the task force. The mountaintops were lost in cumulus towering to 15,000 feet. Colonel Compton decided to lead the 376th over the clouds. He waggled his wings to indicate a straight climb. Colonel Baker, in the lead ship of the Ninety-third Group, just behind Compton's 376th, shot off a flare to alert his force to the same decision. Both groups, on oxygen, holding perfect formation, climbed into the clear at 16,000 feet.

A few miles behind, "Killer" Kane, leading the 98th, decided otherwise. Some of his aircraft, in order to lighten ship, had dispensed with heavy oxygen equipment before takeoff, under the impression that it would not be needed on a low-level mission. A climb to high altitude was thus impossible. Instead, "Killer" Kane led the 98th through the clouds at 10,000 feet. The two trailing groups stayed with him. Because of the danger of collisions in zero visibility, they took the time and fuel to alter their tight defensive formation into one more suitable for penetrating deep clouds en masse.

The same was repeated over a mountain range in Yugoslavia. Here the two high groups, the 376th and 93rd, picked up a tail wind. By the time Teggie Ann descended into the valley leading to the Bulgarian border, the three trailing groups, led by Killer Kane, were sixty miles behind.

In the last B-24 of the trailing squadron of the 93rd—Ass End Charlie—the pilot queried his tail gunner, "Any sign of airplanes back there?"

"Just empty sky, sir."

"Where in hell are they?" The pilot slapped the control column in frustration. The orders mandating radio silence had been explicit. He could do nothing.

Atop the 7,500-foot Mount Cherin just south of Sofia, a German radar unit had cause to be exultant. A year earlier they had hauled, on their backs, a ton of equipment up to the pinnacle. Ever since, they had been living in a lofty isolation of misery and boredom. Nothing ever came their way.

Then suddenly their apathy was shattered as blips appeared on the face of their glowing Wurzburg. A large enemy force was crossing the Yugoslavian frontier into Bulgarian airspace. In moments the air defense circuits came alive. The eight men on the mountain grinned appreciatively at the melodic female tones of a dozen Luftnachrichtenhelferinnen acknowledging their call.

"Big Wings! Zone Twenty-four-East, Sector Eleven. Bearing thirty degrees!"

In the war room at Otopenii, Captain Pitcairn stared at the large map. The Americans had turned east. Brayer had been right. It was to be Ploesti. In an hour, the enemy would be overhead with their bomb doors open.

Fifteen minutes later, "Killer" Kane, leading three groups, came down from the mountains of Yugoslavia. Seeing no one in front of him, he assumed that somehow, inadvertently, he had taken over the lead of the entire mission. Another fifteen minutes were lost as he circled, waiting in vain for the two groups to catch up. In the process, the separation increased to almost a hundred miles.

Up ahead, the leaders, now over Bulgaria, flew blithely on, unaware that mission cohesion was irrevocably lost. The careful planning that would have put five groups over their targets simultaneously had been for nought. Operation Tidal Wave now consisted of two uncoordinated task forces that would hit the target separately at different times.

CHAPTER 5

MARCH 1942

Colonel Edward Greeves arrived at the base hospital with a photographer in tow. The colonel, at thirty-four, was the "old man," the commanding officer of the 287th Bombardment Group. He was tall, grossly elongated; an unstable structure, who, like a flawed military monument, was well rooted in an enormous pair of feet. He loomed over the hospital bed as a nurse jiggled the patient's shoulder to wake him.

Sergeant Abraham Cohen's eyes opened, wavered for a moment, and then, as if radar-guided, locked on the colonel's.

Colonel Greeves rewarded him with a stiff smile. "Thought I'd drop by to see how you're doing, Sergeant."

The sergeant nodded, raised his head to allow the nurse to plump his pillow.

"They treating you okay?"

Cohen, only half awake, nodded again. He sat up.

"Captain Colfax says you'll be out of here in a few days. Then we'll fix you up with a thirty-day furlough."

"Thank you, sir."

Colonel Greeves prided himself on being able to read a man's character at first glance. He ascribed to a theory of physiognomy in which a person's character or temperament was accurately projected by his outward physical appearance. Thus, the colonel was impressed with Sergeant Abraham Cohen who possessed a straight nose, angled at an ideal 140 degrees, and a forehead that was considerably furrowed for someone his age. A strong jaw and bushy eyebrows reinforced Greeves's positive assessment. There was no doubt, therefore, that Cohen was resolute, sensitive, intellectual. But it was the sergeant's eyes that impressed Colonel Greeves most of all. Deep, penetrating, unwavering, they indicated honesty, forthrightness, and strength of character. The man was obviously officer material; a throwback, concluded the colonel, who prided himself on being a biblical scholar, to the small, ancient band of Hebrew warriors who had fought the massive Roman legions to a standstill.

Cohen said, "How's Major Caesar?"

"He's okay. But he inhaled a lot of smoke, and a little phosgene from those damned Halon extinguishers, so it'll be a few weeks before they let him go. God knows we need him." Colonel Greeves folded himself into a chair by the bed. "I'm recommending Major Caesar for the Distinguished Service Cross." He offered Cohen a long Pall Mall, flicked a silver Ronson. "He's already got a DSC from the last war, but an oak-leaf cluster will look handsome on the ribbon. And Sergeant D'Amato is up for the Soldier's Medal."

Over the lighter flame, Cohen's deep-set eyes bored into those of the colonel. "Frank D'Amato will sure appreciate it, sir. It'll look nice next to his Good Conduct ribbon."

Greeves wondered briefly whether Cohen was being a wise guy, but he let it pass. He said, "I'm sure he'll have a few rows of ribbons before this thing is over. We all will." He gestured over his shoulder to the photographer. Sergeant Cohen, seeming to be sitting at attention, said nothing. Colonel Greeves was beginning to find his rigid behavior irritating. He said, "There's something nice in the works for you, too . . ."

There was no response from Cohen, not even the flicker of an eyelid. The colonel felt foolish, wondering what to say next. He was getting weary of maintaining incessant eye contact. He broke it off; allowed his awkward smile to die, transforming his demeanor into one of labored seriousness. It was the moment of truth. He said, "You're being recommended for the Distinguished Service Cross. That's the second-highest honor our country confers on its heros. Had this been a combat situation, I personally would have been proud to recommend you for the Medal of Honor. You deserve it."

Cohen's eyes closed in a sustained blink. It was, thought the colonel, hardly the excited reaction he had anticipated. But at least it indicated that the ungrateful son of a bitch had heard him. Perhaps now was the time to pile it on. "The 415th squadron needs an engineering officer. You're it. You'll be getting a field commission to captain. Since you're regular army, that means a permanent rank of first lieutenant."

The photographer, raising the Speed Graphic to his eye, said, "Look this way, Sergeant." Cohen grabbed a current copy of *Collier's* from his night table and held it in front of his face. He was just in time.

Colonel Greeves, fighting down a rush of irritation, took his time. In a tight voice he said, "What the hell's that all about?"

"I don't want my picture taken, sir."

"Take another one, Corporal."

The photographer ejected the old flashbulb, popped in another; reversed the holder, pulled the slide, cocked the shutter. Cohen held *Collier's* at the ready, saying, "There's nothing in the general orders, sir, that says I have to pose for pictures."

"I could give you a direct order, Sergeant."

"I'd disobey it, sir." Cohen stiffened. "And I don't want the medal."

Colonel Greeves suddenly understood. His expression softened. He waved off the photographer. He said, "Ah, you mean you think you don't deserve it, right?" He smiled sympathetically. "That sort of thing is to be expected; the modest reaction of a true hero." He blew a puff of smoke out through his nostrils. "I'm sure many before you have felt the same way. It's understandable that you're a little overwhelmed." The colonel laid a hand on Cohen's shoulder. "Anyway, it's not for you to judge. In my eyes, you committed the single most courageous act I've ever personally witnessed. And the four officers whose depositions are on my desk at this very moment, they feel the same way. If D'Amato and that fireman hadn't pulled you out of that airplane this decoration would have been posthumous. You would have been cinders—thirty seconds. So don't let it worry you. You deserve it, believe me."

"No, sir, that's not it, I'm sure I deserve the medal. I just don't want it."

"Enough of that, Sergeant, you made your point."

"No, I don't think I have, sir."

"You serious?"

"Yes, sir.'

"You don't know what you're saying." The colonel rose to his massive feet. "If something is bothering you, let's deal with it."

"What the hell difference does it make, sir? I mean Captain Hammond is dead. I blew his head off with his bombardier's GI automatic. My wearing a ribbon on my blouse won't bring him back to life."

"I see. So that's what's bothering you. I think that maybe you need a nice long talk with the chaplain."

"No thanks."

Colonel Greeves looked down on Cohen from a great height. His Adam's apple bobbed twice in quick succession. "Captain Colfax said nothing about you suffering any head injuries, but I can't imagine any other reason for your attitude."

"I'm fine."

"Like hell you are, Sergeant." Colonel Greeves felt a rush of anger. He tried to control it, then gave up the effort. "You're suffering from shock or something. You don't need a chaplain, you need a goddamned psychiatrist! And worse, you're preventing the 287th from receiving a high honor even before we go into combat. Where's your loyalty, soldier? Do you know what that means to the group?"

"I'm sorry."

"Sorry my ass! No one turns down the Distinguished Service Cross! Who in the hell do you think you are? You're insulting the memories of all the men who gave their lives for it!" He paused, breathing heavily, allowing the acid tones of disdain to replace those of outrage. "I would just like to know why. Is it against your religion or something?"

"Maybe it is."

"Bullshit. Other Jews have received this award. You go around talking crap like that and you're going to turn perfectly normal people into anti-Semites."

"Don't put me in for it, sir. And I don't want a commission. I mean, if it's okay, a promotion to tech sergeant would be nice. The extra stripe would give me twenty bucks more a month."

* * *

Colonel Greeves picked up the phone. It was Ralph Willets, squadron commander of the 514th squadron.

"I got a little problem."

"What is it, Ralph?"

"Maguire, he was Hammond's copilot. I raised him to pilot's status, assigned him one of the new airplanes."

"Okay, so if you don't think he has it, bust him back to copilot. We've got plenty of pilots, it's airplanes we need."

"No, it's not that. I checked him out personally. He's an okay pilot. But he came in to see me this afternoon to request I take Sergeant Cohen off his crew."

"Oh Christ, what now . . . ?"

"He doesn't want any Jews on his crew, says it would be divisive."

"That son of a bitch!"

"I mean with Cohen up for a big decoration and a field commision and all that, I thought I'd better kick the decision up to you."

"There ain't going to be no goddamned decoration, Ralph. And you tell that prick lieutenant that he's stuck with Cohen. They deserve each other!"

THE MISSION

AUGUST 1, 1943

Teggie Ann, setting the course for the two groups in the lead, turned a few degrees right at Pitesti, the first initial point. She descended to one hundred feet to fly onward through a series of rain flurries.

Finally, General Ent, standing on Teggie Ann's flight deck, stared down at the village just beneath them and flicked on his throat mike to speak on the airplane's interphone. "Okay, this is Floresti. The railroad's up ahead . . . there it is." A tight grin of satisfaction lit his face. Another right turn along the railroad would put them onto their bomb-run heading. Everything was going perfectly. Not a single enemy shot had been fired at them. They were on the button, as planned.

In the general's headset, the navigator's tone was strident, the tempo of his words emphatic. "We still have about twenty miles to the Floresti initial point . . . This isn't it, sir! This is Targovisti!"

General Ent looked again out the right window. He was sure he was right, certain they had overflown Tragovesti during the last rain squall. The general frowned. Teggie Ann's navigator was a kid, still wet behind the ears, an inexperienced shavetail. The general tapped Colonel Compton on the shoulder. "Keith?"

"I'm with you, General. It's Floresti."

They were close enough to the target now to break radio silence. The general said, "Order a right turn along the railroad."

The flagship turned as the order went out. The formation

turned behind her, following the leader. There was an immediate, simultaneous response by a half-dozen excited pilots over the now-open command channel,

"Wrong turn!"

"Mistake—mistake!"

"We're turning too soon!"

"Not here, goddammit!"

"This isn't it!"

It was too late. Those who realized the error were hemmed in by the tight formation. Only Brewery Wagon was able to break loose and overfly what the pilot knew to be Tragovesti. He continued on the proper, briefed heading to Floresti.

The general was shaken, but the commitment had been made. At an altitude of a hundred feet, the lead elements of Tidal Wave shot through another rain flurry into an all-pervasive purple haze that reduced visibility to less than five miles.

Minutes later General Ent and Colonel Compton lost all doubt as to their error. Had they made the turn at Floresti, they would be over the target. Instead, they could see it on their left, brooding on the horizon under dirty white clouds of defensive smoke. Up ahead, the spires of Bucharest were emerging from the haze.

General Ent weighed his options. There were two. The first of these was to wheel the entire formation back onto its original course in order to attack the target from the northwest, as briefed. But to execute such a corrective turn was a complex maneuver that would surely result in scattered aircraft, possibly collisions.

The second option would have him leading the formation in a simple turn to the left in order to attack the target from the south. However, the original planning had dictated an assault from the northwest because of the perception that the enemy would least expect it from that direction. Since the southern approach was the most direct it was therefore the most obvious and would certainly be the most heavily defended. There would also be a problem with target identification. There had been no aircrew briefings on an approach from the south. The great difference in angle of attack would render most of the individually assigned targets unrecognizable to pilots and bombardiers.

As General Ent agonized over the decision the interphone came alive.

"Tail gunner to pilot . . . the Ninety-third has bandits!"

"How many?"

"I count two . . . no, three. They're attacking the ass end of the formation!"

"What about the other groups?"

"What other groups?"

"Beyond the Ninety-third."

"There's nothing back there."

"Take a good look, Sergeant."

"Nothing . . ."

"Pilot to top turret . . . What about you? You see 'em?"

"Just the Ninety-third."

"There's supposed to be four groups back there!"

"There's only one."

"No pink airplanes?"

"All green, about thirty."

"This is General Ent. Were they with us before we turned east?"

"No way, sir . . . those other three groups haven't been with us since the mountains."

"Pilot to crew. Why the hell didn't one of you say something?"

"There's a B-24 smoking . . . she's climbing . . . someone's getting out—three—four chutes!"

"There goes another one out the nose wheel hatch!"

"She's burning! Jesus! C'mon, you guys!"

"Okay. Cut the chatter."

"The Ninety-third's turning!"

"The whole group's turning left!"

Major Brayer hit the red button to activate the air raid alarms in Bucharest. He alerted flak installations in the area immediately south of Ploesti in case the enemy turned. That done, he turned abruptly to Captain Pitcairn, who was staring down intently at the Wurzburg scope. "Why the city?"

"They've split up," said Pitcairn. "Half of the force just turned north toward the refineries."

"Ah, I see," said Major Brayer. "Bucharest's a diversion." He pulled on his ear. It didn't make sense.

"Brilliant planning," said Pitcairn. "The bombers over the city will draw off a good portion of the fighter defense, while the rest of them hit the real target."

"But they've too small a force to split."

Pitcairn seemed not to hear him. "The aircraft making for Bucharest will probably hold their bombs, swing over the city, and attack the oil fields from the west. A two-pronged attack."

"Only sixty, seventy bombers." said Brayer. "Barely enough for even one prong."

Pitcairn was staring at the big map. There were new markings: three red circles at Lom, just across the frontier in Bulgarian air space. They indicated that an even larger force than the earlier one was approaching on the same heading. He called Brayer's attention to them. "That looks like the main element. There's now enough for a three-pronged attack." He checked the Wurzburg again. A scattering of blips was coming to life on the edge of the scope. He said, "Radar shows them further along; south of Pitesti, about thirty minutes from the target. My guess is they'll turn east at Floresti."

"Interesting tactic," said Brayer, staring at the radar scope. But he wasn't sure. By splitting their attacking force into three parts, each attacking from a different heading, they would indeed, as Pictairn pointed out, also split the German and Rumanian fighter defense, lessening its effectiveness. But at low altitude, the greatest danger to the bombers was flak, not fighters. As flak officer, he knew that a single massive low-level formation could overwhelm the antiaircaft defenses, whereas an attack by three smaller units, coming in at different times, could be cold meat for the flak gunners. Surely the Americans knew this, too. He picked up the phone, passed the order to alert his flak gunners in the Ploesti area to expect separate attacks from three different directions. Then to Pitcairn, "I think the enemy has somehow made a terrible mistake."

Captain Pitcairn ignored the remark. He used the red phone to order half the Luftwaffe fighter reserves to Floresti and the other half to a line: Floresti–Brazi. The Rumanian Air Force could defend Bucharest if they chose. His job was to defend the oil fields.

* * *

In Teggie Ann, Colonel Compton glanced down at the rooftops of Bucharest as he turned left to lead the 376th almost due north. He planned another left at Brazi, which would bring the group over Ploesti from the southeast.

In the near distance, both he and the general could see, on a parallel course, the 93rd, which had split off just minutes before. The 93rd's green airplanes raced through the valley a few feet above fields of corn, wheat, and alfalfa, under intense antiaircraft fire. Beyond them he could make out a large number of small flyspecks turning in toward the target—enemy fighters.

A B-24, with two engines blazing, nosed up in what was obviously an attempt by the pilot to gain enough altitude to allow his crew to bail out. Two chutes emerged as the airplane fell off on one wing to create a lake of fire in the midst of a wheat field. The general watched, his heart sinking as the two parachutes drifted like moths into the flames. Almost simultaneously another B-24 lost half a wing to an explosive charge attached to a barrage balloon cable. A third, like a grounded comet, skidded through the ripe wheat, throwing off flaming bits and pieces of itself. The 93rd was flying through the valley of death.

Then Teggie Ann, having overflown the outskirts of Bucharest, turned left to find itself in the same valley. Compton took her down to the deck at full throttle. The 376th followed. The landscape in front of them was punctuated with flak towers and barrage balloons. Glowing balls of tracer, from guns of every caliber, crisscrossed their path. The flagship shuddered from the heavy chatter of fifty-caliber Brownings as her gunners dueled with the German and Rumanian antiaircraft crews.

Now General Ent could see the 93rd flying into the guns of Ploesti as it overflew the town to hit a refinery target just to its north. A wingless B-24, like some monstrous truck, was skidding down what looked to be the main boulevard. A second, mortally wounded, flew into a three-story brick building—the women's prison—entombing itself in the wreckage. The ensuing holocaust, fueled by a few thousand gallons of hundred-octane aviation fuel, incinerated one hundred inmates in their cells: shoplifters, prostitutes, political critics of the fascist Antonesqu government, farmgirls convicted of watering milk.

The general stared ahead into the mayhem, realizing that on

their current heading, there was little chance of reaching the 376th's assigned target: White One, the Romana Americana refinery, and if they did, there was even less chance of recognizing it from their unbriefed angle of approach. Without further thought, he turned to the radio desk to open the group frequency. He breathed deeply, saying, "This is General Ent. We have missed our target. You are all cleared to strike targets of your choice."

At about the same time that the remnants of the 93rd were hitting their target of opportunity, the 376th came apart. The months of planning and weeks of intensive training were out the window as small groups of aircraft struck out on their own, seeking, as had the 93rd, targets of opportunity. What had started as a well-planned, intensely rehearsed operation descended into chaos.

CHAPTER 6

JULY 1942

Master Sergeant Samuel Fibich stood atop the engine stand, sweating in the hot Florida sun. He and Corporal Quinn, one of his mechanics, were finishing their inspection of number-two engine when he spotted a jeep carrying two officers coming down the line. He hoped it had nothing to do with him.

He wanted to be left alone to work on his airplane. He had been at it for six hours. He was tired. It wasn't like the old days. The army had put weight on Sergeant Fibich. He had a gut. He was flabby, out of shape, carrying forty-five excess pounds.

Twenty-seven years earlier, during the first war, when he transferred from the cavalry into the Army Air Service, he had weighed in at a mere 155. Slim and handsome, he captivated a dozen mademoiselles in the vicinity of the First Aero Squadron base at Saintes. He had long since forgotten the names of the ladies, but he still remembered the French nomenclature of all of the parts that went into the marvelous 135-horsepower V-8 Hispano-Suiza engine that powered the squadron's Spad XIII biplanes.

Later it was the Keystone Bomber and then his favorite, the pretty little Boeing P-12 pursuit, the last of the army's biplanes. In the middle thirties he tended the Air Corps' first all-metal monoplane, the Boeing P-26, "Pea Shooter," a production aircraft that looked and flew as if it had been built for the Cleveland Air Races. Then, up until two years ago, he had crew-chiefed a blue-and-orange twin-engined Martin B-10B. For a year of two it was considered the most advanced bomber of its day, able to outrun most contemporary fighters. It became totally obsolete in four years. He had heard that a few of them were caught on the ground by the Japs at Hickam Field.

Next was the B-18, a potbellied bomber version of the Douglas DC-3 that exhibited few of the stirling attributes of its civilian cousin. Now it was the B-24 and its four big Pratt and Whitney engines. It was a generation ahead of any other bomber in the sky, surpassing, in range and bomb-load capacity, the glamour-girl B-17 Flying Fortress.

After twenty-five years, he was still having love affairs with airplanes, but the B-24 would probably be his last. He was a thirty-year man with only two more to go; then he, too, would be obsolete—retired.

Sam Fibich thought of airplanes as some thought of thorough-bred horses. In action they were all individuals with dissimilar personalities. Even two identical aircraft rolling off the assembly line within minutes of each other could display distinctly different characteristics. Aviation was still as much an instinctive art as it was a science. But there were already signs that soon would change and everything would be done by the numbers. Happily, by then, he would be long gone. Master Sergeant Fibich was an artist. There weren't many left.

Above all, to those who understood them, airplanes, like thor-oughbreds, demanded respect. The lack of respect could turn even the gentlest, most responsive aircraft into a high-strung, can-tankerous creature which, when in the hands of an insensitive— or worse—an uncaring pilot or ground crew, could be just as dangerous as a squadron of enemy fighters.

The jeep pulled up to park in the shade of the wing. There were two second lieutenants. The "fifty-mission-crush" in their garrison caps indicated they were pilots.

The driver disembarked, stood, hands on hips, looking up. He called out, "Sergeant, this number thirty-four?"

"Yes sir. They'll be painting the number on tomorrow,"

"Then it's my airplane. You the crew chief?"

Fibich grunted. They always thought it was their airplane. He said, "Master Sergeant Samuel Fibich, sir."

"I'm Lieutenant Maguire." He gestured toward the figure in the jeep, "Second Lieutenant Deutsch, my copilot."

Fibich turned to Quinn. Quietly, he said, "Put the cowling back and start on number three." He climbed down.

Lieutenant Maguire said, "How is she, Sergeant?"

"She's brand-new. Came in this morning with two lady drivers, fresh from the factory. She has just under fifteen hours logged flying time." Fibich wiped his hands on a greasy rag stuffed in the back pocket of his coveralls.

"Terrific," said Maguire. "I want to do a check-out flight later this afternoon."

"Sorry, sir. No can do."

"What the hell you talking about, Sergeant? I've been assigned this airplane."

"Sir, nobody flies it unless I release it."

"I say I want to fly it, I fly it."

"No, sir. When this airplane is on the ground it's my baby, my responsibility. Not even General Hap Arnold starts up the engines until I give the word." Sam Fibich folded his arms across his chest. "You have any trouble with that, you can speak to the engineering officer, sir."

Lieutenant Maguire seemed about to speak when Lieutenant Deutsch interrupted. "Is something wrong with it?"

"So far," said Sergeant Fibich, "we've had an overspeeding turbo on number-one engine and a screwed-up carburetor on the auxiliary generator. The armament shop found the bomb racks wired in reverse, a bad amplydine generator on the top turret, and the guns ain't been bore-sighted. Sheet Metal has a whole shitpot of their own modifications, and Instruments is going to have to replace the fluxgate compass gyro. We've got the usual hydraulic leaks, stripped threads, missing cotter pins and lock washers, and we've only been at it for a couple hours. I got two more engines to check and a whole lot of other stuff."

"Sounds like a lemon," said Deutsch.

"No," said Fibich. "Just par for the course."

Lieutenant Maguire said, "Okay. How long will it be?"

"Depends on what else we find, sir."

"I mean, a day—two days?"

"Beats the shit out of me, Lieutenant. I ain't through checking, and there are other departments involved. Just keep an eye on the ready chart in operations."

"Christ . . ."

Lieutenant Deutsch, bending to look under the aircraft, said, "Hey, we got us a belly turret."

"Sperry ball turret," said Sergeant Fibich. "First one in the squadron."

Maguire said, "Drag . . ."

"Yeah," said Sergeant Fibich. "From what I hear, when it's extended, you lose maybe ten miles an hour."

"And the weight? I mean with the ammo, the extra gunner."

"We're taking out the waist armor plate to compensate. They tried it over at the 412th and it worked fine."

"Who dreamed that one up?"

"Sam Caesar. He says the protection you gain from the armor plate back there you lose because of the possibility of ricochets. Makes sense. That particular armor plate is facing the wrong way—fore and aft. You get flak bouncing off it can rattle around inside the airplane forever."

"Any other modifications?"

"The bomb-door interlock switches. Major Caesar ordered them removed. If the bomb doors get hung up, you just drop the bombs right through them."

"Through the doors?"

"Yes, sir. Once we're overseas, in combat, there'll be no sense flying all the way to the target then bringing back all your bombs because of a lousy fifty-cent switch. It'll keep the sheet metal shop busy making new doors, but what the hell, there's a war on." Fibich took a plug of chewing tobacco from his breast pocket, bit off a chunk. "We're also installing electronic supercharger controllers and new-type nose-wheel shimmy dampers."

"Sounds like you're rebuilding the airplane."

"Not quite. Just a few improvements."

"Well, I hope everybody knows what they're doing."

"I do." Fibich spat a long stream of tobacco juice over his shoulder. "I've been doing it for twenty-five years, Lieutenant. I'm the best there is. I've lost a couple airplanes, but never due to faulty maintenance. You just fly her and leave the rest to me."

Maguire, looking down at the crew chief's hands, paused for a moment. "Yeah, we'll see, Sergeant."

Lieutenant Deutsch said, "Let's go up on the flight deck."

"Go ahead," said Maguire. "I'll be there in a minute."

Sergeant Fibich said, "Don't turn on any switches, sir."

They both watched as the copilot ducked into the bomb bay.

Maguire said, "We got a squadron artist for a little nose art, Sergeant?"

"PFC Charlie Gordon. You want me to hire him?"

"Yes. I want a woman pulling a wagon with a bomb in it." He handed Fibich a photograph. "I want it to look just like her, and I don't want any of that Petty Girl, *Esquire* stuff. No bathing suit, no tight sweater or bare boobs or any of that crap. Good taste, skirt below the knee. Understood?"

"Roger." The crew chief smiled for the first time. It was ten bucks in his pocket. He said, "PFC Gordon charges thirty-five dollars."

"Fine. And we're going to call her Sally's Wagon, in big blue letters."

Later, atop the hardstand, Corporal Quinn said, "You straightened out his ass, Sergeant."

"I've been doing it for a long time, Quinn. The airplanes have changed, but the pilots are the same. These guys are no different from the ones in 1917. Volunteers. They're here because they want to be. They're crazy and they're young and two thirds of the poor bastards will be dead before it's all over. Guaranteed."

THE MISSION

AUGUST 1, 1943

The air, agitated by a few hundred propellers, was a palpable, churning mass. Sally's Wagon, at the rear of the 287th, stumbled through the rutted slipstream, wallowing like a small, unstable boat in a following sea. Maguire had been at it for over six hours, exerting constant pressure on the controls in an unceasing effort to keep the aircraft straight and level. There were at least seven more hours to go before they would be home. His back was hurting. He gestured to his copilot, Second Lieutenant Jordan Deutsch, to take over the rudder pedals so he could straighten his legs to relieve cramped calf muscles. He clicked on his throat mike. "Everybody stay sharp. The Three Seventy-sixth and Ninety-third are supposed to be up ahead of the Ninety-eighth. Any of you eagle eyes see them?"

There was no reply. Up top, in the tight confines of the upper gun turret, Cohen strained his eyes. Only the desert-pink birds of the 98th preceded his own group. Beyond that, the sky was clear all the way to the horizon. Something had gone wrong. There were two groups missing, almost seventy airplanes.

Cohen's ears told him that they were letting down rapidly. He fumbled for his canteen. The Egyptian rum tasted metallic. He swallowed quickly, taking a perverse pleasure in the shudder that passed through his body. Booze was much more effective at high altitudes while breathing pure oxygen—more bang for the buck. But now they were on the deck, under a hundred feet in an airplane conceived and built to function at altitudes over 20,000.

Cohen twisted the control handles, spinning the top turret to survey 360 degrees of green, gently rolling, Rumanian country-side. The farmland, the golden fields of wheat, the neat villages and tree-lined roads could have been in the Midwest.

Always in the past, the enemy, from four miles up, had been invisible, lost in an impersonal, small-scale map. But now Sally's Wagon seemed to be moving through the countryside rather than above it, much like a train. Cohen loved trains. Unlike airplanes, their passage was preordained, their rhythm invoked a cadence for one's imagination. Airplanes were noisy, shuddering, unreliable brutes, engaged in a relentless struggle to remain disconnected from the earth.

They were up and over a rise in the landscape; revealed seventy-five feet below was the village of Pitesti, their first initial point in Rumania. It was a neat, well-ordered, Lionel-electric-train town with little houses nestled in groves of trees.

A military band played in the town square. Small groups of startled people gaped upward. A woman threw a colorful apron up over her head, an elderly couple knelt in prayer, a group of soldiers bearing long, awkward rifles that looked to be from World War I took hasty aim to fire into the air.

Just outside town, a farmer threw rocks at the aerial intruders, while another dove under a hay cart. Its horse bolted, exposing the terrified man face-down on the dusty road.

There was laughter on the interphone; then Junior Darling was singing. The crew joined in a tinny chorus—"Rose of San Antonio."

Sally's Wagon seemed in the grip of a peculiar euphoria. The mission was proving to be a milk run, a pleasant outing in the country.

At 220 miles an hour, the 287th executed a shallow right turn into the valley toward the town of Targoviste. To the left an aimlessly meandering brook widened into a small lake.

Someone called out, "Women . . . ten o'clock, low!" A trio of young females, wearing bathing suits, stood knee-deep in the water. They were waving, probably, thought Cohen, in response to

D'Amato in the left waist window. Immediately, the interphone came alive with lewd anatomical appreciations of the enemy. Yardbird Smith threatened to bail out. The girls receded quickly into tiny dots and were gone.

The 287th raced through the valley. With his head nestled between twin fifty-caliber Browning machine guns, Cohen surveyed the sky through the Plexiglas dome, wondering about the lack of enemy fighters and antiaircraft fire. Less than a mile behind them was the 389th dressed in the drab green of the Eighth Air Force. Up ahead were the desert-pink aircraft of "Killer" Kane's 98th. The 93rd and 376th were still nowhere to be seen.

They were nearing the target after having flown more than thirteen hundred miles, half of it over enemy territory. Until now the only opposition had been from an old man throwing stones and two soldiers firing at them with ancient bolt-action rifles. It was all too good to be true. Perhaps—miracle of miracles—the low-level ploy to sneak in under the German radar had been successful.

Cohen checked his watch, observing only the second hand. He had no interest in the actual time but only in the rate of its passing. He felt he had the power to will the hand slower or faster; to delay the inevitable or conversely to speed things up and get them over with. He took another swig from the canteen, but a decision eluded him. He watched for a moment as the 389th, behind them, banked left toward their target, the Steaua Romana Refinery, at Campina.

The 287th and 98th bomb groups overflew Targoviste, the second initial point, as briefed. The group's four squadrons broke up into elements of four to six airplanes, each committed to a specific target. There were five others in Sally's element. The aircraft on either side were tucked in tightly: on Sally's left was the flight leader, Betty Boop, with Colonel Greeves in the right seat; then Sassy Suzy and Watermelon Man. Orange Crate and Chloe were on her right.

Farm buildings and haystacks dotted the landscape. They initiated a right turn, exactly as briefed. Up ahead, a goods train trailed a streamer of black smoke. The village of Floresti, the third I.P., lay fifty feet beneath them. As they banked to the right, Cohen could make out, in the distance, a dirty white smudge that was the enemy smokescreen over the refineries of Ploesti. The navigation had been on the nose. They were just where they were supposed to be.

CHAPTER 7

JULY 1943

She stepped out of the olive-drab ambulance that served as her private dressing room. Jack was beginning the show, warming up the audience. Cheers, whistles, and laughter filled the desert night. She turned to stare out at the Mediterranean. A dozen date palms, backlit with the golden light of a rising full moon, lined the shore. Three nights ago she had been viewing a similar scene in Florida. But these stars were much more profuse. As seen through the pure desert air they filled the sky, millions of them. Africa.

They had flown ten thousand miles in a big, brand-new, four-engined Army Air Transport Command airplane featuring seats that made up into Pullman berths. Palm Beach to Caracas, Venezuela; Caracas to Belém, Brazil; Belém to a tiny island in mid-South Atlantic called Ascension; an isolated, barren stopover for airplanes and for thousands of migrating birds. Then from Ascension to Abidjan on the Ivory Coast, and from there, via a Pan American survey station in French Equatorial Africa, to an RAF base at Khartoum, in the Anglo-Egyptian Sudan—all places she had never heard of. From Khartoum it was a matter of a few hours to Cairo and then west to Benghazi.

There were nine passengers aboard the DC-4: her USO troupe of six, a lieutenant general from the judge advocate's office, his aide, and a young *Life* photographer named Frank Howard.

She played gin, drank scotch, took pictures out the window, visited the flight deck to flirt with the four crew members, and on the second night out, as the airplane droned twenty thousand feet over the South Atlantic, she went to bed with Frank Howard. It was a straightforward seduction on his part, aided and abetted by a bottle of New York State champagne. She made it easy for him. There was, noted Frank Howard in a whisper, barely enough room for the two of them plus the bottle in the tiny berth.

The following morning, as the passengers were seated in the lounge breakfasting on powdered eggs and coffee, the young pilot, Lieutenant Crawford, saluted smartly and presented her and Frank Howard with ornately engraved certificates of membership in the Mile High Club. Her immediate reaction was one of flushed embarrassment, but in a matter of moments she found herself laughing along with the others. What the hell, there was a war on.

Out of Abidjan, she remained glued to her window, floating in a cool euphoria orchestrated by the steady drone of the engines. Sipping scotch, she stared down into the deep, sunlit green of the jungle. She played at swinging through the forest in Tarzan's muscular arms. Dozing, off and on, she was amused with the idea of being the glamorous other woman in the ape-man's life while plain Jane was little more than a housewife confined to the arboreal nest. *Tarzan's Great Love.* She, Bonnie Astor, would star in it. It would be a musical. Technicolor.

By afternoon, the forest had begun to thin out into a vast savannah inhabited by herds of elephants and wildebeest. Lieutenant Crawford descended to six thousand feet in order to improve the sightseeing. She trained the general's field glasses on a family of lions refreshing themselves at a water hole. It was all part of a reality she had trouble accepting. The real context for such visual experiences was the Fairmount Park Zoo.

She had always wanted to be a singer. As a little girl, she had imitated the voice of Helen Morgan as played on her mother's Victrola. Later there were voice lessons and other singers to emulate: Lee Wiley, for her way with a lyric; Ella Fitzgerald, for her tonality; Lady Day, for everything.

She quit college to sing with a local band—fourteen men and a girl. It was a Philadelphia regional band, featuring "shuffle-rhythm" swing. They played proms and ballrooms, like the dance shell at Willow Grove Amusement Park. Later it was New York and a gig with the house band at Leon and Eddie's, on Fifty-second Street. And now she was in Africa on the bill with a real star. Africa. It was a marvelous dream, as unreal as the lions.

She awakened as the DC-4 was banking into its base leg for a landing at the Pan Am survey station. A steel mat landing strip and a trio of Quonset huts squatted in the middle of nowhere, the sole human punctuation on a flat, scrubby wasteland extending to the horizon in all directions. Here and there the tortured grotesquery of a large, twisted tree basked in the brilliant sunlight. There was nothing else. As described by Lieutenant Crawford, the place was occupied by a half-dozen native workers and a half-mad Australian station chief named Cliff Dawson. Norm Levine, their accordionist, compared the station to an isolated gas stop on Route 66 in the Arizona desert. She redid her makeup and fluffed her hair, hoping for a shower and an ice chest filled with Cokes.

They taxied off the runway, cut the engines. It looked hot. Someone said they were only ten degrees north of the Equator. She wondered how many miles that represented. She watched as a group of native workers wheeled a Pan Am boarding ramp across the tarmac. In a swirl of dust, a jeep reeled into view to brake sharply just aft of the trailing edge of the wing. A tall, blond-bearded man unfolded from it.

Despite the heat, he was dressed in a decrepit leather jacket, a silk ascot, a pair of khaki shorts, and tennis shoes. His left eye was concealed behind a black eye patch. His legs were scrawny, a disappointment.

His glance swept by, as if he were searching the airplane windows for a familiar face. Then, in an almost comic double take, he turned to look at her. Raising her hand in a friendly greeting, she smiled at him through the window. He remained frozen in place, leaning against the jeep, an incredulous, single eye locked on her face.

Finally, as the cabin door was being opened, he grinned, touching the peak of a battered yachting cap in a casual but gallant salute.

She managed to be the last passenger to leave the aircraft, hesitating at the door to make sure she would have the ramp to herself. He stood below, making a visual feast of her descent. At the bottom he blocked the way, grasped her hand, surveyed her intently from top to bottom. "Almost forgot what you people look like. Sorry miss, I'm a bit surprised to find that women really do exist. I thought it was a false memory."

She laughed. "Poor guy."

"Would you consider doing a small favor for a well-meaning stranger . . . I mean, by way of a charitable act?"

"Try me."

"Well, the front configuration confirms my recollection, but I'm less sure of the rear . . . I mean the back."

She turned a graceful pirouette.

"Thank you, ma'am." With a show of sincerity, he took her hand. "I was right, my faulty memory does womankind an injustice. I'm the station manager, Clifford Dawson, at your service."

"Bonnie Astor," she said, attracted by his air of amiable dissipation. "Is there anything else I can do for you?"

His smile was engaging. "Not at the moment, Miss Astor, but please keep in touch."

She accompanied the other passengers into the relative coolness of a double Quonset hut that bore a hand-written sign identifying it as the Mongoro Ritz. They were each assigned a tiny room and then, according to "hotel rules," were permitted a three-minute shower of cold water pumped by a native from a barrel outside the hut.

She changed into a crisply starched khaki uniform, then joined the others in a large partitioned area—the "lounge"—at one end of the Quonset. It was furnished in decrepit rattan and equipped with a bar, a pair of ceiling fans, a GI Hallicrafter shortwave receiver, and a phonograph. Unlike the water, there was no shortage of scotch.

Dinner consisted of breaded Spam and something that was vaguely reminiscent of sweet potatoes. It was washed down with warm Schlitz. Dawson explained that the beer was from one of four crates just unloaded from the cargo hold of the airplane. Lieutenant Crawford flew in supplies on a regular basis. The current delivery had included scotch whisky, fresh eggs, coffee, condensed milk, canned vegetables, Heinz catsup, New Zealand canned butter, quart bottles of Schlitz and Bud, Chesterfields, and phonograph records.

She danced in turn with each of the men to the slow-tempo

strains of Glenn Miller records. Cliff Dawson was last. She placed her hand on the back of his neck, humming the melody to "Careless" into his ear while he held her close and made no effort to conceal the graphic evidence of his need.

Later, as they lay perspiring on his rumpled bed, exhaling smoke into the slowly revolving ceiling fan, he said, "I've never made love to a woman in uniform before."

"But I'm out of uniform."

"Thank God for that," he said, running a finger down the valley between her breasts. "What does USO mean?"

"United Services Organization. I entertain the troops."

"And a smashing fine job you do of it."

"I sing."

"And the other blokes?"

"Comedians, musicians . . . Jack Benny, he's well known in the States."

"A marvelous way to spend the bloody war, I'd say."

He was, by far, the best lover she had ever had. Their lovemaking had been unhurried, a voluptuous learning experience. He had sought out her secrets and, unlike all the others, had allowed her equal access. Even more unusual, in the midst of everything he had talked to her. He had spoken her name, expressed his pleasure, praised her beauty, elicited her feelings.

Wallowing in the afterglow, she spoke in a small voice. "What happened to your eye?"

"I lost it over Barcelona."

"What happened?"

"A dogfight between myself and a pair of Messerschmitts. It was in '38, I was flying a Potez. That's an open-cockpit French crate that would have been hot stuff in 1928."

"The Spanish Civil War?"

"That's what they called it."

"But you're Australian," she said, hoping he wouldn't talk about it.

He was quiet for a moment. Finally, he raised himself onto one elbow, glanced down the length of her body. "Lovely," he said, quietly. "And you're an authentic blonde in the bargain."

Relieved, she ran her hand through his hair. "It takes one to know one." Unlike some other men, this one didn't insist on going on and on with war stories in bed.

He said, "Where are you from in the States?"

She wondered if he were really interested or just being polite. She said, "Philadelphia."

"The City of Brotherly Love . . . Pennsylvania."

"Ah, you're also good at geography."

"And you're a college girl."

"How can you tell?"

"Education will out."

"Bryn Mawr, ever hear of it?"

"Can't say I have."

"It's a girls' school. My mother pawned the family jewels to pay the tuition. I quit in my junior year."

"And what did you learn at this Bryn Mawr?"

"I learned that young men never marry young ladies they don't respect and they never respect those who give them access below the waist. So I quit, threw away my panty girdles, and became a singer. And I'm finished with young men and all that."

"You're a real lady."

"Thank you." She felt he didn't mean it, but it was nice.

"There are two kinds of women," he said, "ladies and cunts. You're a lady."

"Cunts," she said, savoring the word. It was a man's word, never, except in extreme anger, spoken in the presence of women. There were others, equally taboo, that he had used in the course of their lovemaking. Each had been a separate experience, like a small electric shock. Quietly, she said, "Fuck, cock, pussy . . ."

He laughed. "Diction needs a little work, but you're getting the hang of it."

"How do you tell a lady from a cunt?"

"In bed."

"How?"

"A cunt thinks of herself as an object to be used. A lady participates. A lady is not afraid to express her pleasure and she never lies about it. I've known two, you're the other one. Maybe things will improve after the war."

"And who was the first?" She hoped he wouldn't tell her.

"I've forgotten her name."

"Well," she said, "if I'm a lady, you're one hell of a gentleman."

"I'm not sure of that. Gentlemen are defined a little differently."

"How?"

"A true gentleman never pisses in the shower."

She laughed. "There must be more to it than that."

"Okay." He got up on one elbow to look down at her. "A true gentleman never purposely causes pain. I don't qualify."

"Nobody's perfect." She felt marvelous. She pulled him down, kissed him.

They made love again. This time their coupling was less exuberant but somehow even more intimate.

Afterward, they lay on their backs, holding hands, staring up at the ceiling. In the dim light she turned to look at him. Despite her first impression, he now seemed far from perfect. His nose was crooked, his lips too thin, his face somewhat pinched, almost mean. She was suddenly distant from him, as if they were two strangers thrown together by inadvertence. The only desire she felt was to get into her clothing and leave. She heard herself making conversation. "How long have you been in this godforsaken place?"

"Too long, but not much longer. The war up north is over. Jerry's finished in Africa, so this place is going to be on the way to nowhere. Probably be back in Australia in a few months, stretched out on the beach."

She said, "We'll probably never see each other again."

"C'est la bloody guerre."

"If I write, will you answer?"

He smiled, his one eye gleaming with reflected moonlight from the open window. "Sure."

But she knew he wouldn't, just as she knew she wouldn't write. C'est la bloody guerre.

She left his quarters at about four in the morning to make her way back to the Ritz. She felt empty, depleted, isolated.

Even while making love to Dawson, a sour apprehension had not been too far beneath the surface. *Wham-bam—thank you ma'am.* Warm expectations turned to ice. It hadn't mattered on the airplane with Frank Howard and most of the others before him, but every now and then it hit her like a chronic cold or a stomach cramp. It was probably due to lack of sleep. She'd catch up on the airplane and everything would be fine. She took a deep breath in an attempt to come alive.

Takeoff was scheduled for five-thirty. The night was alive with a rhythmic native chanting. The sound was coming from the DC-4. It was parked nearby, bathed in the yellow glow of work lights. The airplane was being fueled by a crew of natives pumping hundred-octane gasoline by hand from fifty-gallon steel drums. She paused to watch them and to listen. It seemed right out of a Tarzan movie. Moments went by before she realized their native chant was actually a strangely atonal version of a current Andrew Sisters hit: "Rum and Coca-Cola." She felt like laughing but realized, with some confusion, that she was weeping.

THE MISSION

AUGUST 1, 1943

Junior Darling saw them first, a trio of eighty-eights squatting at twelve o'clock on a slight rise bordering a railroad. His voice, on the interphone, conveyed all the fervency of a train announcer.

Cohen, squinting into the glare, spotted them a few seconds later. He depressed his twin fifties as far he could, but unless Maguire lowered the nose it wouldn't be enough.

There was a lot of chatter on the interphone, and the navigator's strident tones peaked in his headset. "We're flying right into them!"

"Okay," said Maguire. "Settle down, everybody. To hell with the guns. Go for the gunners."

Sally's Wagon shuddered from Junior's twin fifties. A second later, Russell Beel's single gun in the nose added to the cacophony.

The distance was closing rapidly. There was nothing Cohen could do but sweat it out. He felt Sally drop until he was sure that Junior's ass, in the belly turret, was dragging the ground. Maguire was attempting to get down below the maximum depression of the enemy eighty-eights, but they were dual-purpose cannon, meant also to be used against ground targets. And, thought Cohen, that's almost what their airplane was at the moment.

The eighty-eights commenced firing over open sights as if shooting at oncoming tanks. It was their specialty, and it was an easy, no-deflection shot, like shooting skeet at the last station. Cohen, holding his breath, slumped down in the turret. At the same time, Sally's guns were joined by a cat's paw of tracer from the other airplanes of the formation. Twenty heavy machine guns were firing, churning up the ground around the target.

Cohen counted the enemy muzzle flashes: two, three . . . four. Then Sally's Wagon was over and past. Finally allowing himself to breathe, he whipped the top turret around. He could depress his guns sufficiently now. He joined Sally's tail guns, adding to the shambles of the enemy battery. A half-dozen bodies were scattered about. One of the enemy guns was pointing skyward, its muzzle split open like a daisy, as if it had been spiked. Another was traversing, its lone gun layer working the azimuth crank furiously. Cohen walked his fire across the ground just in front of it. Then suddenly the man was moving in a disjointed jog through an obscurity of dust and debris. In seconds, he fell to his knees to be torn to pieces.

Sally's Wagon picked up a few feet of altitude as the interphone came alive. *"Tail turret, what's the status?"*

"They're out of business,"

"Okay, stay sharp, everybody."

"Jesus! Betty Boop's been hit!"

Cohen turned to his left. Betty Boop, the element leader, a veteran of over seventy missions, one of the few remaining original aircraft, was climbing out of formation. Colonel Greeves, the 287th group commander, had chosen it as the airplane in which he would fly the mission. As was his tradition, he sat in the copilot's position. A tongue of flame licked around its wing root. The pilot was obviously attempting to gain sufficient altitude to bail out his crew.

As Cohen watched, Betty Boop climbed to four hundred feet to hang on one wing, seemingly forever. A figure emerged from the waist window. The parachute opened immediately, much too soon—the shroud lines became entangled in the tail structure. Two more figures emerged, one from the ball, another from the waist.

Betty Boop, glowing like a giant firefly, straightened out, then dropped rapidly to within a hundred feet of the ground, trailing the entangled chute. There was a brilliant flash as the residual gasses in her empty bomb bay tank ignited. Her left wing folded upward as if it were hinged. A sudden buffeting threw Sally's

Wagon to the right, almost causing her to collide with Orange Crate. Betty Boop was gone before she even touched the ground, transformed in less than a millisecond into bits of white-hot metal, oily smoke, shards of flesh.

D'Amato, in the waist, reported the safe descent of two of the three men who had bailed out. As neither of them had exited the cockpit hatch, or the bomb bay, Cohen realized with a shock that Colonel Greeves had bought the farm. A few moments later, Sally's Wagon moved up to take over as lead ship in what was now a formation of five.

CHAPTER 8

JULY 1943

And I heard that whenever an important civilian shows up—a congressman for instance—you fellows paint brassieres on certain airplanes. You know the ones I mean." It got a big laugh. Everything was working. He had expected a tough audience but was surprised and delighted to find it one of the most responsive he had ever experienced. The 287th Bomb Group had lost twenty-one men that afternoon on a mission over the marshaling yards at Milan and now, less than four hours later, they were laughing at his jokes. He had led off his opening monologue by saying how privileged he felt to be here. He was surprised to find that for once he really meant it.

He looked out over a sea of faces, estimating the audience at well over five hundred. Included, he had been told, were about a hundred men from a nearby RAF installation and some doctors and nurses from a British base hospital. A few dozen patients sat in wheelchairs or were propped up on stretchers. The brass were seated up front on a row of benches. Everyone else sat on the ground or on blankets. The stage had been constructed from a half-dozen maintenance stands. The lights consisted of Jeep headlight lamps mounted high on engine stands and powered by a distant putt-putt generator. Barely visible, beyond the lights, Benny could make out the bombers squatting, like winged elephants in the moonlight. They reaffirmed the war which still seemed distant to him. But it was real. Men were dying . . . kids.

Rochester said, "Mr. Benny, the Four-Thirteenth Squadron is

taking up a collection for a beer run to Cairo. I told them you'd contribute five dollars."

"Rochester!" He wrung his hands. "You know beer doesn't agree with people in hot weather."

"There's a cold snap coming, boss."

"In the Sahara Desert!"

"Looks like Atlantic City to me, Mr. Benny, except for the palm trees."

"It's a long way to the boardwalk, Rochester."

"Then we'll drive, boss. I guess we'll have to—ah—borrow some gas for the Maxwell. And she's burning a lot of oil, too."

"Enough, Rochester . . ."

"Enough oil would be about fifty gallons, Mr. Benny. She's burning about a quart a mile."

"Rochester . . ."

"And that coconut oil we used last time isn't working so good. The rear end sounds like a marimba band."

"Rochester!"

"I'm getting tired of squeezing them coconuts, boss."

"Well, there's a war on."

Rochester pointed to the audience. "I'll bet *they're* not squeezing coconuts."

Benny waited for the laughter to die. "Enough of that, Rochester. We've got more important things to do than trying to be funny."

"What things, boss?"

"Serious things, like introducing the men of the great Two-Eighty-seventh and their guests to our songbird, little Miss Bonnie Astor."

It was her cue. For an instant she thought he was going to say "Little Miss Round Heels." Jack had been referring to her that way since takeoff from Mongoro that morning. He seemed good-natured about it—just kidding—but it made her nervous. It was impossible to have a private life. Some one must have seen her leaving Dawson's quarters last night. She was sure everyone knew. Nevertheless, except for Frank Howard, the photographer, they had all behaved like gentlemen. Howard had been surly, ugly, had not spoken a civil word to her all day. He had turned out to be one of those terrible, possessive men who equated what they called a quick roll in the hay with lifetime ownership. She was relieved that he had disembarked at Cairo.

She gathered herself together, then stepped out into the lights, blowing them all a kiss as she ascended the stage. She had chosen the gown carefully. It was bright red, sequined, clinging, low-cut. Mr. Luciano, a true gentleman, had paid for it. A gift. It made her feel like a star.

Jack put his arm around her waist. "I just want you men to see what you've been fighting for."

It brought down the house. She grasped the mike with one hand, waved with the other, displaced a hip just enough to lend her body a supple S curve. "Hi'ya fellas!" She revealed a leg to mid-thigh through the slit in her gown.

The audience exploded in applause, cheers, whistles, shouts of "hubba-hubba." She was awash in a palpable wave of joy. It left her light-headed. She stood silently, hands on her hips, a ghost of a smile lighting her face, waiting for silence. Then, as Tony Franks played his lovely guitar intro to "Melancholy Baby," she scanned the sea of faces. On the left, about a third of the way back, for just an instant, she caught one that seemed familiar. It left her with a vague feeling of apprehension. But there were too many, and she lost it. For a moment the glare of the lights caused her to squint unbecomingly.

She relaxed her facial muscles, threw her eyes out of focus, smiled softly at her audience, and opened with the verse. She loved doing verses, particularly those that were rarely sung. Their lyrics were quite often more expressive than those in the choruses, lending themselves to even more eloquent readings.

Despite a husky quality her voice possessed a good range, and she had learned how and when to lag the beat, to create lyrical tension and then pay it off in just the right place. Her phrasing, unusual for a white singer, was rooted in the blues. Jazz musicians liked working with her, and after only a year in the business there were already a few who considered her one of their own.

She followed up with "Darn That Dream," "Sleepy Time Down South," "It Had to Be You," "The Lady Is a Tramp," "Stardust," "I Get a Kick Out of You."

Halfway through her duet with Rochester on "Jeepers Creepers," she spotted the face again. It turned from the person on its right to stare back at her. It looked like Mike. She felt herself go cold. She glanced away, then back again. Now she wasn't sure. Her vision was not good enough, and there was glare from the lights. Besides, it would be too much of a coincidence, the sort of thing that happened only in the movies. The figure clasped its hands in front of its chin and with the church steeple of two index fingers rubbed the bridge of its nose. It was not one of Mike's familiar gestures.

She turned to find that she had missed her cue, but Rochester, with a comic gesture of confusion, picked it up for her. She threw him a quick, apologetic smile, then made it up to the audience with a wriggle of her hips. When she looked again for the guy who resembled Mike, he was gone. He had been, she concluded, an apparition, a trick of the light or of the quick scotch she had had in her ambulance dressing room.

She went off with a standing ovation. As encores, she sang "White Cliffs of Dover," which she dedicated "to our gallant British allies sitting out there," and finally, "I'll Be Seeing You."

She took three curtain calls and was trading wisecracks with Jack, when Colonel Greeves, the 287th group commander, mounted the stage. He was dressed in knife-creased "pinks" and one of the new and still rare Eisenhower jackets.

A corporal ran out to raise the mike as the colonel held up both hands for silence. "Gentlemen," he said. His voice was loud and clear, a deep, handsome, if somewhat pretentious baritone. "I have just received word from Wing that tomorrow is to be another maximum effort. Because of that we are going to have to cut short these delightful proceedings." The response was a universal groan accented with isolated boos. Once again the colonel raised his hands, waited patiently for silence. "But I'm sure Mr. Jack Benny will be happy to do another show tomorrow night. Reveille will be at five, breakfast at five-forty-five, briefing at six-fifteen. You armament chiefs will have your bomb-load postings in about thirty minutes." He paused for a moment, staring out at them. Then, raising his voice over the general hubbub, he said, "Once again, I'd like to extend an invitation for our British friends to join us in the festivities tomorrow night."

Someone called out. "What's the target, Colonel?"

"The goddamned enemy . . . excuse me, ladies."

The audience laughed, breaking the tension. Colonel Greeves, playing it straight, said, "War is hell, gentlemen."

THE MISSION
AUGUST 1, 1943

The double railway line was on their left, where it was supposed to be. Captain Maguire checked the compass, then clicked on his throat mike. With some effort, he kept his voice cool and precise. "Taylor, give me the target heading."

"We're right on course, Captain." Maguire squinted into the deep purple haze for the target that lay directly ahead of them: Red-Three, the Adina Primari refinery complex.

They were in farm country. From an altitude under fifty feet and at a speed of 210 miles per hour, he registered fleeting impressions of pastoral farm houses, barns, haystacks. In the distance a white curtain of fog hung over the target heading. Smoke pots, he thought.

Maguire wriggled about in his seat in order to stretch his muscles. The cockpit was sweltering in ground-level August heat. He was sweating profusely under heavy flying clothes that had been designed for high-altitude temperatures of twenty below zero.

He felt a vague uneasiness, a concern that some of his reactions might have become imprecise; his thinking clouded with a growing apprehension. He thought, for a moment, of Sally, felt himself growing heavy with depression. He shrugged it off, then stood outside himself attempting to evaluate his own fitness. With a nod to Deutsch, he released the control yoke, tore off his gloves. His hands were wet, hot, as if they had been immersed in warm, brackish water.

He felt dazed, somehow removed, momentarily unsure of where he was. He watched with little comprehension as, in a matter of seconds, a magical change occurred simultaneously in a half-dozen haystacks within his view. As if in response to a conjurer's wand, they split open; collapsed before his eyes to reveal twin 37mm batteries, agile, fully automatic, quick-firing, antiaircraft cannon, probably the best of all possible weapons against low-flying aircraft. The deadly guns began firing even before they were completely free of the hay.

Sally's reaction was immediate. All of her guns, except for the tail turret, responded. The interphone came alive with gunner's chatter, calling targets around the clock. Once again, hundreds of heavy fifty caliber rounds from the small American formation were churning up the rich Rumanian topsoil, taking their toll of enemy guns and gunners.

The antagonists seemed evenly matched. The flak gunners were seeking out their fragile targets, bracketing them from three different angles with balls of fire strung along glowing threads. To Sally's left a rustic barn dropped its siding to reveal an eighty-eight.

Maguire was aware of Sergeant Cohen's voice from the top turret peaking above the others. "Forget the eight-eight! Go for the fucking haystacks!"

Cohen was right. The unwieldy, single-shot breech-loading eighty-eight-millimeter cannon fired a massive, exploding shell, deadly against targets at high altitudes or coming head-on as they had been just minutes ago. But the big guns could not be tracked fast enough or loaded quickly enough for accurate fire against high-speed airplanes flying low-level at even a small angle of deflection. At the moment, the greater danger was from the rapid-firing smaller guns.

Maguire shook himself. Sally's Wagon was his. He came erect in his seat, fighting muscle cramps and fatigue. He breathed deeply, tensed his muscles, arched his back till he thought it would break.

He sensed a welcome charge of adrenaline. His buttocks were again the center of his being, sensitive to every movement and tremor of the aircraft. He was one with it.

He tried thinking again about Cohen, but found he didn't really give a damn. The knowledge seemed to liberate him. The only thing that really mattered was his airplane. He was suddenly elated . . . his airplane.

He placed his hands on the yoke, signaling with a slight jiggle that he was taking over from his copilot. Then, quite suddenly, they were past the haystack guns and Sergeant Smith in the rear turret reported over the sound of his own twin fifties that only one enemy battery was still firing.

"Orange Crate's feathered number two."

"She's leaking gas."

Maguire tightened his grip on the wheel. The cloud hovering over the target was no longer the white smoke of enemy smudge pots and smoke generators. A dirty boiling gray, it loomed larger as they approached; seemingly impenetrable. He wondered what had caused it.

A glance to the right convinced him that Orange Crate was fatally wounded. Hundred-octane aviation fuel was flowing from her wing root, forming a vaporous tail that streamed for a half-mile behind the stricken airplane.

The whole formation was loose, too spread out, thought Maguire. The tighter the formation, the more concentrated the defensive fire. The target area was a corridor, three hundred feet wide by a thousand feet deep.

Maguire felt the edict against radio silence no longer applied. It was ludicrous, he concluded, to try to keep one's presence secret from an enemy who was already shooting at you.

It was time to execute command over the formation. He motioned to Deutsch to switch on the command set, then wiggled Sally's wings to signal the other aircraft to do likewise.

He spoke in calm but decisive tones. "All right, let's tuck it in." Straight ahead, in the distance, a series of airborne dots coalesced into about a dozen B-24s flying a southerly course. He checked to his right. The 98th was where it was supposed to be, just within view; flying parallel to him. But the aircraft up ahead were not supposed to be there. Was it the 376th? The 93rd? Something was very badly screwed up.

Maguire got Orange Crate on the command set.

Harry Orange said, "A voice from outer space."

"You got a two-mile tail of hundred-octane, Harry."

"Roger. What else is new?"

"You going to bail out your crew?"

"Number one's running hot. I go for altitude I'm liable to end up trying it on two engines."

"Oh, Christ . . ."

"The percentages," said Lieutenant Orange, "are with keeping it straight and level. Four of us voted to stay with it till the target, then set it down, nice and easy."

"Four?"

"I got three dead and two wounded, Mickey. I'm the boss, and according to my rules, they don't vote."

Maguire clenched his teeth, ventured a quick glance to his left. Sassy Suzy was in place, neatly tucked in. Watermelon Man was off her left wing. On Sally's right, Chloe hovered about 150 feet off their wingtip. The intervening space had been vacated by Orange Crate. He said, "Woike, give me the word on the Crate."

"Roger. She's fallen back about two hundred feet; two engines feathered. She's still throwing gas."

Maguire raised the nose, throttled back a little, until the airspeed indicator dropped from an already sluggish 170 to 150. It was about 45 miles an hour slower than he had planned. They were going into the target like a slow freight, but Orange Crate was slipping back into isolation. Maguire was trying to give her a chance to catch up. Without the guns of the formation the wounded Liberator could be dead meat for ground fire or marauding fighters.

He switched to the command transmitter. "Okay, let's get down to bombing altitude . . . and keep it tight right into the target. Then we'll spread out for maneuvering room."

Orange Crate had once again crept into his peripheral vision on the right. If she blew, she'd probably take Sally and Chloe with her. He shrugged off the thought, adjusted the throttles, letting the airplane settle to what he judged to be forty feet of altitude. A little jogging had the five Liberators tightly spaced, line abreast once again in shallow V.

Maguire stared ahead into the looming chaos. He could make out details now. A storage tank blew its top silently, beneath the roar of Sally's engines; a brilliant Roman candle orchestrated with billows of heavy black smoke.

There were airplanes over his target. He could just make them out in the distant smoke: desert-pink B-24s that should have been elsewhere—over their own targets, as briefed.

Clyde Taylor's voice was an irritating presence in Maguire's headset. "It looks like the biggest snafu since Wrongway Corrigan! What the hell are they doing there?"

"Somebody's been sleeping in our bed!" D'Amato was a regular Bob Hope.

Maguire was aware that his right hand, seemingly of its own volition, was reaching to shove everything forward to climb the hell out. With a conscious effort, he fought the impulse; he put an unlit cigarette between his lips, then proceeded to chew it to bits.

CHAPTER 9

JULY 1943

Ten minutes after the theatrical spots were killed, Bonnie Astor found herself in the mess tent surrounded by avid young officers. She signed autographs, engaged in good-natured banter, accepted a cigarette and a drink poured into a canteen cup from a priceless bottle of Old Grandad. She said, "What's maximum effort mean?"

"It means getting every airplane into the air that can make it to the runway."

"And some that can't."

"The War Department insists we earn our pay."

The prospect troubled her. She had taken keen delight in being a rare commodity in a devil-may-care world. Now, suddenly, she felt upstaged by other realities. It was an annoying intrusion. War would be a marvelous way of life, ideal if they could somehow do away with the killing.

One of the men was taking pictures. She posed with each of them, and in various combinations, their arms about her waist, until the photographer ran out of flashbulbs.

Finally, she said, "Any of you guys know a Lieutenant Michael Maguire?"

"A pilot?"

"Yes, about five-ten, sandy hair."

One of them said, "Sure. You must mean Mickey Maguire. We're in the same squadron, the Four-Fifteenth. I'm his navigator." Suddenly possessive, he put his hands on her waist. "My name is Clyde Taylor. Wow, what a small world! You a relative?"

She smiled, prettily. "Not exactly. I mean we're old friends."
She felt suddenly chilled. It actually had been Mike in the audience.

Somebody said, "Lucky guy."

She searched for a way to change the subject. "It's not important, really."

"If it were me who was your boyfriend," said one of the others, "you wouldn't be here with this pack of wolves."

Over the laughter, she said, "Where would I be?"

The young officer, at a loss for words, blushed. She took his hand, kissed him lightly on the lips. They all applauded. She loved it, but it was all mixed up with anxiety about Mike. She said, "We should really call it a night. You guys have to go to work in about five hours."

She sang a good-night song for them, unaccompanied, standing on one of the mess tables. Her audience swayed back and forth in tempo as if they were dancing with their girlfriends. A few had their eyes closed. She wondered which of them would not be alive to see the show tomorrow night. *Shine on harvest moon . . .*

Lieutenant Taylor and two of his friends, their silver wings glowing in the moonlight, saw her to her tent. It was situated in a grove of palms, just behind the beach; a white British desert tent, like all the others, canopied for air circulation, dug in to a depth of about two and a half feet to create headroom and to function as a kind of slit trench in case of enemy air attack.

Taylor said, "Mickey's probably in the sack, but I'll tell him you're here. I guess he wasn't at the show. Maybe he's duty officer or something. Wow, will he be surprised."

As brightly as she could, she said, "Very nice of you, but please don't wake him up special, there's plenty of time."

She awakened in the middle of the night, aware of a presence. She held her breath, fighting to come fully awake. There was the click of a Zippo, a momentary flare of light. It was Mike. He had a mustache. She focused on the glowing tip of his cigarette. From its position she could tell he was sitting on the footlocker to the left of the tent flap. She had been expecting him. She breathed his name. "Mike?"

"Hello, Sally. Were you expecting someone else?" His voice was husky with suppressed anger. He added, "Bitch." The word jolted her.

The fiery spot, as if under the influence of a magical levitation, rose into the air. Momentarily, it glowed even more brightly, highlighting his eyes. She followed it, as it descended rapidly in a shallow arc to the tent floor. Once again, all was darkness unrelieved by even that small beacon of orientation. She steeled herself against a sharp pang of fear, saying, "It's a small world, Mike." Her tone was honeyed in an attempt to defuse his anger. "Imagine running into you in the middle of nowhere. How are you?" There was no response. She breathed deeply, fighting to contain the fear.

Then suddenly, like a punch to the solar plexus, the full weight of his body rendered her breathless. A hard shoe skinned the length of her shin. A loose belt buckle pressed into her belly flesh through the thin silk of her pajamas. He pulled the bottoms down over her hips, then ripped them off. There were no preliminaries, no words, no foreplay. He was inside her before she could maneuver her limbs to accommodate him. The unrelenting power of brutal, dry thrustings drove her repeatedly into the taut canvas of the narrow cot.

She managed to liberate her legs, wrapped them around his waist; forcing him higher, embracing him, changing the angle and depth of his thrusts in order to deny him the satisfaction of inflicting pain. She gained control of her anguished groans, adroitly changing their pitch and timbre into moans of ersatz passion. He remained silent, intent on reaching the finish line—a sprinter rather than the long-distance runner she remembered from other days.

Sensitive now to all the nuances, she became aware that his breathing was growing shallow. Seeking control, she rotated her hips in order to hasten the process, get it over with. His hairy chest pressed down on her face, crushing her nose till she thought it might break. His limbs stiffened, his body seemed to grow rigid. The rhythm of his movements became erratic, uncoordinated. She jerked upward in a series of short, quick strokes; contracting and releasing secret muscles. He shivered, exhaled explosively, and as suddenly as it had begun, the ordeal ended. She was free of his weight. He was gone. She pulled up the sheet. He would calm down now. He always had.

The sudden light blinded her. She squinted upward to find him standing in the ugly glare of the overhead bulb. He was grinning, buttoning his fly as if he had just finished at the urinal.

Breathing heavily, he said, "Best grudge-fuck I've had in years."

She looked directly into his eyes. An acid aftertaste of anxiety was all that remained of her fear. She said, "It's not the best I've had."

The slap came as a shock, almost knocking her off the cot. His mouth was twisted, his eyes unblinking. "Cunt!"

The memory of Cliff Dawson's use of the word left her feeling cool, disconnected. She heard herself say, in calm and clear tones, "Does the Army Air Force consider rape a crime?"

He stood over her, the anger draining from his face to be replaced with a rueful astonishment. In a tight voice he said, "You're really something." His laugh was ugly. "It's a general court-martial—five, ten years in Leavenworth."

"Then all I have to do is scream." She touched her lip, it was bleeding.

"But it wasn't rape."

"What would you call it?"

He reached down, grasped her cheeks in the fingers of one hand, and squeezed till she thought he'd rip her face apart. "I'd call it a woman performing her wifely duties." The kiss on her involuntarily puckered lips was painful, opening the cut. "Love, honor, and obey, remember?" He released her.

Painfully, she said, "That was then and this is now . . ."

"It's still "then," bitch. You're still Mrs. Michael F. Maguire."

"But the annulment . . . ?"

"It didn't come through."

She closed her eyes, echoing him, with equal emphasis on each word. "It didn't come through . . ."

"They turned it down."

Till death do us part. Aloud, she said, "God, I hate you." She breathed deeply, expecting another vicious slap, or worse.

Seconds went by. She waited, her muscles taut, the tension building in her body. Finally, she opened her eyes to find him looming over her, twisting off the cap from a fifth of Kasser's rock and rye. It was as if she were trapped in a deep pit staring up at him.

He said, "Why did you darken your hair?"

"I got tired of looking like a cheap blonde."

"It didn't help." He took a deep swig and passed it to her. She sat up, swallowed a mouthful. It left her feeling as if her esophagus had been burnt out. She coughed explosively, then, with tearing eyes, fell back onto the bed to stare at the ceiling. "God, that's awful."

"Relax. You have to get used to rotgut if you're going to be a camp follower." His voice had lost its edge. Grinning, he sat on the edge of the cot, took the bottle from her. "What's this Bonnie crap?"

"Sally sounds like a cheap blonde."

"Bullshit." He drank deeply, cleared his throat, and said, "And Astor, what in the hell is that all about?"

"It's my stage name."

"What was wrong with your real name?"

"Sally Shank on a marquee? Are you kidding?"

His voice went soft. "No, I mean, Sally Maguire."

"I wanted my very own name."

"It's a joke, like you're named after a hotel or a movie theater."

"Are you going to . . . you know . . . tell everybody we're married?"

"Hell, no." His laugh emerged from a tight grimace. "I know you. Before you leave, you'll probably get around to screwing half the squadron. You know what that makes me?"

"Can I have a cigarette?"

He lit a Camel, got it going, and placed it between her lips. "Stupid broad. Why did you do it?"

The tip of her cigarette was blood-stained. She sighed, wondering if her lip would be swollen for the show tomorrow night. It could have been worse, but at least it was over. She'd get some ice from the mess tent in the morning. She said, "It's almost two years. Let's not get into it."

"My best friend . . ."

"I'm sorry, Mike." She was surprised to realize she meant it. "But I guess it turned out that he really wasn't your best friend."

He paced the length of the tent, stamped out his cigarette, lit another. Finally, he stood looking down at her. "We had good times together." He took her hand. "I treated you okay. You were my girl. Right?" There were tears in his eyes.

Against her better judgment, she was touched. She said, "You were terrific, Mike."

Staring down at her, he said, "And now you're big time and they love you."

"You mean it?"

"You're a star."

She smiled, shyly. "I didn't really think you'd understand."

"My airplane is named after you—Sally's Wagon."

"My God, it is?" She placed her hand on his arm.

"There's a picture and everything."

He upended the bottle. She watched his bobbing Adam's apple. He was a bastard, but once again, he was her bastard. And she was a yo-yo—from love to hate and back again. No, she thought, not love, something else. When she figured out what it was she'd sit down and write herself a letter.

She would, more than likely, hate him again in the morning, or maybe even before the night was over. In the meantime there was a war on. She grinned up at him, saying, "You're still an animal."

"A tiger."

She managed a pout. In a little girl's voice, she said. "If you promise to take your shoes off this time . . ."

THE MISSION

AUGUST 1, 1943

Copilot Lieutenant Jordan Deutsch in the right seat could make out three—five—barrage balloons, like plump groupers floating in the thick air. There were others, barely visible in the hazy distance. The heavy cables anchoring them to the ground were designed to tear the wings off airplanes; some of them were strung with explosive charges. They had been informed at the briefing not to worry, as the cables would be easily cut by B-24 wings. He wondered how the brass had tested the concept.

He had no faith in such pronouncements. The S-2 officer had also predicted "light to medium flak." It was obvious that reconnaissance had discovered nothing but a few antiaircraft guns and a few dozen ineffective barrage balloons hovering over a bucolic landscape dotted with peace-loving haystacks and innocent farm buildings.

Deutsch wondered why he had opted for flight training. He had a law degree. With a little maneuvering he could have gotten a cushy deal with the judge advocate's office, and a nice tailor-made uniform in which to survive the war without ever hearing a shot fired in anger. But the silver wings beckoned . . . *Off we go into the wild blue yonder.*

Why? You had to be crazy to fly in the goddamned things. Yet everyone who did was a volunteer and a lot of guys were waiting in line. It was a sucker's game. The pay was lousy, the food was lousy, the hours were lousy, and if you flew bombers, even the flying was lousy. Bomber pilots were no more than truck drivers, crazy truck drivers, and before it was over they'd all be dead; their crews, also volunteers, along with them.

It was hot. He squirmed in his seat, recalling the briefing film they had seen just a few days before. For some reason, it bore the title *Soap Suds.*

The movie had been narrated by a typically constipated news-reel voice. It consisted of film footage and still photographs. It was obvious to Deutsch, from the vintage of the cars and trucks, that some of the scenes had been shot as long ago as the early thirties. They included views of the Ploesti complex and other refinery installations. The narrator indicated that much of the intelligence came from Allied agents on the ground in Rumania. *". . . The defenses are nothing like as strong as they are on the Western Front. The fighter defenses at Ploesti are not strong and the majority of the fighters will be flown by Rumanian pilots who are thoroughly bored with the war.*

The antiaircraft defense of Ploesti is estimated at eighty heavy AA guns and one hundred-sixty light AA guns. These again have largely been disposed for a night attack coming from the south along the railroad. The heavy ack-ack should not trouble you at low altitude. All the antiaircraft guns are manned by Rumanians, so there's a pretty good chance there might be incidents like there were in Italy early in the war, when civilians could not get into the shelters because they were filled with antiaircraft gunners.

Reports have been received that machinery for making smoke-screens has been installed. Smokescreens have not, however, proved successful against daylight attacks. The defenses of Ploesti may look formidable on paper, but remember, they are manned by Rumani-ans. . . ."

Lieutenant Deutsch wiped the sweat from his brow with the back of his hand. "Bullshit." He spoke the word aloud. There was the dry taste of fear in his mouth.

Once again they were being fired on. From all around the clock, glowing streams of tracer were seeking them out. Sally's Wagon, at an altitude of fifty feet, was bracketed. The voices of her gunners, spotting enemy gun positions, resonated in Lieuten-ant Beel's head-set. The airplane shuddered with the recoil of their weapons.

Beel stood and grasped the handles of the heavy fifty-caliber machine gun mounted in a ball and socket near the top of the aircraft's Plexiglas nose. He had a panoramic view.

Someone was calling out a target at two o'clock. He yanked the charging handle back, released it. A cartridge slammed into the chamber as the bombardier swung the gun around.

He was aware of Clyde Taylor standing to his left in the tight confines. The navigator was firing a "cheek" gun mounted in a Plexiglas extension just aft of the greenhouse.

The heavy gun jolted in Beel's hands. He held the trigger down with his thumb, squinting through the ring-sight, walking the tracers along the ground to the target: a duet of twin twenty-millimeter cannon and a tripod-mounted light machine gun at an initial range of about 250 yards. The enemy were in his view for a matter of seconds, but to Beel, time had slowed. He had plenty of it, there was no hurry.

The perspective was flattened. As they got closer, he could see the sharply etched results of his efforts, as if shuffling through a sequence of high-contrast stop-action photographs delineating the blood, the agony, the dismemberment of the enemy.

Ten seconds later, Sally's Wagon had run the gauntlet. Her guns were silent once again. The copilot was checking the crew on the interphone. Both airplane and men remained intact—not a scratch on any of them. They were inviolate, sacrosanct.

Lieutenant Beel found himself in the grip of a burgeoning optimism. He would live forever. He was indestructible. The current ordeal would be over in a matter of hours and there was little doubt that the larger one, the war, would be over by Christmas. *After-the-war* would find him capable of anything. He would make his fortune, enter politics, be a great lover. *After-the-war* would last a long time.

Up ahead, the dark cloud came into sharper focus. A flickering red forest lay at its base. It became clear to Beel that the enemy smoke pots had little to do with the smoke. The target was burning. He caught fleeting glimpses of low flying B-24s, little more than black dots flitting in and out of the smoke. They were not supposed to be there. They were dropping bombs meant for another target.

The meticulous planning, the precise training missions over the simulated desert Ploesti seemed to be down the toilet. It was a screw-up. Wide-eyed, unblinking, he stared into the approaching target, the euphoria he had felt just seconds earlier dissipated. In minutes, if they made it that far, Sally's Wagon would be less than fifty feet over the random blasts of delayed-action bombs and the debris and deadly flames of an exploding oil refinery.

He ventured a quick glance over his shoulder at Clyde Taylor seated at the navigator's desk. Taylor, a cigarette dangling from his lips, was hunched over, toying with his map. The navigator looked his way. Beel, managing a shaky frown, pointed toward the target. Taylor grinned, gestured knowingly, pointing downward with his thumb.

Lieutenant Beel's hands were trembling. He studied them as if perhaps they belonged to someone else. The optimism of moments before was gone. He prayed his death would not be painful . . . the agony of fire . . . disembowelment.

He closed his eyes, searching for some secret internal compartment in which to tuck away the fear, hide it from himself and the world. In the process, a terrible pain tore at his stomach.

CHAPTER 10

JULY 1943

The mission, that morning, had been scrubbed. As explained to Bonnie Astor by a handful of adoring second lieutenants, the problem had been bad weather over the target: the Fiat factory at Milan. Southern Europe was socked in. The 287th, they estimated, would probably be standing down for three or four days.

Earlier, the Jack Benny troupe had gone on again as Colonel Greeves had promised the previous night. She had used some special material, including nine different choruses to "Let's Do It," naughty Noel Coward lyrics to the marvelous Cole Porter original. It had brought the house down.

> Sikhs do it,
> Sheiks do it,
> Nice young men
> Who sell antiques
> Do it . . .

The temperature, for once, was bearable. Stretched out on her cot she realized that, for the first time since stepping off the DC-4 two days earlier, she wasn't perspiring. She lay awake, staring out the raised tent flap, feeling at one with a landscape gone silver in the moonlight. She thought of the one-eyed Australian, a romantic encounter; like so many others, consummated but unfulfilled. *Little Miss Round Heels.*

So many others. She closed her eyes to see their faces. Despite the moonlight, the reminiscences left her feeling stale. She had a bad memory for names.

She assumed that Mike would, as he had the night before, materialize in her tent. It was an expectation colored with both dread and a disturbing, perverse desire. As the night wore on, the prospect dimmed. By eleven, she felt relieved, but twenty minutes later, still wide awake, she was wallowing in a vague disappointment. She tossed about in a fit of gritty restlessness. Finally, she gave up.

She stripped out of her silk pajamas, got into crisp khakis. She applied a dab of lipstick and fluffed her hair. A little walk in the moonlight might do the trick.

She strolled up the beach about two hundred yards into an invisible cloud of sandflies. In a few seconds her arms and legs suffered a myriad of bites. The tiny bugs were everywhere, in her eyes, her ears, her nostrils. She ran from the beach, finally stood, breathing heavily, scratching her arms. Fortunately, sandfly bites were not persistent; the tiny welts would be gone in a matter of minutes. There was, however, a danger of sandfly fever, whose symptoms were akin to those of malaria. She walked on through a palm grove in which were dispersed a large number of personnel tents.

"Halt! Who goes there?"

Bonnie Astor paused in mid-step. "It's only me." She smiled at him: a skinny private holding a carbine to his shoulder. Its muzzle was pointed at her mid-section. She assumed it wasn't loaded. He was just a kid.

The guard stared at her with wide, unblinking eyes that strayed downward. "Holy cow, I mean, I thought you were a man." Looking flustered, he lowered his weapon. "I'm sorry, ma'am . . . I mean, what with the pants and all."

She smiled at him. "I guess there's a first time for everything."

His face lit up with sudden recognition. "Wow! I saw you in the show last night . . . Bonnie Astor! You were terrific."

"Thank you." He was cute. She managed a coy pout. "I was just taking a little walk."

"I really loved the way you sang and everything. I mean I really did."

For want of something better, she said, "Where you from, soldier?"

"Dalhart, ma'am. It's in the Panhandle—Texas."

"That's nice."

The young guard said, "I don't want you to think I go around pointing guns at ladies."

"And what's your name?"

"Private Buster D. Dalton, ma'am. The D is for Dustin. They call me Dusty—Dusty Dalton."

"Nice to meet you, Dusty."

"Likewise." The shy smile lighting his face dissolved into perplexity. "There's nothing in the General Orders about female-type civilians. I mean, maybe I'm supposed to call the sergeant of the guard."

"I don't think you have to do that. I mean, it doesn't make sense. I'll just go back to my tent."

"Yeah, well, nothing makes sense in the army, ma'am. But I guess it's okay."

A trio of tugs passed nearby, each towing a line of carts, nestling large, olive-drab cylinders.

She said, "What's that?"

"That's ordinance delivering bombs. I guess they must be loading up for a mission tomorrow."

It occurred to her that the young officers who had told her the standdown would continue had been mistaken. In the morning, they would be flying to the war after breakfast. It was as if they were suburban commuters, except that some would not be home for dinner. She felt a stab of anxiety as the tugs passed behind a grove of palms.

The guard was saying, "This is the first time I've ever been close to an honest-to-God celebrity."

She took his hand. It seemed flaccid in hers. For an instant she flashed the tactile image of a limp penis. She said, "Nice talking to you, Dusty."

"Likewise." His hand in hers suddenly stiffened, then pulled away. He twisted to the right, raised his carbine, and called out, "Halt! Who goes there?"

"Friend . . ."

She turned to see a figure backlit by the moon. It stood, legs apart, hands in hip pockets. It spoke in a strong, resonant voice, "Tech Sergeant Abraham Cohen. Four Fifteenth Squadron."

"Advance and be recognized."

He took a half-dozen paces forward. He was of about medium height, slimly built, almost skinny, with a sad face that sported bushy eyebrows shielding deepset, probing eyes. He awarded her a perfunctory nod, then glanced away. She was surprised to note that his eyes did not fall and rise on the inevitable tour of inspection.

The guard said, "Okay, Sergeant." He turned back to her. "Could you do me one little favor?"

"What's that?"

"An autograph?"

"I'd be delighted," she said. The sergeant was firing up a cigarette. She turned to smile at him. "Could you spare one of those?"

The sergeant removed the cigarette from his lips and handed it to her. It was an intimate act by a total stranger. With wide eyes focused on his, she placed it between her lips. She drew deeply, then handed it back. The tip was lipstick-smeared.

She said, "Thanks, but I wouldn't want to smoke your last one."

He took a deep drag. "It's not my last." Once again, with his eyes probing hers, he handed it to her.

Dusty Dalton, patting his breast pocket said, "I don't have a pencil or anything."

"Neither do I," she said.

The sergeant shrugged.

She said. "If you tell me how, I'll get it to you tomorrow, an autographed photo if you'd like."

"A photo? Yes ma'am. That would be terrific. Thanks. You could leave it at the Four-Thirteenth orderly room . . . PFC Dalton. Write something—well, you know—nice on it."

"I will." With her hand on his arm she glanced at the sergeant. Again, their eyes met. She said, "Good night, and thanks for the cigarette." She turned and started toward her tent. She could feel their eyes on her back.

"Miss . . ."

She smiled to herself. Tech Sergeant Abraham Cohen was right on cue.

He offered to escort her back to her tent. She accepted, graciously.

On the way, she said. "I couldn't sleep. Thought I'd take a little walk." She laughed. "I guess I forgot there's a war on."

They walked in silence. She noted three more tugs pulling bomb carts. Outside her tent, he put two cigarettes between his lips, lit them, and handed one to her.

She said, "You have a way with cigarettes."

He said, "You have a way with 'Melancholy Baby.' "

"Thank you."

"I've never heard it sung that well."

"It's sweet of you to say so, Sergeant."

"Call me Abe, Miss Astor."

"Hi ya, Abe. Call me Bonnie."

"Have you been out on the line yet?"

"The line?"

"That's where the airplanes are parked."

"Well, no . . ."

"It's only a short walk."

"I'd love to."

They stopped by the 415th Squadron Operations tent. He showed her the "board," a wall-sized chart listing the status of the squadron's nine aircraft. He explained it to her, pointing out that there were six marked "A" for available. One of them was Sally's Wagon. Two sported red X's. Number 27, Apple Crate, was undergoing an engine change. Number 18, Sassy Suzy, was down with shot-up hydraulics.

"And that one?" she said, pointing to the bottom of the chalkboard. "Thirty-three? It doesn't say anything."

"Fearless Freddy," he said. "She's an LB-30, an early model B-24, built for the British. No superchargers, no tail-gun turret. We got her from the Aussies—sort of reverse lend-lease. She doesn't fly combat. She takes guys on leave—Cairo, Alex, Tel Aviv. But mainly, she chills beer. Load up a few cases, take her up to about twenty thousand where it's nice and cold, tool around for a half hour, and you got yourself a cool brew."

On the way out, he picked up a piece of chalk. She wondered what he intended to do with it. She liked him.

"TO ADOLPH." She wrote in big letters, using the white chalk on the olive-drab steel casing of the thousand-pound demolition bomb.

Abe Cohen stood over her as she knelt at her task under the wing of the desert-pink Liberator. Her sleeves were rolled up neatly, revealing slim, graceful arms in the harsh glare of the work lights. He noted her long, red, impeccably manicured fingernails. ". . . WITH LOVE FROM BONNIE ASTOR AND HER GI FRIENDS." A gentle waft of her scent tinged the night air. She was, he felt, the kind of woman who would be wearing silk underwear beneath her GI suntans.

There were a half-dozen armament men gathered around. Hers was the fifth of eight bombs they would load into the airplane. She glanced up at them—her audience—a grin lighting her face. With a final flourish that jingled the bracelets on her wrist, she signed her name. "I never thought I'd be doing this. I mean, just a month ago—two weeks—nobody told me I'd be autographing a bomb."

One of them said, "Yeah, I know how you feel. I mean, fifteen minutes ago, if someone said there'd be a beautiful dame out here, I would have put him in for a section eight." They laughed good-naturedly.

Cohen took her hand, helped her to her feet. She held the contact for a few seconds longer than necessary, relinquishing it with a brief squeeze.

They entered the aircraft through the waist hatch in the belly. Cohen went first, then grasped her under the arms to pull her up. He was aware of her body heat through the khaki fabric. Then, for an instant, they stood close, her body pressed tightly against his. She pulled away, her hands gripping his arms, her head tilted back, parted lips gleaming in the moonlight from the open waist windows.

She was good, he realized, very good—perfect. But there was no hurry. He preferred to savor the hors d'oeuvres, cultivate his appetite.

A trio of armament men entered the waist, turned on the compartment lights, and began loading ammunition into the two gun turrets and the long troughs that fed the single, flexible waist guns. Cohen grasped her arm to guide her forward around the ball turret so they could stand out of the way in the bomb bay hatch. They watched as her bomb was rolled into position. An armorer locked a shackle to the twin lugs, and with one man guiding, the other cranked the bomb up into the airplane. He attached the shackle to the top station of the left rear rack. One of them screwed the yellow, boxlike tail fin assembly onto the hanging thousand-pounder while another bomb was rolled into position. She said, "They ever go off accidentally?"

"Once in a while."

He left her standing there, climbed onto the half-deck over the wing to retrieve a pint bottle of rum hidden behind the command transmitter. He put it in his hip pocket.

It required ten minutes to finish loading and ten more to screw in the fuses. Moments later, the work lights blinked out. Cohen stood with her in the waist window watching as the armament crew drove away in their weapons carrier to the next aircraft up the line. He removed the cap from the bottle, wiped off the top with his handkerchief, and offered it to her.

"Lovely." She tilted the bottle up for a deep swig. He watched her, admiring her courage. She lowered it, gasping for breath. "God, that's awful!"

He helped himself to a mouthful, smacked his lips. "Genuine Egyptian rum. It's guaranteed."

"You sure know the way to a lady's heart." She seemed out of breath. "But you should have warned me."

"It's much better with ice."

She said, "Are you a flier?"

"Yes," he removed two cigarettes from the pack in his breast pocket. "I'm a flight engineer."

"What does a flight engineer do?"

"He takes care of the airplane, makes repairs in flight, keeps an eye on the engines, transfers fuel from tank to tank to keep things in trim, stuff like that." He lit the two cigarettes, handed one to her. "On my crew, he's also the top turret gunner."

"Sounds like you're a busy man."

"Keeps me out of trouble."

"You ever fly it? I mean, like a pilot?"

"I say a prayer every night that I'll never have to."

She was quiet for a moment. "You flying tomorrow?"

"This is my airplane."

"What do they call it?"

"Sally's Wagon."

She hesitated, an expression of surprise lighting her face. "Sally's Wagon?"

"Yes."

She took a deep drag on her cigarette, erupted in a brief fit of coughing. He slapped her on the back and was surprised to find she was laughing.

"What's funny?"

She laid a hand on his arm. "I don't know, I guess it's these cigarettes. It's hard to believe, but they're worse than the rum. I mean, they're so terrible that they're funny."

"They're Indian, standard issue to British forces." He showed her the pack, a small cardboard box emblazoned with a large V. "We get them from the RAF guys. They refuse to smoke them so we trade cans of C-ration. Anyway, someone had the cigarettes checked out—an English politician. I read about it in the *Palestine Post.* The guy found they were twenty-five percent cow dung."

"C'mon . . ."

"I wouldn't kid you. Take a drag, let the smoke roll around over your tongue."

With wide eyes she followed his suggestion, swirling the smoke around in her mouth as if she were testing wine. She exhaled through her nose, closed her eyes to simulate deep thought.

"Well, what do you think?"

"I think you're right Abe, it's cow dung, about twenty-five percent, give or take." She reached up to undo one of his shirt buttons. "I'd recognize the stuff anywhere."

"From the best cows," he said, placing both hands on her waist.

"If that's what the Indians put in their cigarettes, I hate to think what the Egyptians put in their rum." She blew smoke in his face, unfastened another of his shirt buttons. "I've got a question."

"Name it."

"Why don't you smoke American cigarettes?"

"Can't get them."

"That's funny," she said. "Less than a week ago I was in New York, and you have to have a connection to get a carton of cigarettes there." She ran her fingers through his hair. "They say all the cigarettes are going to the brave boys in the service."

"Not these brave boys." He pulled her close. She leaned back, traced his lips with the tip of her finger. He said, "We never see American cigarettes or American Coca-Cola or American apple pie or American girls."

"Poor guy." She put a hand inside his shirt.

"It's been hell, Bonnie."

"How come you don't wear an undershirt like all the other guys?"

"I don't like undershirts. How come you don't wear a girdle like all the other girls?"

"How come you're so sure I don't?"

"You're not the type." He reached behind her, slipped his right hand under her belt into her slacks. He had been right about silk underwear. He squeezed gently, taking delight in the pneumatic reaction.

She said, "Fresh." She put her arms around him, rested her head on his shoulder.

He withdrew his hand. She nibbled on his ear as with a single-handed show of dexterity he unhooked her brassiere through the khaki fabric of her shirt.

She spoke in a whisper. "You're a real expert, a mechanical genius."

"I'm a flight engineer."

She pulled out his shirttail, ripping off the last button in the process. Then reaching down between them she unbuckled his belt.

He pulled her onto the bomb bay catwalk. Piece by piece they undressed each other.

They made love on the narrow catwalk, squeezed between the two rows of fat bombs. For three days afterward her buttocks were to be marked with a series of horizontal welts impressed there by the corrugated metal decking.

Afterward, Cohen cranked up the auxiliary generator, then

hoisted her, still naked, into the top turret. She operated the control handles, spinning herself round and round like a kid at an amusement arcade.

He switched on the small speaker Charlie Crenshaw had installed on the radio desk: tuned the Hallicrafter liaison receiver to the German overseas wavelength. Axis Sally's late-night English language propaganda broadcast was featuring Tommy Dorsey records. Bonnie Astor came down from the turret. He took her in his arms to stand and sway to Frank Sinatra singing, "I'll Be Seeing You."

He took delight in inhaling her scent, burying his face in her hair. He had never experienced a woman so adept at sensuous nuance, or so vocal with both appreciation and encouragement. It had been, he realized, among other things, an exquisite learning experience.

Finally, seated on his lap, sharing the rum and a cigarette, she said, "Pilot or copilot?"

"What do you mean?"

"Who sits here?"

"It's the left seat," he said. "The pilot always sits on the left."

"Captain Michael Maguire."

"Bingo! Give the little lady a Kewpie doll."

She said, "He's your pilot, right?"

"Right. So okay, how do you know?" Despite the rum he experienced a sour taste. "How do you know he's my pilot?"

"He talked about his airplane in bed." She looked directly into his eyes as if she were describing the weather. "Most men talk about their airplanes in bed; or their cars or whatever it is they drive. But anyway it wasn't a bed, it was more like a cot."

"I think it's time we got our clothes on and got the hell out of here."

She ran her hand through her hair. "Do you like him?"

"Who?"

"Maguire."

"He's a good pilot."

"No, I mean as a man."

"Look," he said, placing both hands on her naked shoulders. "Why do you want to ruin a perfect night?"

She grinned. "I can do anything I want. I'm Sally and this is my wagon."

She was, he decided, drunk. He grasped her under the arms, lifted her off his lap. "That's it," he said, standing. "Time to go."

She said, "My maiden name is Sally Shank, my married name is Sally Maguire. You've been screwing your boss's wife, Sergeant Cohen."

Cohen searched her eyes. "You're drunk, Bonnie, or Sally, or whatever the hell your name is."

"Of course I'm drunk. You got me that way so you could do it to me. I know your type." She pinched his cheek. "And call me Sally."

"You're not kidding me?"

"We were married in Philadelphia, New Year's Day, 1941. Easy to remember for anniversaries. There was supposed to be an annulment, but it didn't take. I mean, a girl can't have everything, right?"

He held her at arm's length. "You're a slut, a real slut."

"Is that the same as a cunt?"

"Yes. Get your clothes on."

"I mean," she said grinning. "That's funny. A gentleman of my acquaintance, an Australian type, just recently called me a real lady."

"How many people around here know you're married to him?"

"You and me and him."

"How come? I mean why doesn't he advertise it?"

"He suspects I sleep around, and as my old grandmother used to say, doesn't want his horns to show. I'm sure he figures that given half a chance I'd put out for every good-looking guy in the outfit. He's wrong, I'm not going to be here long enough. The Benny troup's pulling out in a day or two."

"Why are you telling me all this?"

"Because I hate him," she said, her voice low-pitched. "And I like you . . . I mean, a lot. You want me to tell you what a bastard he is?"

"No."

"Okay, then, would you like to hear what a freak he is? He likes wearing women's underwear. I have pictures back in New

York." She laughed. "That's not nice. I shouldn't have told you that. But he's such a bastard, I feel I want to get even."

The radio clicked off in the middle of Bunny Berigan's "East of the Sun" solo. Cohen twisted around. Sergeant Fibich stood there, hands on hips, like a schoolmaster.

"What the hell is going on?"

Cohen grinned at him. "What's it look like, Sarge?"

"It looks like you're making a whorehouse out of my airplane!"

"A boudoir, Sergeant," said Sally. "Have a heart."

"Sorry Miss . . . Cohen, you got sixty seconds to get your clothes on and get your Jewish ass out of here or I call the guard." He appeared to be on the edge of apoplexy.

"You want me to take the lady or leave her?"

"Okay, wise guy, that's it." Sergeant Fibich crossed the flight deck, removed the flare pistol and one flare from their stowage on the bulkhead. With his eyes on Sally, he loaded the flare and opened the overhead hatch.

Cohen said, "Okay, Sarge, you win." He helped Sally to her feet. "Our clothes are in the bomb bay."

Sam Fibich's face glowed red as the naked Sally squeezed by him to get to the hatch. He said, "You're crazy, Cohen, you know that?"

"Have a drink," said Cohen, offering him the bottle.

Master Sergeant Fibich took a deep breath, shook his head. "I got to check out this airplane sober." With Sally off the flight deck he seemed to have calmed down. He restowed the flare pistol. "You ought to read your general orders. Only officers and gentlemen are allowed to use government property for screwing. They'd bust you down to zero. You'd be flying combat as a fifty-buck-a-month private."

A graceful arm, draped with Cohen's clothes, materialized in the hatch. Fibich passed them to Cohen, who said, "What is this crap, Sarge? For a year I've been listening to your cock and bull about Mademoiselle Fifi and Mademoiselle Babette and all those other French cookies from the last war. You telling me you would have fired that flare pistol?"

"What's in the bottle?"

"Rum." Cohen handed it to the crew chief. "You would have pulled the trigger and got me busted?"

Master Sergeant Fibich upended the bottle. His Adam's apple bobbed twice. He lowered it, coughed, smacked his lips. "Good stuff . . ."

"You like it, there's more behind the transmitter, up on the half deck. Help yourself to a bottle."

Fibich breathed deeply, released the air in a lengthy sigh. "Okay, Cohen, I'm sorry I was so chickenshit. I mean, let me put it this way. If your woman had been a little less beautiful I would have been a little less pissed off. I'm not as old as I look." The crew chief watched as Cohen got into his underwear. Finally he said, "How the hell you ever get the name Abraham Cohen?"

"That's what I'd like to know." It was Sally's voice. She stood fully dressed in the bomb bay hatch.

"Master Sergeant Fibich," said Cohen. "Meet Sally Whatsername."

"Enchanté, mademoiselle." Fibich bowed at the waist.

"Likewise, I'm sure," said Sally, executing a mock curtsy.

"This is her wagon," said Cohen.

"No kidding?" Sergeant Fibich seemed impressed.

"Is there a picture?" said Sally.

"Yes, it's on the left side of the fuselage," said Cohen. "That's why you missed it."

"It does kind of look like you, at that," said the crew chief. "Except the artist really didn't do you justice . . . I mean, you know."

They watched her as she went into the bomb bay, dropped down to the ground, and ducked out.

"That's one hell of a classy-looking dame you got there," said Fibich, helping himself to another slug from the bottle. "I mean, she looks almost as naked with her clothes on, if you'll pardon me for saying so."

"Listen, Sarge," said Cohen, buttoning what was left of his shirt. "Can you get hold of Charlie Gordon?"

"Sure. What for?"

"A little nose art."

"On this airplane?"

"Yeah."

"We already got a picture on this airplane. I just met the little lady in person."

"Right. I just want to improve the art."

"You mean bare-assed?"

"Like a jaybird."

"I always said you were the best flight engineer in the outfit."

"Thanks, Sarge."

"But Maguire will have a fit. I gotta tell you, I overheard some of your conversation."

"Just get Gordon over here with his little paint pots and don't worry about it, Sarge. You just deny everything."

"Okay. When?"

"Tonight, right now."

"You're out of your fucking mind. It's almost one in the morning."

"A hundred bucks says it's not too late."

THE MISSION
AUGUST 1, 1943

*T*aylor, give me the time to the target."
    "About three—three and a half minutes."
"Okay, everybody, watch out for fighters."

For the moment, no one was shooting at them. Abe Cohen lit a cigarette, then realized the danger, crushed it against the housing of the left-hand gun mounted just inches from his head. He stared forward into the maelstrom. Fed by burning oil storage tanks, a broiling pillar extended upward for two thousand feet. As he watched, a pair of B-24s materialized out of the storm of smoke only to disappear a second later. There were others—mavericks, screw-ups—who weren't supposed to be there.

The sky ahead had turned from gray to black. Every few moments it flashed an orange glow as another bomb detonated. At their present heading they would go right through the center of it. Their target was pinpointed by three tall smokestacks, set in a triangle. He began to look for them.

His muscles were stiffened with apprehension, but he had learned to control his fear by deferring it, putting it off, tightening up the way one might attempt to control a bodily need such as hunger, thirst, or the need to urinate. It could be an exhausting procedure.

Where others might let go and defecate in their pants, Cohen, more often than not, suffered from constipation.

He rotated the turret. Far to his left a formation of B-24s was turning into its target. Beneath the distant aircraft, a fiery bowling ball rolled along the ground.

Orange Crate hovered a few feet below and slightly behind Sally's right wingtip. The rear portion of the aircraft was a sieve. Cohen could make out holes through which one could toss a basketball. There was no one in the waist window. It was hardly likely that the three gunners back there could have survived. About one third of Orange Crate's left vertical stabilizer was shot away. One engine had a prop feathered and another looked as if it might be windmilling. The stream of gasoline was now even longer: a trailing mist, visible a mile beyond her tail.

Up top, Orange Crate's Martin turret was traversing. If the guns were fired anywhere but directly forward, the tracer rounds would undoubtedly provide the detonator that would transform the airplane into a fireworks display. As the turret came around, Mike Musielski's head and shoulders were visible under the Plexiglas dome. With a toastlike gesture he raised a canteen to his lips. Cohen mimicked a response. Staff Sergeant Mike Musielski was a big man who, before joining the Air Corps, had won a regional championship as a Golden Gloves middleweight. He played spirited fraternity house piano, was a good flight engineer, but above all, the best poker player in the squadron—a gifted man.

Further forward, visible through the flight deck side panel, Captain Harry Orange sat hunched in the driver's seat; his thin, old-fashioned flyer's mustache ornamented an upper lip beneath which a cigar butt was clenched between big white teeth so perfect they seemed false. The thirty-two-year-old captain had been known to insist that aerial warfare was too serious an endeavor for sartorial slobs and therefore, just as he had on all his thirty-seven missions, he sported a class-A uniform complete with a white shirt and two rows of ribbons. However, his GI garrison cap insignia displayed not the golden eagle of the Great Seal of the United States but rather the red and white insignia of TWA. The dapper Captain Orange had worn it for two years as a DC-3 copilot for Transcontinental Western Airlines out of Houston. His crew, in a show of deference toward their pilot, had taken to a similar mode of formal combat dress and they too affected individual, nonregulation enhancements: silk scarfs, Belém boots, Boy Scout merit badges, and in the case of one of the waist gunners, a GI steel derby, circa World War I.

Cohen continued around. The sky was empty between the large ovals of Sally's twin rudder. Up ahead, to the right, a cluster of about a half-dozen dots seemed to be heading at right angles to their course, hugging the ground—friend or foe? If they were friends, they were in the wrong place at the wrong time, just like the Libs over their target a minute earlier.

Sally was gaining rapidly on a train running the track about three hundred yards to their left. It pulled four identical freight cars. Even at a distance they seemed newly painted, like toys. Cohen wondered why it was speeding, at about sixty miles an hour, into an erupting refinery area during the course of an air raid. It smelled wrong. Real freight trains were much longer, the cars not so evenly matched, not so perfect a set.

Once again, unable to depress his guns sufficiently to deal with a nearby ground target, he clicked on his throat mike. "Top turret to Ball . . . Junior, how about putting a couple of bursts into that train at eleven o'clock? Go for the locomotive . . ."

"Hold your fire!" It was Maguire's voice. "We ain't got ammunition to waste on choo-choo trains."

The words were barely out when the aircraft pulsated with the recoil of the belly turret's twin guns. They were joined by D'Amato's single fifty in the left waist.

Cohen observed the tracer streaking toward the target. The first few rounds were long, striking the ground on the other side of the track, forward of the locomotive. The gunners corrected quickly. In a matter of seconds its boiler was holed by armor-piercing rounds. The engine erupted in billows of steam.

As if on signal, the sides of each of the boxcars dropped down to reveal antiaircraft guns. D'Amato called out, "Q-Train at nine o'clock!"

The two B-24s to their left joined in a response to the enemy fire as the train, its locomotive kaput, came to a stop. Once again the air-ground battle was joined.

Earl Woike's voice was pitched almost an octave higher than usual. "Bandits, four o'clock high!"

Cohen twisted the control to the left, whipping the turret around to the target heading. There were three of them, line abreast; coming in from about 3,500 yards, diving steeply. At first they seemed to be German Folke-Wolfe 190s. As they got closer, he realized they were a breed of enemy fighter he had not seen before; radial-engined, offering a minimal silhouette. The briefing had mentioned a Rumanian fighter, the IAR-80, describing it as not overly fast, but maneuverable and heavily armed with four light machine guns and two twenty-millimeter cannon.

The Rumanian fighters, thought Cohen, were either foolhardy or grossly inexperienced to be flying into their own flak from the train. They were sliding back toward five o'clock, but were dropping too fast and would probably undershoot. He tracked them, holding fire till they would come well into range.

From the tail-gun turret, Yardbird Smith's voice on the interphone was a piercing squawk, barely decipherable. "I got them now . . . they're diving like fucking rocks."

"Take the one on the right," said Cohen.

One of the other B-24s in the formation was firing. It was premature, a waste of ammunition. The range, at almost 1,500 yards, was too long for accurate fire from the American machine guns but not too long for the Rumanian cannon. Closing rapidly, the leading edges of their wings sprouted winking fire. Cohen prayed that none of their shells, or those of the defenders, would pass through Orange Crate's hundred-octane vapor trail.

The IAR-80s began leveling a thousand yards out. It was a tricky procedure for a fighter pilot to recover precisely from a power dive at an altitude of less than seventy-five feet while holding a target in his gunsight. It was a maneuver requiring talent, experience, and, not least of all, courage. The three Rumanian pilots seemed well endowed with the necessary courage; the next ten seconds or so would determine whether they possessed the other two qualities.

Cohen held his breath. Then, with the range down to about 800 yards, he coolly opened fire with a series of short bursts. From the gunner's point of view, the IAR-80's pursuit curve presented a frontal view that slid back toward the B-24's tail. Cohen disregarded the misleading tracer, tracking the optical reticle on a theoretical point, about a third of the way between the attacker and Sally's tail in order to allow for his own relative airspeed. Initially he allowed about two rads of elevation, or double the diameter of the projected circle in his optical sight. Within three seconds he was down to one rad, dropping progressively and decreasing the azimuth deflection as the enemy got closer.

The Rumanian marksmanship was erratic as the trio attempted to pull up and come out shooting. Two of them, overcautious, ended nose-up in near-stalls, fifty feet too high. The third, over-eager, flew into the ground.

The two surviving fighters, on the edge of stalling, slowed till they seemed to be hanging in the air. For an instant they were almost stationary targets. His Rumanian slid back into the stream of bullets, shedding pieces of itself. It executed a series of snap rolls as its propellor spun off, windmilling upward like a child's toy. One of its wings slapped the ground. The IAR-80 folded itself up into a mass of wreckage that skidded across a wheat field, scattering flaming bits and pieces over a dozen acres.

Cohen turned his attention to the third Rumanian. He was in a near-vertical climb, trailing smoke. Both Yardbird and one of the other Liberators were scoring hits. At about four hundred feet, he fell off on one wing. A figure emerged, plummeting halfway to the ground before the parachute deployed in a long streamer. It never had the chance to blossom into a full canopy.

"Wahoo!"

Cohen's response to Yardbird's triumphant shout was cool and precise. "The poor bastards were amateurs, Yardbird. Save your breath for the professionals." He depressed the guns while rotating the turret to the left. The train was a few miles behind them now, shrouded in steam.

There was a sudden jolt, like a car at high speed hitting a bad pothole. Out of the corner of his eye, Cohen saw the steel barrage balloon cable strike Sally's wing just outboard of the number-one engine. He turned quickly to see the rubber deicing boot that lined the leading edge of the wing flapping in the breeze. Overhead, the balloon, released from its anchor to the ground, shot skyward like an airborne sausage. Sally's wing had cut the cable.

A crisscross of tracer filled the sky. Enemy fire seemed to be coming from all directions. Sally's gunners were no longer calling out flak positions. There were enemy machine guns and 37mm and 40mm guns firing from all points of the compass.

Maguire reduced altitude till it seemed they were running on wheels. The other three B-24s followed their leader down, spreading out a little to give themselves maneuvering room for individual bomb runs. Some of the enemy guns, mounted atop hills, ridges, buildings, and other structures, were now perched higher than the attacking aircraft.

The four Liberators were in the smoke, speeding through a gray murkiness punctuated with dark wisps that momentarily blocked the view ahead. Here and there, thick black plumes climbed a few hundred feet to merge with a murky ceiling that cut off the daylight. Patches of fire provided the only color.

Despite the confusion, Cohen picked his targets carefully: tracking, when he could, from way out; holding fire as he worked on the ballistic problems; lining up precisely, then squeezing the trigger as they crossed the edge of effective range. He preferred it that way, was good at it. Long-range gun laying gave him more time to exercise control, seconds rather than the mere milliseconds allotted when shooting from the hip at close, fleeting targets. It was, for him, a simple conscious equation: control was an antidote for his greatest fear, not of dying but of panic.

He listened as Maguire reminded the waist gunners about the three boxes of British incendiaries in the waist. Altogether, they numbered about 150 one-pound sticks of thermite, deadly and effective, particularly in the presence of combustible materials. The waist gunners would toss them out over the target area. Every little bit helped.

Maguire executed a shallow three-degree turn to the right. Dead ahead now, lined up, though barely visible in the smoke, lay a refinery, a cracking plant; a few acres of complex plumbing and squat buildings, some of them partially surrounded by twenty-foot high concrete blast walls.

Because of the extremely low altitude, the pilot rather than the the bombardier and his Norden bombsight would be executing the bomb run. But the trio of tall smokestacks—Sally's pinpoint—was nowhere in sight. It should have been.

Cohen centered his optical gunsight reticle on a three-story rooftop from which a duet of tripod-mounted heavy machine guns were firing at the oncoming bombers. Initially the range was nearly fifteen hundred yards. He took his time, three whole seconds, to edge the turret slightly left and upward to compensate for deflection and bullet-drop. He squeezed off a few rounds for ranging. The heavy, high-velocity, armor-piercing bullets pulverized the brick a few yards below the roof line. Azimuth was perfect but he was low . . . he wondered how long it had been since the squadron armament shop had boresighted the guns.

Holding the firing switch down he allowed the closing range to walk the stream of heavy slugs up to the roof. In an instant there was a dead machine-gunner slumped over his gun. The ammo feeder stood and turned; then he too was dead. With the range closing rapidly, Cohen twisted the control grip about an inch to the right and slightly downward to seek out the second gun.

There was a sudden burst of light, as if someone were taking a picture with a gargantuan flashbulb. For just a second, the gray vista was rendered in full color. A portion of the ground was momentarily airborne as the building collapsed into itself. An instant later all that remained was a heap of dust-shrouded rubble.

There were two others in quick succession: delayed action fuses were detonating the bombs dropped by the aberrant airplanes that had earlier, for whatever reason, hit the wrong target. Fuse settings for Tidal Wave ranged from forty-five seconds to two hours.

"Bomb doors open . . ."

The smoke had thickened. Dark billows obscured the target area.

"Bandits . . . eight o'clock . . . level!

"They're hitting Watermelon Man! Three 109s!"

Cohen whipped the turret around. Watermelon Man was on the far left, on the other side of Saucy Suzy. The three attacking Messerschmitts were wingtip to wingtip, about 800 yards beyond Suzy, their wing-mounted guns winking and blinking. Cohen instinctively chose the one in the middle, getting off two short bursts.

There was another bright flash, much closer this time. For an instant, the air turned to fire. Then once again they were in the smoke. Watermelon Man was gone. She had disappeared along with the three enemy fighters—winked out. Now they were four.

"Okay, everybody, keep your eyes open for three smokestacks . . . close together in a triangle."

Most of the enemy flak was now coming from the flanks. Cohen whirled the turret to the right, squeezed off a short burst at a Bofors battery at about 150 yards. It would be all short bursts from here on. Ammunition was limited and they had another 1,300 miles to go, give or take; half of it within range of enemy fighters. He continued around, searching the sky. There was a loose formation of Messerschmitt 109s, about four o'clock high at five or six thousand feet, about ten of them. For the moment they were circling, unwilling to fly down into the cauldron of their own flak in order to attack the bombers.

A half-mile ahead and less than fifty yards to the right of their flight path, a large oil-storage tank, one of a few dozen grouped together on the edge of the refinery complex, was bleeding fire through a jagged gap. A broiling red pool surrounded its base, sending out flaming tributaries.

Orange Crate hovered slightly behind, just off Sally's wing. A long stream of hundred-octane gasoline continued to trail the intrepid bomber. But she was still in business. Her bomb doors rolled open.

Cohen's cheeks flushed with a sudden rush of heat. Sally's Wagon was suddenly fifty feet higher, nose up, one wing low. Now, a few hundred yards away, the shattered storage tank blew, taking others with it. Three massive fireballs soared upward like fiery balloons.

Orange Crate was lifted by the same thermal. The airplane's vaporous tail came to fiery life as if someone had put a match to an acetylene torch. The stricken airplane was ablaze aft of her waist windows, trailing fire for a hundred yards. A stream of black, oily smoke lengthened to half a mile.

Cohen closed his eyes in a sustained blink and prayed for a miracle. Orange Crate's flaps came down, bomb doors rolled open. The airplane was still under control, still alive.

Her bombs salvoed out of the open bomb bay. Harry Orange was lightening ship, fighting for a few hundred feet of altitude to enable his four surviving crew members to bail out. Seconds later, Cohen found himself craning his neck to stare up at her; the stricken airplane had picked up a hundred and fifty feet. A figure emerged from the bomb bay. Spread eagled, the man fell, the white silk shroud trailing behind him. At the last possible moment, the chute filled with air. Moments later, the parachutist was on the ground, rising to his knees to release the harness.

As Captain Maguire got Sally's Wagon down, once more, to bombing level, the miracle died. Orange Crate lost the little altitude she had gained. Streaming flame, she was once more off Sally's wing. Cohen couldn't get his eyes off Staff Sergeant Mike Musielski, still seated in the top turret; firing his guns, chopping up a string of tanker cars parked on a rail siding. The stricken Liberator, airborne through the sheer will of her pilot, dropped an additional thirty or forty feet to within inches of the tangled spaghetti of refinery piping. Now, with both wings trailing fire, she clawed upward once again, fighting for yardage. Clearing a low building, she executed a shallow right turn. For a few seconds it seemed as if a wingtip was about to drag the ground. Then the flaming wreck flattened out to hurtle unerringly for two hundred yards toward a large brick power house. It was, realized Cohen, her pinpoint. Orange Crate was still doggedly in the war.

She hit her target square on, penetrating the structure as if it were made of wax. The big Liberator was gone. Then, a second later, the fuselage, minus its wings, emerged through the other side. In slow motion, the building dissolved into a pile of fiery debris.

Delineated by fire, the wingless Orange Crate streaked for another half-mile till there was nothing left of her but a shapeless mass of flame. Then, finally, as if the subject of a diabolical stage magician, she dissolved into a puff of smoke that dissipated rapidly into the grimy atmosphere.

Cohen whirled the turret around. They were only three now.

"Where in the hell's our pinpoint?"

"Beats the shit out of me . . ."

CHAPTER 11

JULY 1943

Abe Cohen picked a few dead bugs out of the coarse bread. The mess sergeant called it raisin bread and maintained, with a straight face, that it was the source of vital protein. Cohen savored it. It was fresh, delivered daily from a native bakery in Benghazi and was meant to be eaten with canned butter from New Zealand that tasted vaguely of cheese.

The squadron mess tent was not a proper tent, but rather a series of overlapping canvas canopies. Half-awake combat crewmen filled it, along with weary mechanics and armament men who had been working all night readying the squadron's aircraft. The men huddled quietly with their own, sipping coffee and toying with scrambled eggs and fried bully-beef.

"You look awful," said Staff Sergeant Alexander Darling, Jr. He leaned forward to stare at Cohen. "Your eyes are all puffy."

"Another cup of coffee will fix me right up."

Junior took his canteen cup. "I'll get it for you, old buddy. You don't look like you could make it to the chow line."

"Three sugars." Cohen managed a weak smile. He liked Junior Darling. The little guy was very obliging, constantly doing him favors.

Junior returned with a canteen cup filled to the brim with black coffee and another helping of scrambled eggs for himself. Cohen glared at the stuff, unable to conceal his distaste. It was concocted—congealed—from powdered eggs floating in a pool of water of its own making. He watched with growing nausea as Junior doused it with ketchup.

"How can you eat that goddamned garbage?"

"The Lord's name, Abe . . ."

"He's not my lord." Cohen grinned. It was a game they played. "And why me all the time, Junior?"

"You're special. I want to save your soul."

"I don't give a damn about my soul, why should you?"

"That's blasphemy. You're a good man. You'll be the first real soul I ever saved."

"Bullshit. You try to convert every Jew you run across. Someone must be paying you for them."

"I never saw one before I was in the army, I mean, up close. You're the first, Abe." Junior wiped his plate clean with a piece of bread. "My Dad told me that the Jews own all the money and run everything."

"You believe him?"

"He's my Dad, he never lies to me."

"Your Dad's crazy. I don't have any money."

"And I thought you people had horns. I mean, I did, really." He grinned, reached over to part Cohen's hair by way of mock examination. "Zero horns, and Roosevelt doesn't have any either unless they touch up the pictures."

"But we do," said Cohen. "Mine just never grew in." He sipped the hot coffee, hoping it might ease the throbbing vacuum in his head. He said, "And at Passover I used to gag on that awful Christian blood. My dear old mother even tried mixing it with honey, but I still couldn't stand the taste. She thought I was some kind of freak."

Junior laughed, revealing a set of teeth so big and perfect they seemed false. Cohen had taken a liking to him back in Florida. The little guy earned his living curled up for hours, fetuslike, sighting between his knees inside a small, retractable bubble suspended beneath the airplane. The entire turret rotated in both azimuth and elevation like a thrill ride at an amusement park. With his head nestling between a pair of twin fifties, he handled his ball turret as if it were an extension of his body, much as a good pilot handles an airplane. A small picture of his bride was taped up on one of the Plexiglas panels.

There was barely room enough in the Sperry-made power-operated ball for Junior, his Bible, a chest chute, and a few of his favorite K-ration chocolate bars. He was probably the only living GI who had ever finished one, often trading K-ration Wings or Marvel brand cigarettes for the unpopular concretelike confection.

They rinsed out their mess kits and made their way toward the group briefing tent. Halfway there they halted in the dull bluish light of the false dawn to stand side by side and urinate. Cohen found himself tracing the name *Sally* in the thirsty sand.

He said, "I'll tell you what, if I get through my fifty in one piece, I'll convert."

"You will?"

"Fucking-A," said Cohen. "My word of honor. But if I buy the farm and you live through it, you've got to swear that you'll become a Jew." His bladder was emptying, there wasn't going to be enough to get past the second l.

"You mean," said Junior, "that if you live, you'll become a Christian, and if you die and I live, I become a Jew?"

"Right." Cohen had no intention of honoring the bet. He'd brought it up only because Junior Darling loved the subject. It pleased Junior to think that he might be responsible for claiming Cohen's soul for Christ, even if the little guy had to die for it.

"How do you become a Jew?"

"There's a Hebrew chaplain attached to Ninth Air Force headquarters in Benghazi. He'll take care of everything. A deal?"

"Of course."

Cohen grinned. "Okay, you're betting your foreskin against my soul."

"Right, I guess I am. I'll pray for you." Junior Darling's face took on beatific glow. He laid his hand on Cohen's arm. "I have faith that the Lord Jesus will prevail."

"Amen." It was all crap. The guys who got prayed over, who made church call every Sunday, who were blessed by the chaplain before takeoff went down with their flaming airplanes just as readily as the guys who screwed their neighbors' wives and never made it to confession. In fact, thought Cohen, the sinners probably had the edge. Dependency on something outside yourself when you were being shot at was a sucker's game. If a guy believed his faith could stop bullets, he might forget to duck.

There was a series of backfires, small explosions, then a sustained, ragged roar. One of the crew chiefs on the line was cranking up an engine. It subsided into a series of pops and, finally, a single loud bang.

Cohen said, "They should send that one back to Pratt and Whitney for a refund."

Junior buttoned up. "Maybe it's ours."

"I fucking-well hope so."

"Why? If we abort this one, we'll have to fly another. No matter how you cut it, Abe, we've got nine more to go. I'd just as soon get it over with and get home."

"Not me, sweetheart."

The briefing tent, like the mess tent, consisted of overlapping canopies, closed off on two sides with hanging flaps. It was hot, and as it filled with men, it would get hotter, and dense with the smoke of hundreds of cigarettes. Cohen took an aisle seat in the last row near the open end. Junior sat next to him. The makeshift stage, deserted at the moment, was highlighted with spotlights. There was a table, a blackboard, and a large wall map, currently curtained off with drapes fashioned from a pair of GI blankets.

In twos and threes, sergeants and officers were drifting in. They were ragtag, hardly two of them dressed similarly. They could have been a road gang in hand-me-down work clothes: coveralls, suntans, ODs, fatigues, light leather jackets, British battle jackets, heavy fleece-lined flight jackets, field jackets, GI shoes, side-buckled loafers, flying boots, sneakers, leather flying helmets with the ear flaps pulled up, fatigue caps, khaki overseas caps. A few sergeants, for reasons known only to themselves, wore Class A's, and about half the officers sported garrison caps from which the wire stiffeners had been removed, creating a dashing "fifty-mission-crush" in order to facilitate the wearing of headphones.

The laconic attitude they had displayed earlier in the mess tent had been transformed into one of hard-boiled, devil-may-care joviality. It was, thought Cohen, pure bullshit. They were frightened. They were sweating out the mission even before they knew the target. There was hardly one of the three hundred and thirty who wouldn't happily trade a year of his life to be somewhere else. He had shared the feeling time and again, but now he was too tired to care. The ten-minute walk from the mess tent had been the last straw. He slumped in his seat, shut his eyes, betting to himself that he was the only guy on the base who'd been laid last night.

Despite the noise, he dozed off, savoring graphic mental images of a naked Sally, her breasts, her firm buttocks, her eager sensuousness. He had never before been with a woman so free of the stock inhibitions, so ardently lecherous.

A hush fell over the briefing tent. The sudden quiet opened his eyes. Colonel Edward Greeves, the 287th group commander, had mounted the stage, a blackboard pointer nesting under his arm as if it were a swagger stick. He was wearing coveralls that appeared to be hand-tailored.

"Good morning." His tone made it more a statement of fact than a greeting. He stepped briskly to the edge of the stage, where he faced them as if from a greater height. "We've got us a nice one today, gentlemen." He paused sufficiently to allow the suspense to develop. "Our target is the railroad marshaling yards in Rome."

The colonel, cued by the inevitable universal groan, turned abruptly to pull the drape cord, revealing, beneath a sheet of Plexiglas a large map of southern Europe stretching north to the borders of Germany and south to the North African coast. In red crayon, he encircled the city of Rome. Then, in a single rapid, slashing gesture, he drew an almost straight line, connecting it with a dot on the Libyan coast that was Benghazi. His action resulted in a general hubbub of subdued conversation accented by the almost simultaneous clickings of a hundred Zippo lighters.

The red line crossed the Mediterranean to bisect the heel of Italy at Ugento. It delineated a mission of about eight hours round trip, three quarters over enemy territory.

Junior Darling, leaning forward, his eyes locked onto the map, spoke in a loud whisper. "I'll bet there's going to be a lot of heavy flak."

"Right," said Cohen.

"Jesus, save us."

"The Lord's name, Junior," said Cohen, not fully awake.

"But not in vain, Abe."

Using his pointer, Colonel Greeves struck the encircled city with a force that should have cracked the Plexiglas, a pistol shot that sharpened their awareness. Once again the tent was dead quiet, a church in which the colonel was about to deliver the sermon. "This is the main railroad junction in Italy. Everything passes through it, particularly German troops and equipment bound for Sicily. It's a vitally important mission. If we bring it off, we'll not only save Allied lives but will shorten the war." The colonel paused as if expecting applause. Instead, he was rewarded with the rustling of over three hundred bodies shifting about on their hard, narrow, uncomfortable benches.

Cohen slumped even lower. They had all heard this sort of thing before. Every mission was going to shorten the war. It should have been the shortest war in history. Home by Christmas . . .

The colonel went on, his body rigid, only his eyeballs moving as he surveyed the congregation. "The good news, gentlemen, is that, for the first time, we're to have little friends. Two brand new groups of P-38s from Pantelleria will escort us as far north as their fuel will hold out; maybe, with a little luck, all the way to Rome. But don't get too used to the idea. Those 38s are needed for tactical missions in Sicily and soon, God willing, in Italy."

Cohen leaned forward. It was good to know they'd have fighter escort at least part of the way. The 287th had never before been afforded that luxury. But his interest centered on the colonel's voice rather than on his words. It was pitched somewhat higher than usual, less dramatic; colored with the kind of intimate, good-natured intonation that might be used by an experienced salesman selling a snappy-looking used Packard convertible. Cohen prided himself on knowing a snow job when he heard one. They were being conned, softened up for even more bad news.

"Okay," said the colonel. He paused for effect. "The object of this mission is to destroy the Italian transportation network, not to kill Italian civilians. And of almost equal importance is to avoid the Roman art treasures and monuments. This group has never had a more sensitive target, so we will not be bombing on the leader today. The final responsibility rests with you individual bombardiers. We want all our bombs on the target and no where else!—all of them! The reputation of high-altitude daylight precision bombing is at stake. If the Brits were doing this, they'd do it at night and destroy the whole damned city of Rome. Let's show them how it's done."

The CO was doing a Gipper locker-room routine. Cohen felt nauseous. It was probably the coffee.

"And there is one more thing, gentleman." His voice grew softer. "Under no circumstances will there by any overflights of the Vatican. In order to avoid any possibility of this, we will circle the city to approach our target from the north. It will add thirty, maybe forty-five minutes to our flying time, but it's absolutely necessary." *By all means, lets be sure and preserve an institution that was helping the Krauts knock off the Hebes.*

Cohen lit a cigarette and tried to pay attention. He wondered just how much additional flak this tactic would expose them to.

"Aborting or disabled aircraft will fly a course at least forty-five degrees off the Vatican heading until well past it." Smoke from the colonel's Egyptian cigar wafted upward to merge with the blue haze. "And lastly: if there are any Roman Catholics who take exception to this mission they may speak to the chaplain after this briefing. But keep in mind that anyone excused today will have two missions added to their tour. Replacements, if any, will come from the five standby crews whose aircraft are grounded."

Colonel Greeves waited patiently for the hubbub to die down. "Takeoff is scheduled for eight hundred hours. Altitude over the target will be twenty-two thousand. The Four-Fourteenth Squadron will lead the group. It and the Four-Twelfth will be high squadrons. The Four-Fifteenth and Four-Thirteenth will be low. I'm sure that Captain Cory will be happy to hear that I'll be flying with him today."

A deep baritone from the third row said, "Welcome aboard, Colonel."

"Thank you, Captain." The Group CO used his cigar for emphasis. "Our visitors from the Eighth will be flying today. The mission will be composed of five groups formed into two combat boxes. The Two-Eighty-seventh will comprise the last element of the second box."

Cohen had been expecting bad news and here it was. Across

the aisle someone said, "What do I have to do to get out of this chickenshit outfit?"

Their fate was sealed—officially. The 287th was to take up the rear, they were to be "Ass-End-Charlie," the most vulnerable position in the bomber stream. The 415th, Cohen's squadron, was to be the trailing element of the 287th. The enemy fighters and destroyers traditionally concentrated on the trailing elements, where they had plenty of free maneuvering room. To make things even worse, the flak gunners would have the fuse settings worked out by the time they were in range, and circling Rome was going to keep them in range for a hell of a lot longer than would a straight run-in.

Cohen glanced around. The earlier bravado was gone. Half the men in his row of seats were staring, unblinking, at the map. The others were studying their hands. Reality had set in. The time for useless pissing and moaning was past.

"Let's not get carried away because of our fighter escort. Defensive fire is still important, so keep formations tight. Bomb loads for the Four-Twelfth and Four-Thirteenth are five-hundred pounders, the Four-Fourteenth and Four-Fifteenth are carrying thousand-pounders. Fuse settings are zero delay, nose, and one-point-five, tail."

The colonel glanced down at the Rolex watch on his left wrist, raised his other hand and extended a finger. "On my count, gentlemen, synchronize your watches to six-twenty-four." He counted off fifteen seconds as officers and men adjusted their timepieces, then, bringing his left hand down sharply, he called out, "Woof."

The weather officer, Captain Clarence "Sunny" Day, using a map pointer, spoke of scattered thunderstorms at about five to seven thousand feet over southern Italy and drifting toward the Adriatic, extending from the Gulf of Taranto to a line just south of Rome. "In addition, you can depend on a five to seven tenths altocumulus at twelve to seventeen thousand, to help obscure your vapor trails. It will clear to about ninety percent visibility when you reach the target. Real lucky today."

Next, the flak officer, First Lieutenant Irwin Stern, read his briefing from a sheet of paper. It was, thought Cohen, a kind of cop-out to impersonalize bad news. Stern predicted flak at the target to be moderate to heavy. In briefing parlance, the term "moderate to heavy" had evolved into a euphemism for "devastating."

Cohen, still fighting drowsiness, looked up to find Captain Kramer briefing them on fighters. "There's a squadron of Italian Folgores at San Pancrazio, near Leece. If the area is clear of thunderstorms, they might be waiting for you. They shouldn't be too much of a threat, but don't underestimate them. A little farther north, at Foggia, the Luftwaffe has recently based about forty to sixty FW-190s from I and J Gruppe, JG 92. Here, too, the weather might keep them down, but don't count on it. The Luftwaffe has also been moving stuff into the Rome area, ME-109s and ME-110s with rocket tubes. The 110s are cold meat for your escort, but if the P-38s burn a lot of fuel in combat farther south, they might not make it that far. There are also assorted Italian squadrons all up the boot, but just the presence of our P-38s should scare them off. You're carrying chaff to be dropped just after you cross the coast. With luck, the stuff will screw up the Kraut ground controllers with a false radar reflection. Take off is scheduled for eight hundred hours. Good luck."

After the general briefing, there were specialized briefings for pilots, bombardiers, navigators. In the meantime the sergeant airmen picked up their parachutes and other flying gear, then made their way out to the line.

In the contrasty, low-angled light of morning, the crew, sweating in their sheepskin-lined leather flying pants were sprawled under the wing, some propped up against the landing gear, others stretched out full-length, using their flying jackets as pillows.

"I want to know who did it," said Maguire. His voice, though emphatic, demonstrated none of the anger displayed in his reddened face.

Sergeant D'Amato said, "I don't know who did it, Captain, but it sure is a hell of an improvement."

"Okay, that does it. Everybody on their feet." Maguire snapped his cigarette to the ground, twisted it angrily into the lose sand with the toe of a flying boot. "Attention, goddammit!"

The sergeants came to their feet slowly. They stood, arms at their sides, shoulders slumped, feet apart, like men who had just run a ten-mile race.

He picked one of them at random, "Woike, who's responsible for this?"

"Beats the shit out of me, Captain."

Maguire's voice was a hoarse shout. "Fibich!" He waited impatiently for a few seconds and was about to call out again when the crew chief emerged from the bomb bay.

"Yes, sir?"

"Okay, Sergeant, what do you know about it?"

"About what, sir?"

"You know damned well, about what!"

"No, sir."

"The naked broad on the nose of my airplane!"

"Oh, that." Fibich spat a stream of tobacco juice. "I figured that was your doing, Captain."

"You know damned well it wasn't."

"I guess I do now, sir."

"It wasn't here yesterday . . ."

"Right, and it wasn't here last night. But when I came out this morning, about an hour and a half ago, there she was. I mean, you can see, the paint is still sort of tacky."

"It looks like the work of PFC Gordon."

"No, sir. Charlie Gordon always signs his masterpieces with his initials and there ain't no initials on this baby. There's another nose artist over at the 413th, a Polish guy."

A flare, trailing a tail of smoke, arched up from the control tower to burst finally into a glowing yellow ball. Maguire said, "Okay, let's get aboard." He turned to Fibich. "I want that damned thing removed as soon as we get back, Sergeant."

"Sorry, sir, I got nothing to do with nose art. You'll have to arrange with the sheet metal department to get it painted over."

"You bastard . . . you take care of it or I'll have your fucking stripes!"

"You'll have to arrange that with the engineering department, Captain."

Lieutenant Deutsch grasped his pilot's arm. "We got to crank up engines, Mickey."

Maguire allowed himself to be pushed into the bomb bay. He hoisted himself up onto the catwalk and then through the flight deck hatch. He removed the clipboard from his seat and settled himself in. It was going to be a long trip. Almost nine hours would pass before Sally's wheels would touch the ground. He glanced down at the clipboard to check the 1A form, and saw the envelope. It carried a crossed-off logo of Shepheard's Hotel in Cairo. His name was penciled in large block letters. He ripped it open, impatiently. The note was printed in pencil.

> Dear Captain Maguire:
> Your wife, Sally Shank, Sally Maguire, Bonnie Astor (have it your way), has told me everything. She has even supplied me with a photo of you wearing ladies' underwear. Pretty. I'm sure that the squadron photo lab would gladly make 8x10 glossy copies for posting on the orderly room bulletin board.
> Danny
> P.S. She likes the new nose art. So do I. So does the crew. Leave it alone.

Maguire crumpled the note into a ball, was about to toss it out the cockpit window, but changed his mind. Instead, he dropped it into the pocket of his flying jacket. Then, swallowing rapidly in an attempt to fight down a sudden fit of nausea, he started on the preflight checklist with Deutsch.

Through the windshield he could see Cohen, standing, one arm raised with three fingers extended to indicate that the crew chief was standing by number-three engine with the hand fire extinguisher at the ready. It was the engine of choice for start-up as it powered the hydraulic pump. He heard Deutsch repeat for the third time, "Ignition switches on."

Captain Maguire fought to clear his mind of all but the matter at hand. He had a mission to fly. *Who the hell was Danny?* He poked his head out the cockpit window, called out, "Clear." Deutsch did the same on his side. Whoever he was, the bastard had known about her appendectomy scar.

Deutsch was looking at him, his eyes curious, his mouth frozen in a frown. Captain Maguire nodded, watched as the copilot primed with one hand, fired up number three with the other. Maguire ascribed his nausea to too much GI coffee. His chest was constricted. There was a picture on his airplane to remind him that some bastard named Danny had plumbed her depths. How many others? He should have been enraged. He was only annoyed.

The starter whined up the scale. The big engine farted twice, then came to life with a full-throated roar. It was, as always, beautiful music to Maguire's ears. He brought the mixture control back to auto-rich and leaned to his right to watch the oil pressure rise on the gauge. He was once again where he belonged: in charge of an airplane. He was on his way to Rome. Problems on the ground were insignificant. Fuck 'em. They would just have to await his return to earth.

It was the Jack Benny troupe's third and last day with the 287th. In a few hours they were to be trucked over to the 98th, about five miles up the Coast Road. In the meantime, they had been invited by Colonel Greeves to watch the takeoff. They crowded the control tower, a makeshift open-air forty-foot wooden belfry topped with a windsock that at the moment hung forlornly uninflated.

The air pulsated with the discordant music of 120 Pratt & Whitney 14-cylinder, 1,200-horsepower Twin Wasps. The thirty serviceable Liberators of the 287th Bombardment Group, checked out the night before by their resolute crew chiefs, trundled out of their revetments, stirring up clouds of dust. Patched, battered, oil-streaked, pregnant with bombs and fuel, they trundled across the uneven ground, bobbing and weaving, to the sound of squealing brakes and gunning engines.

The civilians watched from the tower, unconvinced that any of the squat, corpulent beasts could ever leave the ground. They didn't look like airplanes in the way that Spitfires, P-38s, or B-17 Flying Fortresses did: gracefully streamlined, sleek, seemingly airborne even when on the ground. The big, awkward Liberators moved heavily, nose to tail like tired old elephants groping their way to the burial ground.

Sally used a pair of borrowed field glasses to search for her namesake. It was one of the last in line. She was pleased with the new nose art, feeling that it suited her and the airplane much more than had the previous dowdy, joyless woman pulling her miserable wagon.

She found it hard to believe that less than a week had passed since leaving New York. Her life had been changed irrevocably. She felt a stab of fear for the three hundred men of the 287th, who were lining up below her to face the enemy on its own turf. Though she had only been with them for three days, she felt it was her outfit. Would it be the same with the 98th and the others to follow? Would they all look alike, act alike? How many of the names would she remember ten years after it ended? She went cold with the sudden conjecture that somehow it might all be interchangeable.

The big airplanes queued up. They stood quivering, their engines growling, creating a storm of Sahara sand. The crews, on a fine edge, waited at their takeoff stations. Pilots and copilots were poised to shove everything forward. It was a moment shared by everyone on the base: mechanics, grounded air crews, medical officers, supply sergeants, cooks and bakers, clerks, first sergeants, S-2 officers, everyone. Go or no-go? It was a question to be answered now by the lone Liberator that had taken off over an hour before to check en-route weather.

At precisely eight-sixteen, the tower operator, Tech Sergeant Joe Boundary, stepped to the rail with a flare pistol. A flare arched high into the air over the runway, leaving a trail of smoke. Mug Shot, the lead ship of the 415th squadron, gunned all four engines. Like an angry dog pulling against its leash, it stood trembling at the head of the runway. As the flare burst into a glowing green ball, Captain Bill Blanchard came off the brakes. Mug Shot, sporting twenty degrees of flaps, fought to overcome the inertia of its 69,000 pounds.

Slowly at first, the lead ship, at full throttle, hauled itself forward. It gained speed reluctantly. At the half-mile mark its manifold pressure read 47 inches, its props were spinning at 2,600 RPMs, its airspeed indicator registered 65 mph. All was as it should be. Gently, the pilot raised the nose just enough to take the pressure off the nose wheel.

At this point, the second ship in line, the 415th's Bluebell, began its trip down the runway. Fifteen seconds passed, then Mug Shot, a mile from her starting point, hauled herself off the ground at 135 indicated. A few seconds later she tucked in her wheels.

With reduced drag and increased speed, Mug Shot became an

airplane. She retracted her flaps. The ugly duckling transformed into an eagle; granted, not the most beautiful of eagles, but nevertheless a deadly one that was in its rightful element.

The lead ship started a climbing turn at a thousand feet. She would continue to circle as the four squadrons of the 287th Bombardment Group joined her. Over the Med they would tack themselves onto the tail end of the other four groups of the Ninth Air Force, Bomber Command. The mission to Rome was underway.

CHAPTER 12

JULY 1943

A half-mile below, a brilliant white cloud cover blanketed the toe of Italy. To the south, long, billowing contrails marked the presence of the American bomber stream. It was just where the German radar station at Crotone said it would be. They were turning northwest, onto a direct heading for Rome. Major Roberto Bianchi led his squadron of Macchi 202 Folgore fighters into a climbing half-circle in order to get the sun behind them.

The Folgore was a thing of beauty, the pride of the Regia Aeronautica: light of line and substance, graceful, elegant. As an airplane it was a thoroughbred, a joy to fly: fast and responsive. As a fighter it was impractical and therefore, in Major Bianchi's eyes, a typical example of Italian design. It was grievously underarmed. Like the fabric-covered Spads and Fokkers of an earlier, less sophisticated war, it mounted only two machine guns beneath a cowling just forward of the windscreen, synchronized to fire between the propellor blades. To Bianchi, it was as if the bastards were unwilling to spoil the clean Italian line of the Folgore wing by adding a few more 12.5 machine guns or, better yet, twenty-millimeter cannon, an esthetic desecration they probably equated with wearing black shoes and tan slacks.

He and his *pop guns* had been at it for two years, first against the British and their eight-gunned Spitfires, then against the aggressive, cannon-bearing Russian Yaks and Migs. For a short while in the very beginning, in Spain and later over Britain, it had been sport: talented gladiators, one on one, locked in chivalrous combat. A personal duel between two officers—gentlemen. The prize was awarded for skill, experience, courage, mental agility, and lightning reflexes. The loser, more often than not, died. But bombers were different. Hardly sport, bomber hunting was little more than butchery. The fighters had the decisive edge. Wrenched apart, the big airplanes would flutter to earth with folded wings or broken backs, their large, anonymous crews trapped in a deadly inertia. Or they disappeared in an instantaneous flash of high-explosive gasoline, oxygen, and human flesh; thirty-five tons of airplane and as many as ten men gone instantaneously. It had nothing to do with sport. And it was the wrong war against the wrong enemy. Bianchi had lost his stomach for the game.

Beneath him, the Americans were growing closer, filling the sky almost to the horizon. Over a hundred individual aircraft paraded against a pure-white cloud bank, stretching for miles: a thousand highly trained men, over a million pounds of demolition bombs, a thousand heavy Browning machine guns, almost a million rounds of fifty-caliber ammunition, a half-million horsepower. Italy was countering with twelve underarmed fighters, twelve men, twenty-four guns. A pinprick, a joke.

Major Roberto Bianchi pushed the throttle forward, kicked left rudder, eased the stick forward and left. The Folgore rolled into a dive. He freed his mind of doubt and conjecture, permitting professional instincts to guide his actions. His target, the trailing element of nine B-24 Liberators, was three thousand feet below and four miles to the west. They flew a tight, mutually supporting formation, stepped down to give each aircraft a maximum overlapping field of defensive fire. With the sun behind him, he would attack at an angle of forty-five degrees in order to present the squinting American gunners with a deflection problem.

Swiveling his head, Bianchi checked his squadron. They were diving with him, staggered in tight formation. His wingman was tucked in nicely—a twenty-year-old from a well-to-do Milanese family, a natural pilot, green but eager. The major liked to keep the new chicks by his side. The wingman's job was to protect his leader's tail, but so far, in eleven such actions, the enemy bombers had flown unescorted by fighters.

The four-engined Liberators resembled ugly, oversized railroad boxcars suspended from incongruously graceful, long, narrow wings. They were purely functional machines, crewed by ten professionals, dedicated to a single purpose: to deliver bombs to a distant target with great accuracy in broad daylight. Each was defended by ten, sometimes twelve, heavy machine guns. The gunners were alert now, like ancient knights defending a fortress; readying themselves for the onslaught. The Plexiglas domes of their power turrets gleamed in the sunlight, turning, elevating their twin guns. Single waist guns, protruding from open hatches, swung about and upward.

The Americans opened fire at about twelve hundred yards. They were aiming not at the attacking Italian fighters but at a point in space where they would be, where bullets and target would converge. Their survival depended on a constantly changing estimation of the target range, their own speed, the angle of fire relative to their line of flight, the rate of target approach. The fighters, with fixed guns firing forward along the axis of flight, had a much simpler equation to solve. They had only to aim their aircraft, lead a bit for apparent speed differential, and allow a bit of elevation for range. But bringing down a four-engined B-24 Liberator bomber with the Folgore's inadequate armament was like downing an elephant with a pistol; possible, but very difficult. Bianchi's method was to go for an engine. Loss of an engine could force the bomber to leave its formation, salvo its bombs harmlessly into the sea, and fly home, its mission aborted but, with luck, its crew of ten intact.

He hunched his shoulders forward, slumped lower in his seat as enemy tracer from thirty heavy machine guns crisscrossed the intervening space: deadly, glowing tentacles searching for the Italian kill. He held his fire. If the enemy wanted to waste its ammunition with long bursts at an impractical range, that was their business.

His squadron peeled off in elements of two, each seeking a separate target. With his airspeed indicator reading 365, Bianchi flattened his dive. He tensed his stomach muscles to counter the G forces of the pullout. With a quick glance out the corner of his eye to confirm the presence of his wingman, he zeroed in on the desert-pink leader.

At eight hundred yards he sighted on the Liberator's outboard port engine, then brought the Folgore's nose up slightly and tapped left rudder to allow for deflection. He caught a fleeting glimpse of a naked woman seated in a champagne glass and of his wingman's bullets stitching the large oval of the vertical fin. He squeezed the firing tit on the control stick. The twin guns chattered; their rate of fire slowed by the interrupter cam that prevented their bullets from striking his own propeller blades. At three hundred yards, there were hits around the enemy's wing root. He had overcompensated. He dropped the nose slightly to correct.

There was no time to observe the results. In an instant he was above and beyond his target, his headphones filled with the garbled chatter of his squadron. Hauling back on the stick, he pulled up, banking sharply to come around again for a second pass.

There was a brilliant flash to his left. A sudden buffeting almost wrenched the controls from his hands. His wingman was gone. The airplane and its young pilot had disappeared, transformed in less than a millisecond into a few thousand shards of hot metal, shredded flesh, and an ugly puff of black smoke. A freezing wind filled Bianchi's cockpit, whistling through the wreckage of the Perspex side panel just inches from his head.

He wheeled through the sky, checking engine instruments, aileron, and rudder controls for damage. Only one Italian fighter was in view. It was twenty-five hundred feet below; it was burning, tumbling end over end. In the same quadrant of sky, a Liberator was trailing smoke in a shallow dive. He counted five parachutes. A sixth man, looking like a tiny stuffed sack, fell into the clouds.

Bianchi froze all conjecture, focusing his mind on the second-by-second manipulation of the controls. He pushed the stick a few inches to the right, snapped into a ninety-degree bank, and with perfect timing flattened out to find another Liberator engine centered in the projected retical of the Folgore's optical gunsight. He brought the nose up slightly, tapped the rudder, then squeezed the firing tit. There was the whir of the gun camera, but the guns themselves remained silent. Bracketed by tracer, he climbed away, punching the charger solenoid switch to no avail. It was clear that the gun circuit had been cut or shorted. He throttled back to cruising speed, turning due north. He was a gunfighter without guns. It was time to go home.

The Folgore jerked as if it had hit a bump. Tracer grazed the wingtip. There were two loud bangs. He had been hit. Instinctively, he pulled the throttle back into overboost. (Italian throttles worked backward.) He banked sharply, looking over his left shoulder into the inevitability of sudden death. Unarmed and alone at 21,000 feet he was under attack by two American fighters.

Achilles Panzeri, mayor of San Pancrazio, levered his considerable bulk to a standing position. Across the spacious office, Benito Mussolini glared at him from a framed poster behind the desk. The mayor shut his eyes, pulled in his belly, and proceeded to squirm into his corset.

Mayor Panzeri had marched into Rome with Mussolini in October of '22, a glorious day, explosive with promise. Now, more than twenty years later, most of the others, their black shirts replaced by the gilt of rank, were misgoverning provinces or leading armies to glorious defeat, while he languished in a provincial southern town. He inhaled deeply, sucking a final centimeter of belly up into his chest while taking a small measure of satisfaction from the knowledge that Il Duce, too, wore a corset.

As a young man, typical of his sophisticated, Milanese peers, the term "south" had always applied to Naples or Sicily. What lay between was a non-place, a vacuum, the heel and toe of a paralytic who had long since lost all awareness of those appendages. But he had made the best of it. Now the era was coming to an end, and he would make the best of that, also.

He turned to stare at Signora Carlotta Tiboldi. Till now he had not seen her simultaneously vertical and fully naked. It was an unpleasant surprise. Her body had always seemed much fuller, more voluptuous when horizontal. It was a common understanding amongst men—real men—that women's natural state was one of fleshy rotundity. Anything less was a perversion of nature more suitable to the cold, hard, miserly anatomy of American or English women. The mayor surveyed Signora Tiboldi carefully as she turned away to retrieve her clothing. Her buttocks lacked the essential meaty plumpness, her hips were bony, her shoulder blades conspicuous. Over a period of months he had made use of her on the battered leather couch a few dozen times but had somehow been too preoccupied to notice those unfortunate shortcomings. He sighed, aware now that his physical satisfaction was the result of a self-delusion. So be it, but if Signora Carlotta Tiboldi were his, he would feed her as one feeds a pig for market. Her unusual attribute of silent enthusiasm easily justify the expense.

He stared out the window. On the edge of town a swath of green dominated the landscape: a vineyard, the largest in the area. Row on row of tall vines were hung with clusters of ripe red grapes looking like Christmas ornaments. Here and there, between the rows, small groups of pickers, colorless stick figures, were loading the harvest into donkey carts.

Beyond, the narrow rutted washboard of a road snaked through an eroded gray landscape punctuated with a million bone-white stones. A few years earlier, short stretches of the road had been filled with gravel. The improvement constituted Impresa Moderna, part of Il Duce's much publicized program to raise living standards in the south. In an attempt to prove the effectiveness of the program, the official road map of the area, more a political document than an aid to motorists, showed the wretched road in the bright orange that was meant to indicate major highways.

In the near distance, the flatness of the land was broken only by low-lying scrubby hillocks punctuated here and there by groves of olive trees. The tiny village of Sarentina squatted naked, out in the open. Beehivelike dwellings of uncemented stone clustered about the mother beehive of the church. On its outskirts groups of peasants labored in the rock-strewn fields. Harvesting or planting? The sole evidence of a crop seemed nothing more than patches of low-lying scrub.

India, thought Mayor Panzeri, or the famine-stricken plains of China. But no, neither of those. He recalled a newsreel he'd seen six or seven years earlier, when he was still in Rome. Seated comfortably in the dark, he had observed the victorious Bersaglieri in their rakish pith helmets and tropical uniforms marching triumphantly to a martial sound track. The field around them had been littered with twisted corpses of the enemy: jet-black, spear-carrying Ethiopians, slaughtered by Fascist mustard gas and artillery. The sound track bellowed, "Viva Duce! Victory! Viva Italia! Abyssinia is ours!" There had been cheers, close-ups of grinning Italian soldiers. Then the camera panned about to reveal a dead landscape almost identical to the one he now viewed through his lofty town-hall window.

The British and Americans had landed in Sicily. Everyone knew that soon—weeks, perhaps days—they would have Messina, the gateway to Italy.

He whispered, "Abyssinia . . ." This time the newsreels would be shown not in Rome but in London and Chicago: the grim landscape not African, but southern Italian; the triumphant soldiers not Italian, but Anglo-American; the twisted corpses not Ethiopian, but Italian. His might be one of them.

It was foolishness. It was not yet time for him to die. The war would surely end before he had the opportunity to hear a shot fired in anger—a matter of weeks. He would surely live well into his nineties, his virility intact. He knew it in his bones. The thought cheered him. He caught Signora Tiboldi's eye to smile at her. She hesitated for a moment in a show of flustered surprise at the rare and gratuitous pleasantry. Then, shyly, she smiled in return.

They were the first fighters Major Roberto Bianchi had seen during the month he had been flying against the American bombers. Lockheed P-38 Lightnings; twin-tailed, armed with twenty-millimeter cannon and fifty-caliber machine guns. Two engines gave them a forty-mile-an-hour advantage. They possessed almost double his firing range and could catch him in a climb. He could neither outrun them nor dive to safety.

The only advantage held by the Italian Folgore fighter was its superior maneuverability. Under ordinary circumstances Bianchi would be attempting to turn inside the attacking Lightnings in order to get on their tail. In an unarmed fighter, such a tactic was meaningless. Once again he hit the gun-charging switch to no avail.

Less than fifteen hundred meters behind, the Americans had him bracketed. They were holding their fire, toying with him, waiting to get in close for a sure kill that would expend a minimum of ammunition. Despite the freezing wind blowing through the shattered side canopy, a stream of sweat ran down his cheek. He could neither fight nor run. But he could hide.

Eight thousand feet below, the clouds offered a haven. It was simply a matter of getting to the hiding place in one piece.

He fought to compartmentalize his fear, trade it off for cold mental action. Holding to his course he breathed deeply, counting the seconds aloud into his oxygen mask. The closer the enemy came the less time they would have to react to a violent maneuver. With proper timing, he could outguess them, force them to overshoot and thereby increase the range.

On the count of twelve, using all his strength, he shoved the stick forward. He was an instant too late. There was a flash of tracer, another jolting bang. A pattern of neat holes punctuated his starboard wing. Blood sang in his ears as the Folgore fell like a stone.

His eyes flicked over the instrument panel. The altimeter was unwinding with blurred rapidity. The airspeed indicator crept upward: 275—385—400—425—435. He was well over the red line. He wondered briefly if anyone had ever dived a Macchi-202 Folgore under power at that speed and lived to tell of the pullout. The G forces could rip the wings off. The airspeed indicator passed 445. He slowed his breathing, diverting a panic welling up in his belly. He was committed. His fears were academic. There was no other game to play. Swiveling his head he could see that both Lightnings had followed the angle of his dive. The range had increased by five hundred yards, but they were still with him and slowly gaining. The pair of twin-tailed devils were lined up, one behind the other. The enemy pilots were good at their job.

The leader's nose winked fire. A salvo of explosive cannon shells and alternating fifty-caliber tracer, incendiary, and armor-piercing rounds streaked just inches to the right of his cockpit. In a near-vertical tail chase, gravity favored the attacker; effective range was increased, and the problems of deflection and bullet drop were nonexistent. He had gained a few seconds, but the next burst would be at a shorter range and was sure to blow him out of the sky. With his prop turning at 1,400 revs he gave her full manifold pressure and closed the radiator shutters to get the last iota of power from his overheated engine.

At 455 miles an hour he kicked hard left rudder and prayed the Folgore would hold together. The machine turned on itself and snapped into a roll. Impassively he watched the aluminum skin of the wing rippling to the increasing G forces. Both the flesh of his face and that of the airplane seemed about to crack under the strain, to peel back like the skin of an orange. For seconds— an eternity—peripheral vision deserted him. He was peering through a narrow black tube, his head in an iron vice. It was the moment of truth—live or die. He rolled ninety degrees, put the Folgore on its back, and pulled the stick into his belly. There was a roaring in his ears as the blood was forced from his head down into his flying boots. Blindly, he kicked left rudder again.

The Folgore had lost altitude and had turned 180 degrees, heading southwest. He had performed a brutal maneuver that the Americans' slower turning rate could not match. He observed both fighters pass beneath him, going the other way.

Bianchi had earned a reprieve. As always, he was surprised at his calmness, his ability to think clearly. Despite the pounding in his head, he experienced a keen, almost euphoric gratification. Against desperate odds, he had kicked the winning goal, won the tennis match . . . that and more. He was still alive, his airplane was miraculously in one piece, and the sanctuary of the clouds was now less than a mile below.

Keeping his descent shallow, he opened the radiator cooling shutters, eased up on the throttle—housekeeping chores. He checked his instruments. Oil pressure was down, but not dangerously. Engine temperature was above the red but slowly falling. The radio was out. He twisted about to glance out the top of the canopy toward the tail. The antenna was gone, shot away. But he had no real need of it. He was perhaps seventy or eighty miles southwest of the field at San Pancrazio. Below the clouds, navigation would be simple.

But the clouds had grown ugly. He stared down at a boiling

white mass. Despite its movement, it seemed solid, a kind of animated concrete. Sporadic internal flashes lit a metropolis of monumental pillars pushed aloft by powerful vertical winds.

Fortunately, the storm was localized. In order to circle it he would continue on a southern course, away from the bomber stream and its fighter escort. He became aware that rudder control was less responsive than it should have been and reasoned that the vertical stabilizer had been hit.

Once again, he felt the jolt, heard the impact of an explosive cannon shell. A large hole opened in the previously damaged starboard wing. Instinctively, he banked sharply into the good wing to find that one of the Lightnings had completed a turn in his direction. The frustrated American, now minus his wingman, in a desperate and angry last effort was on overboost and firing from extreme range. Like a punch-drunk fighter, Bianchi weaved the Folgore from side to side. For the moment it seemed the only thing to do. He was certain that his damaged wing could not sustain another abrupt maneuver. A steep dive now could be suicide.

With a dogged show of tenacity, the American, alone now, was once again riding to the hounds. Major Bianchi cursed himself for his arrogance in assuming he had outfoxed the fellow. Fox indeed. If he were a fox—a wily fox—who valued his life, he would have been rotating his head every ten or fifteen seconds to search the lethal heavens for killers. He was getting too old for this sort of thing.

The Folgore was showing a marked tendency to drop its starboard wing and skew right. A quick glance confirmed that the cannon wound was festering. Aluminum skin was peeling back into the slipstream, bleeding off lift, creating drag. Without thinking about it, he unlatched the canopy, pulled off his oxygen mask, and tightened his parachute straps: precautions that would save vital seconds if and when he left the cockpit.

The clouds were now about two thousand feet below, the deadly American was less than half that distance and rapidly reducing the range. A matter of seconds, one way or the other.

Major Bianchi banked left just in time to observe the Lightning's muzzle flashes. There was a sound of rocks dropping onto a tin roof. The Folgore bucked. He felt the impact on the reverse side of his armored seat back. His airplane had been hit by machine-gun fire, just aft of the cockpit. There was no alternative now. Piece by piece, the machine was being eaten alive. Again, despite the danger, he executed a split S into a dive, pointing the Folgore's nose at the tempest and the invisible ground beneath it.

It seemed an eternity of seconds before he passed into the maelstrom. He could see as far as his wing tips but beyond that was an impenetrable, swirling gray. The Folgore was subjected to a wild buffeting that increased, as slowly, with wary eyes glued to the damaged wing, he leveled out. The wing stayed on.

Now, no longer merely an object dropping through space, he was once again airborne. But the air that bore him had gone mad. It flung the Folgore about as if it were a child's toy. Then suddenly its buoyancy disappeared altogether, sucked away by a giant inhalation. His head struck the canopy as the Folgore dropped from under him. He opened the throttle fighting for lift.

The airplane struck bottom with a jolt that rattled its bones. Knowing what was to follow, he throttled back. An instant later, he was rising—an innocent leaf in the clutches of a tornado. The translucent gray was slashed with a sporadic series of lightning bolts as he raised the nose slightly to drain off some lift. At the top of the rise, he reversed the procedure to prevent a stall and then flicked on the instrument lights.

Within such angry turbulence one could be on his back and be unaware of it. He was flying blind. Only instruments could provide orientation. His eyes completed a circuit every eight or ten seconds: compass, engine-RPM, turn-and-bank, rate-of-climb, artificial horizon, airspeed, altimeter, radiator temperature, engine temperature, oil pressure . . . With one hand grasping the agitated control stick and the other at the ready on the throttle, he awaited the next downdraft. Instead, the battered Folgore was subjected to a brutal buffeting that almost wrenched the stick from his hands. The turn-and-bank indicator informed him that he was in a thirty-degree bank. He corrected. In the process he turned onto a northeastern heading, began a shallow descent, estimating less than a minute to break out beneath the clouds.

Then, suddenly, a blurred and ghostly image flashed onto his windscreen. Almost instantaneously it resolved into a monstrous whalelike hulk floating, serenely unaware, in a murky sea. He was approaching it broadside—an American Liberator. There was barely time to shove the stick forward.

The Folgore seemed to take forever to respond. His mind registered details. *A feathered propeller, blades turned into the slipstream to keep it from windmilling . . . a silhouette of the pilot in the cockpit window . . . a naked woman seated in a champagne glass . . . large, blue, upper-case letters spelling out words:* SALLY'S WAGON. Instantly he was beneath it, looking up through the canopy at the ball turret slung from its belly. A matter of inches, of split seconds, then it was gone.

Locked in the constricting embrace of aftershock, it was moments before he realized his dive was over sixty degrees and growing steeper. His airspeed read 320. It was obvious he was in another downdraft. The airspeed indicator was, at least momentarily, useless. He estimated his speed relative to the ground to be a monstrous 500 miles an hour. He minimized his throttle setting, then dropped undercarriage and flaps to induce drag and act as air brakes. A few seconds passed before he felt, in the seat of his pants, the inertial sensation of reduced speed. Gingerly, he attempted to flatten the dive against the brutal force of gravity. He sensed, rather than heard, a deep groan as if the Folgore was experiencing mortal pain. Twisting his head to stare out the shattered side canopy he could see the wing was failing under the increasing load. A wide crack had opened just outboard of the gaping cannon wound.

Simultaneously, using both hands, he struck the quick release on his seat harness and pushed upward against the overhead canopy. It required all his strength to move it a mere two inches against the slipstream. He braced his back against it as a loud snapping sound, a hideous whistling, marked the imminent departure of the starboard wing. The canopy was jammed. He reasoned quickly that an errant piece of disfigured metal—battle damage—must have formed a deadly latch for which he had no key.

With a monstrous lurch she gave up her wounded wing. The Folgore was no longer an airplane but rather a dead weight falling through space; turning end over end, tumbling, twisting on three separate axles. He was merely a loose object rattling about inside, his head battering the overhead canopy, the windscreen, the instrument panel. He kicked out desperately, repeatedly in all directions. For an instant he perceived, out of the corner of his eye, a flickering—fire. A throatful of acrid smoke cut short a scream he realized was his.

Then, curled in a fetal ball, he was free, ejected from the dead fighter through the imploded side canopy; his life a gift from his wingman whose wreckage had shattered it earlier. A lightning flash turned the gray opaqueness into a brilliant but momentary luminescence. Breathing deeply of the cold rushing air, he straightened, fumbled for the ripcord, and pulled. With a sharp tug, the parachute blossomed.

He swung in its harness as the grayness dissipated. Looking down between dangling legs, he could see the coastline through a few wispy strands of cloud. A narrow beach stretched beneath a ragged cliff. He pulled the shroud lines to spill air, directing his descent inland.

Below and to the west, the Folgore, trailing flame and smoke, cartwheeled silently into the Straits of Otranto. To the northwest a gray town squatted near the horizon—San Pancrazio or Manduria. It occurred to him that the wounded B-24 in the cloud had been the very one he had attacked. *A naked female in a champagne glass.* With an engine out, the big Liberator had been separated from its formation and, taking advantage of the cloud sanctuary, was headed home to its base in Libya. Though he no longer cared about that sort of thing, the disabled American would count as a "kill" to be credited to him; his twentieth or twenty-first, he'd forgotten, lost count. He felt like laughing and wondered why. He was trembling. Perhaps, he thought, it would be a good idea to include whiskey flasks in parachute packs to protect ejected pilots from cold rain and panic. Foolishness . . .

He twisted about, facing north. A pillar of smoke was rising from the town. Even as he watched there were three bright flashes and more smoke. It took him a moment to realize that the crippled enemy bomber, deep in the clouds, had blindly salvoed its load of bombs in order to lighten ship. The bastards could have dropped them "safe." A mere expediency, the arming wires re-taining the little fuse propellers, preventing them from spinning off and freeing the firing pins, a flick of the bombardier's finger on the arming switch.

The innocent town was smothered in dense smoke, highlighted, here and there, by an orange glow. He turned away to stare out to sea and was not surprised to find that he was trembling un-controllably.

Fully dressed, Signora Carlotta Tiboldi waited patiently. The mayor took his time. There was no one in all of the Province of Pulia who took more pride in his appearance. He surveyed the effect of each item of clothing in the gilded cheval mirror. His riding breeches were cut from closely woven English gabardine; his silk foulard was from prewar Paris; his vest and jacket hand-tailored in Rome only three years ago. The best of everything was his natural due. He prided himself on impeccable taste, on an innate sense of quality.

Mayor Achilles Panzeri spread brilliantine in his palm, then rubbed it vigorously into his hair. He brushed thoroughly, creat-ing a high pompadour. He coiffed his mustache, just so, using a miniature ivory comb carved in the form of a woman's leg.

Finally, satisfied, he turned to present himself to Signora Ti-boldi. She nodded approval. He withdrew the usual envelope from his breast pocket and handed it to her, an act of casual delicacy in which neither of them had to handle or even acknowl-edge the passage of money. Smiling weakly, she accepted the of-fering without comment, then was gone.

At his desk, he swung his chair about to stare out the window. Only the nearby church steeple had a higher vantage point.

The town of San Pancrazio, like an underdeveloped photo-graph, lacked shadows and contrast. The houses lay inside what appeared to be long, gray, creviced walls, accented every three or four meters by a door sporting a black pennant. The pennants had been hung to honor family who had died within. Many of these grim decorations had hung for decades, braving the elements that had eroded them into little more than withered rags.

He was about to swing his chair around when the Fiat garage

across the square disappeared in a blinding flash. There was a monstrous roar, a blast of air that shattered his office windows. Almost simultaneously, the usually opaque stained-glass windows of the church burst into a glorious translucency. The mayor of San Pancrazio was unaware of the third bomb, only of the sky being blotted out and an immense pressure on the small of his back. Then, nothing.

CHAPTER 13

JULY 1943

The taxi driver wore a skullcap, a yarmulke. He looked over his shoulder. "Bist a yid?" Puzzled, Cohen threw a glance at the second lieutenant with whom he was sharing the cab.

The young lieutenant said, "How can you tell?"

The driver turned again, a grin lighting his face. It was, thought Cohen, like the weathered face of a fisherman. Bushy eyebrows framed dark, deep-set eyes. "I have what you call a sixth sense." The words were colored with a nondescript, guttural accent. "And your friend?"

The meaning of the question was suddenly clear to Cohen. Shrugging off a fleeting apprehension, he eyed the driver in the rearview mirror. "I'm a yid from way back."

"We're all from way back, my friend." With a single squawk of the horn, the driver swung the 1937 Vauxhall onto the shoulder and around a British army lorry that insisted on occupying the center of the road. He said, "You're the first American soldiers I've seen. It's good to see Americans, especially when they're Jews."

Cohen said, "There were Americans stationed right here at Lydda, last year—a heavy bomb group—Liberators."

"Yes, my friend, so I've been told. But I wasn't in Palestine last year."

"Where you from?"

"Poland." He lit a cigarette. Cohen noted it was from a pack of Vs.

"Poland," said the lieutenant. "That's a long way."

"So is America," said the driver. "But here we are in Palestine." He paused for a moment, exhaling a cloud of smoke. "You know what's happening in Poland?"

"Nazis," said the lieutenant. "I mean, everybody knows that."

Once again, from under a sheltering ridge of bushy eyebrows, the driver's deep-set eyes engaged Cohen's in the rearview mirror. He was about to say something, then seemed to change his mind. Instead, he nodded his head. His smile revealed a flash of gold.

Cohen felt it was a knowing smile. The driver could probably see right through him. Perhaps the "real" Jews, the ones who wore skullcaps and spoke with an accent, actually did possess a sixth sense. The thought made him uneasy. He stared out the window. The arid countryside was punctuated here and there with patches of green. They passed an Arab leading three camels along the side of the road. The animals were laden with an enormous number of bulging sacks.

The driver seemed intent on making conversation. "I see you've got wings on your tunics. You're flyers?"

"Yes," said Cohen. "I'm a flight engineer."

"I'm a pilot," said the lieutenant.

"Jewish flyers," said the driver. "Imagine . . ."

"Americans," said the pilot by way of clarification.

"My name is Josef Meyerwitz," said the driver.

"Abe Cohen, nice to meet you."

"Second Lieutenant Walter J. Blum."

Cohen said, "How about your serial number?"

"Don't be a wise guy, Sergeant."

The driver said, "You going to be in Tel Aviv long?"

"A few days," said the lieutenant. "Is there a beach?"

"A nice beach with a very nice hotel. You want me to take you there?"

"How much will it cost?"

"The whole trip from the airport will cost one dollar if you have American money."

"No, I mean the hotel."

"About one pound a night, including breakfast."

"Okay."

Cohen said, "Anything cheaper around? I'm not interested in the beach."

"I know a nice little hotel just off the Allenby Road," said the driver. "About fifty piasters a night. How long you going to be staying?"

"A few days in Tel Aviv, then Jerusalem." He had at least a week. Sally's Wagon had been shot up by Italian fighters during the Rome mission and had been forced to abort with a dead engine and other damage. She was grounded for repairs and maintenance. The crew, with eight-day passes, had flown out, along with twenty other guys on the beer plane—Fearless Freddy—for Cairo and Alexandria. Cohen had remained aboard to the end of the line: Lydda Aerodrome in Palestine. The decision to spend his leave in the Holy Land was motivated by a desire to get away from his crew for a week.

"It's Friday," said the driver. "I would like to invite both of you to my house this evening for Shabbat dinner."

They were entering the outskirts of Tel Aviv. The neighborhood looked newly constructed, dusty, unfinished. The houses were white stucco, modernistic, with squared-off balconies and much in the way of glass brick.

The lieutenant said, "It's nice of you to offer, Mr. Meyerwitz, but . . ."

"Think nothing of it, my friend. I won't take no for an answer. It is the least one can do; a Jewish duty to offer hospitality to the lonely traveler on Shabbat. I'll drop you at your hotels, then pick you up at four o'clock. There'll be plenty time. It gets dark late at this time of year. I live with my aunt, she's a marvelous cook, believe me."

"Thanks a lot," said Cohen, squirming in his seat. "That's very nice of you." Despite a hollow uneasiness, he had a hunch that the evening would probably be interesting—educational. He glanced over at the lieutenant, who raised his eyes and spread his hands in a gesture of resignation.

Cohen had developed a distinct dislike for the lieutenant and wondered if the driver had seen the gesture in his rearview mirror.

THE MISSION
August 1, 1943

"**W**here in hell's the pinpoint?"

Captain Maguire leaned forward in his seat. Visibility was restricted by a sulfuric haze and, for periods of seconds, totally obliterated by billowing plumes of greasy black smoke. There seemed to be as much of the stuff inside the airplane as outside. A few of the crew had taken to oxygen masks.

"We'll give it fifty more seconds, Beel, then we'll find us an alternate. Cohen, keep your eyes open up there. Okay, Woike, D'Amato, you can toss those incendiaries out the belly hatch, now. Looks like good stuff down there."

"Roger wilco."

"D'Amato to pilot, Suzy just feathered number three."

"Pull up! Pull up!"

Cohen's alarm jolted Maguire into shoving the throttles forward. Almost instantly, a smokestack materialized directly ahead. It filled more and more of the windshield; a giant club racing to smash them. He pulled the yoke back. They were close enough for Maguire to count the bricks. He twisted the wheel to the right, kicked right rudder, prayed that Chloe would get out of the way in time. There were two other stacks just to the left, forming a triangle—their pinpoint.

"Bombs away!"

Maguire felt the inertial weight in his buttocks, as Sally's Wagon, under full throttle and rid of her heavy load of bombs, reared upward. Out of the corner of his eye he perceived the left wing coming up, slowly, almost too slowly. He willed Sally skyward, every sinew of his body straining. The smokestack was about 200 feet tall; her left wing cleared it by three.

Maguire and Deutsch got her straight and level at 350 feet. Maguire breathed deeply, pressed the throat mike against his neck.

"Okay, look sharp, watch for fighters . . . the bastards are out there. Cohen, I want you down here on the flight deck. Crenshaw, replace him in the turret. Yardbird, some of those detonators got about twenty—thirty—seconds to go. Keep your eye on the target and let me know."

"Roger wilco."

"Bomb doors closed."

"Suzy's got number three feathered and an engine fire in number four."

"How bad?"

"Lot of smoke."

"Haney, this is Maguire."

"I read you."

"You going to make it?"

"I got one feathered. I think we got the engine fire doused but I got a runaway prop on number two."

"Can you make it to Turkey?"

"Damned wing's liable to rip off before I get a third of the way."

"Get some altitude and bail out your crew."

"No can do. I'm going to set it down. I got me an unconscious copilot and my engineer's in shock. He's missing an arm . . . Jesus . . ."

"Wait till you're well out of the target area. You got hydraulic pressure for flaps?"

"Yeah, got the auxiliary going."

"Good luck, John."

"I'll send you a postcard. Over and out."

"Taylor, give me a heading the hell out of here."

"Come around to two hundred and ten degrees."

"We got bandits at two o'clock high. Eight—ten—of them. They're just sitting up there, about four thousand feet . . . ME-109s."

"I see them."

"They're just staying out of their own flak."

"Fuck 'em, feed 'em beans!"

"*Keep your eyes on them and calm down, everybody, we got a long way to go. Crenshawe, what's with Chloe?*"

"*Off our port wing, Captain, looking okay.*"

"*Yardbird, those bombs blow, yet?*"

"*Can't tell for sure, sir. Can't make out a fucking thing through this fucking smoke except flashes every now and then. But I saw the bombs go in. They were right on the fucking button . . . I mean, hot shit!*"

"*What about you, Junior?*"

"*Confirmed, Captain. I saw it too. I counted three of them inside the blast wall.*"

"*Good bombing, Beel. Nice work. I'm glad we didn't come all this way for nothing . . . unless the damned things were duds.*"

They were suddenly in the clear, out of the smoke and mayhem. A patchwork of wheat fields stretched, like a shaggy carpet, ahead of them. Maguire motioned to Deutch to take over the controls. He squirmed about, flexed his muscles, stretched his legs, massaged his aching calves

Two or three miles ahead, three pink B-24s who shouldn't have been there crossed their path at right angles. To their right, a large target area was burning. Twisting around in his seat, he glanced back out the bubble built into the cockpit window. Sassy Suzy now lagged a hundred yards behind them. Her flaps were down.

As he watched, the big airplane let down slowly. Nose high, she seemed to skim the ground forever. Finally in a flurry of dust and alfalfa chaff she touched down and passed out of Maguire's view. It was, he observed, a textbook example of a wheels-down B-24 crash landing. John Haney was good, real good. Unlike most other AAF aircraft, the procedure for crash landings in a B-24 called for the landing gear to be in the down position.

Suzy's made it okay. There are guys getting out. Two . . . three . . ."

"*You see any fire, Smith?*"

"*No, captain, no smoke, nothing . . . one more coming up out the flight deck hatch . . . they're getting two wounded guys out the waist window . . . seven . . . eight . . . nine.*"

"*Jesus, they're waving good-bye.*"

"*Wave back, D'Amato, we're going home.*"

With Chloe off her right wing, Sally began the long climbing turn, back to Africa.

Captain Pitcairn stood in the open doorway to the ops bunker, a pair of Zeiss binoculars to his eyes. To the northwest what seemed to be almost two hundred big American bombers, many less than fifty feet off the ground, were weaving erratic patterns through the smoke over the Ploesti refinery area. He noted two flights of German ME-109s approaching from the west. A third flight, consisting of sleek Rumanian IAR-80s, were diving into the melee, disregarding their own antiaircraft fire.

Pitcairn watched as a B-24 struck an explosive-laden barrage balloon cable, and was instantaneously transformed into a ball of fire and debris. Another nosed up, its right wing root puffing flames. An instant later, the wing itself folded upward, as if hinged. A mile away, to the west, a Rumanian fighter, taking punishment from a trio of pink B-24s, streaked like a comet into an oil storage tank which, two seconds later, erupted into a monstrous pillar of fire and smoke, winking out one of the B-24s as if it were a moth in a flame.

The big, low-flying bombers were enmeshed in an intricate spider's web of tracer rounds—thousands of deadly, glowing red balls. Hundreds of guns of every caliber were pinpointed by their muzzle flashes. They were firing from everywhere: entrenched, sandbagged positions; rooftops; and hundred-foot flak towers from which the gunners had the unusual luxury of firing down on their airborne targets.

The big Liberators, at minumum height, sped through the holocaust, their gunners answering the antiaircraft fire with devastating results.

Pitcairn was awed by the Americans. Their tactics in the face of overwhelming odds were complex, daring, carried out with unimaginable skill and precision. As he watched, two flights of B-24s approached head-on. Collisions seemed unavoidable. At the last instant, one of the flights—five aircraft—ducked under the other to skim twenty-five feet above the burning target to safety. Simultaneously, a third flight crossed at right angles, forming a triple tier. It was a flawless maneuver, more appropriate to a well-rehearsed air show than to the confusion of battle.

Major Brayer was standing beside him. Pitcairn handed him the binoculars, saying, "It's the charge of the Light Brigade, and we're playing the part of the Turks."

"Well put," said Brayer, peering intently through the glasses.

"In all my life as a pilot," said the Luftwaffe officer, "I've never seen such skill, or such precise tactics. The Americans are superb!"

"Yes, and no doubt the Turks at Balaclava were impressed, just as we are," said Major Brayer, handing back the glasses. "Of course, they had no way of knowing that the classic British charge had been the result of a monstrous error. The same might very well be the case here, with the Americans. This may not be exactly what they had in mind."

Captain Pitcairn seemed suddenly deflated. "Perhaps, but somehow I'd hate to think so."

"A moot point, Captain." The Rumanian major turned to go back into the bunker. "The fact is, as we can plainly see . . . *Ploesti is burning.*"

CHAPTER 14

JULY 1943

There were seven of them at dinner. Josef Meyerwitz's Aunt Sarah spent more time serving and fussing than she did eating. Cohen sat directly across the table from Natalie Marek. She was in her early twenties. Her sun-darkened skin was set off by a simple, crisp, white linen dress and jet-black hair, cut short. Except for a bit of lipstick, she wore no makeup. The lipstick, thought Cohen, was superfluous. She needed no enhancement.

Cohen, in an attempt not to be obvious, surveyed her out of the corner of his eye. She caught him at it and smiled. She was the most beautiful woman he had ever seen.

Her brother, Uri Marek, was seated to Cohen's right. He was tall, equally tanned; dressed in British army uniform, sporting sergeant's stripes.

Over the soup course, Josef Meyerwitz, the cab driver, taking notice of Cohen's obvious interest in Miss Marek, said, "Natalie is also in the military. She's a corporal in the WAAF, Woman's Auxiliary Air Force."

Cohen smiled at her. "Your uniform's very attractive."

She smiled back. "I'm on leave."

"The women's forces are fortunate," said her brother. "They're not required, like the rest of us, to wear their uniforms off duty."

"I'm in favor of that," said Lieutenant Blum.

Cohen, seeking a way to extend his dialogue with her, said, "Where are you stationed, Corporal Marek?"

"Please call me Natalie. I'm at RAF headquarters in Cairo—weather section."

"My sister," said Uri Marek, "helps decide whether or not you gentlemen will fly."

"My brother likes to flatter me. But I don't really decide anything. I just transport paper from one place to another on a motorbike."

"We all do our part," said Blum.

She said, "Where are you from in America, Lieutenant?"

"Cleveland, Ohio," said Blum. "A place called Shaker Heights. My father's a judge." He stated it as if it explained everything. Cohen hoped he wouldn't talk about his experiences in the Boy Scouts or on the high school tennis team.

She turned to him. "And you, Sergeant?"

"Call me Abe."

"Abe . . ."

"I'm from New York."

"Brooklyn?" asked Meyerwitz.

"Manhattan, an area called Hell's Kitchen."

Serving the pot roast and kasha, Meyerwitz's aunt paused for a moment to converse briefly with her nephew in a language that sounded to Cohen like German. Finally, in English, the cabdriver said, "You don't speak Yiddish, Sergeant?"

"My parents did."

Meyerwitz said, "My aunt thinks that's a funny name for a Jewish district—Hell's Kitchen."

Cohen grinned up at the elderly woman, "Well, it's not exactly what you would call a Jewish district." She smiled back at him as her nephew translated. He would have to be more careful. He brought the wine glass to his lips, remembering, with a flash of painful guilt, how his teenage gang used to brutalize Jewish kids who were foolish enough to stroll into the neighborhood. He said, "It was tough." He felt himself flush and turned to Uri Marek in an effort to switch the subject. "How long have you and your sister been in Palestine?"

"We were born here; we're native Palestinians."

Natalie said, "Sabras." She smiled. "That's Hebrew for 'cactus.' "

"What about the Arab Palestinians?" said Lieutenant Blum.

"They don't like being called Palestinians."

"Our grandfather walked from Kiev to Haifa in the 1890s. The Turks were the rulers then."

"Uri and I are kibbutzniks," said Natalie Marek. Then, noting the puzzled expression on Cohen's face, she added, "A kibbutz is a kind of cooperative farm . . . well actually, more than just a farm. Ours is called Ramat Sharon." She went on to describe briefly the workings and social structure of their kibbutz.

Cohen barely heard her words as he fought valiantly against a preoccupation with her eyes, her lips, her eloquent hands. When she concluded, he nodded, searching for a response. He could think of nothing. He heard himself say, "You speak very good English."

"Uri and I have been speaking it since we were children. And working with the British every day, I get a lot of practice."

Lieutenant Blum said, "Are you people Communists?"

There was silence for a moment, then Josef Meyerwitz said, "You're asking about kibbutzim?"

"Well, yes. It sounds sort of communistic to me."

"Nothing is more democratic than a kibbutz," said Meyerwitz, quietly. "Not even in your own country."

Blum seemed flustered. He said, "No offense. I was just curious . . . I mean the Russians are communistic and they're on our side in the war."

"No, Lieutenant," said Meyerwitz, pouring more thick brown pot-roast gravy onto his kasha. "I think you got it backward. You're on *their* side."

After dinner, they all moved into the parlor. Sarah Meyerwitz, a lace shawl covering her gray hair, was lighting the Sabbath candles, nodding over them in prayer. Natalie Marek, carrying a brandy tray, threaded her way through the small room with a supple elegance that left Cohen breathless.

There was barely enough room for the six of them. Josef Meyerwitz was sprawled out on a large pillow, his back against the side of the upholstered chair in which Lieutenant Blum was seated. He reached out, slapped the lieutenant's leg, saying, "I'll make a bet that's the first home-cooked meal you've eaten in a long time."

"Eight or nine months," said Blum, accepting a brandy snifter from Natalie Marek.

She said, "But American rations must be good, no?"

"We get mostly British rations," said Blum.

"We also eat a lot of sand," said Cohen.

Uri Marek laughed. "One would think the Americans would feed all their troops on a diet of beefsteak and plum pudding. But it's good to know that everyone's equal out in the blue."

Cohen said, "You fought in the desert, Uri?"

"I did. Got my fill of it from '41 on . . . Bir Hakim, Mersa Matruh. Alamein, the lot. I was hit, so I'm home for a while."

"Badly?"

"In the leg."

"Sorry to hear it," said Cohen.

"It wasn't so terrible," said Uri. "I gave up the cane last week. Actually, it was what you call a lucky wound. I'm needed here. We're going to have our own war one of these days."

Cohen wondered what he meant.

Lieutenant Blum said, "What do you mean, your own war? Against who?"

"The Arabs."

"But what Arabs?" said Lieutenant Blum. "I mean the Arabs haven't got any armies."

Josef laughed. "They had two the last time I counted them. The Egyptians have the biggest and the Trans-Jordanians have the best. When the French leave the Middle East after the war there will probably be two more."

"But the British are here," said Cohen.

"The British will leave Palestine after the war, and it will become a battlefield," said Josef. "That's why men like Corporal Marek are important to us. He has the experience to train our people."

"But why will the Arabs attack?" said Lieutenant Blum.

"To drive us off the land—kill us."

"That's the first I've heard of anything like that."

"Well, now you know, Lieutenant," said Uri Marek. "Hitler is not the only one who wants to slaughter Jews. Arabs have been at it for a few hundred years or so. They sell us land they consider arid and useless and after we cultivate it they try to murder us and take it back."

"If that's the case," said Lieutenant Blum, "why don't the Palestinian Jews just leave?"

"And go where?"

"To America."

Josef Meyerwitz grinned. "It's nice of you to offer, Lieutenant. As an American I'm sure you know all about your country's history: Washington, Jefferson, Thomas Paine, your Constitution and so on. As a Jew what do you know of Herzel, Weitzman, Jabotinsky, Zionism?"

"My father has always given to the UJA."

"That's very generous of him."

"My family has even contributed money to plant trees here."

"Very nice, Lieutenant. Making the desert bloom is very nice indeed . . . but we have more important problems."

"Well, everybody has problems, Mr. Meyerwitz. I mean, we do what we can, but there's a war on."

"How true. And there are some battlefronts you maybe don't know about. For instance, the Nazis are at war with the Jewish people. And it's a war they are winning, particularly, at the moment, in Russia and Poland. Their aim is to destroy the entire race."

"You're exaggerating," said Blum.

Meyerwitz came to his feet. "I have some things to show you that might change your mind."

Cohen felt at a loss. He sipped his brandy and hoped he wouldn't be drawn into the discussion. He watched as Josef Meyerwitz retrieved a large envelope from the bookcase.

The envelope contained about forty photographs: glossy 8x10s, printed on flimsy single-weight paper. Josef pulled them out to hand half to Cohen and the other half to Blum.

Cohen stared down at the one on top. It pictured a group of more than a hundred men and women standing along the lip of a deep, open trench. They ranged in age from children to elderly men and women. Each wore a six-pointed star on his or her clothing. Facing them, on the other side of the ditch, with submachine guns at the ready, stood at least a dozen German soldiers. The next photograph showed the same scene, with the captive civilians in the process of removing their clothing. It was part of a consecutive sequence culminating in a picture of them standing naked, clothing piled at their feet. Cohen made note of the fact that the soldiers were wearing greatcoats. It was obviously cold. Looking down at the pictures, he himself felt chilled, his full stomach growing increasingly sour with nausea.

The print now atop Cohen's stack was a full-length vertical of a young woman who was clearly pregnant. She stood ankle-deep in mud, her facial features and limbs stiffened, rigid as if carved from gray stone. He stared down at her face, unable to look away. Her eyes were wide, beseeching the camera, her lips locked in a grotesque grimace as if the photographer had asked her to smile.

There were other photographs: full-lengths and close-ups of naked women. Cohen, his stomach churning, found them difficult to look at.

Lieutenant Blum's voice was higher pitched than usual. "What's this all about?" Abe Cohen glanced his way. Blum's face had assumed the color of pasteboard. His eyes avoided Cohen's. Meyerwitz switched the two groups of photographs.

Now the trench was filled with naked bodies. Soldiers stood on the edge, their submachine guns and rifles pointed downward, firing. There were close-ups of female dead stiffened in agony. Cohen spoke quietly, hardly recognizing his own voice. "Who are they?"

Josef Meyerwitz said, "They're Russian Jews."

"The pictures? Who took them? Why?"

"The photographer was an oberleutnant in the Waffen SS. I met him in Warsaw." Josef Meyerwitz emptied his brandy glass with one gulp. "He was an amateur whose hobby, as you can see, seemed to be taking pictures of nude women. I offered him money, but he was reluctant to part with his collection of negatives. It was necessary to slit his throat."

Lieutenant Blum said, "But I don't understand. I mean, why . . . ?"

"As I said before, the Nazis intend to kill every Jew in Europe. These pictures are over a year old and show them at work in Russia . . . just one of their methods. They had also taken to using vans in which the exhaust pipe was fed back into the rear compartment. Efficient. During a one-mile drive they could do away with as many as thirty or forty Jews at a time."

Cohen found himself with nothing to say, no comments or

questions to ask. Natalie Marek stood in front of him, the cognac bottle tilted to freshen his drink. He placed his hand atop the glass, inadvertently catching her eye. He glanced away abruptly, suddenly and strangely empty of any desire to look up at her.

Lieutenant Blum broke the silence. "They've got to be fake. It's too horrible. I can't believe it."

Cohen said, "Shut up, Lieutenant." Then in a softer voice, "I'm sorry."

"The unthinkable," said Josef Meyerwitz, "has become even more unthinkable. The Germans are now applying Teutonic industrial efficiency to the logistics of mass murder. Since these pictures were taken, they've constructed killing centers—huge camps—built around gas chambers and connected to the rail system . . . factories of death with the Jews as raw material. The Germans call it 'the final solution.' "

Lieutenant Blum said, "How do you know all this? I mean, there's been nothing in the papers."

Uri Marek stood, hands at his side. "We have people who report to us. Josef is one of them."

Meyerwitz said, "I've been back and forth to Poland three times since the war started. I have a way of getting in and out. The first time was in '39 when I brought family out: my aunt and my sister, who is now at a kibbutz in the Negev. The last was two months ago." He leaned back, stared at the ceiling. "There's been an uprising in the Warsaw Ghetto, a handful of underarmed Jews against regular German troops armed with tanks, flamethrowers, even Stukas. The Jews held out for a month, inflicting many casualties." His voice dropped in tone almost a full octave. "At one time, there were four hundred thousand in the ghetto—most of them dead now—shipped to places like Treblinka to be gassed, including the children. The Poles did nothing to help, nobody did. Goyim, they're all the same. Except for the Danes, nationality makes no difference. They're rounding up Jews in Paris, Rome, Amsterdam. There are thousands of Ukrainians and other Europeans in the SS. It's almost an international endeavor. The one thing Christians have in common is their hatred for us. All over the world."

"No," said Lieutenant Blum. "Not in my country."

Josef Meyerwitz said, "True, but you commit other evils. I've seen pictures. In the south of your country, men in white robes burn big crosses and hang black men."

"Yeah," said Cohen. "They march around with American flags and cut off Negro balls with rusty razor blades in the name of America the beautiful and Jesus Christ the Savior." He squirmed in his seat, taken aback by his own words.

"But that's different," said Lieutenant Blum. "And it's only in the South. I mean, an occasional Negro, but not Jews."

They were silent for moments, then Natalie Marek said, "We need your help."

"Sure," Lieutenant Blum seemed relieved by a change in the subject. "Anything," he said, expansively. "Just ask."

"We need weapons," she said.

Lieutenant Blum stared at her, his face empty of comprehension.

"For the Palmach," said Uri Marek. "It's a Jewish fighting force, the future army of a future Jewish state. Soon, my friends."

"A Jewish army?"

"And God willing, a Jewish air force and a Jewish navy."

"You're pulling my leg."

"Whatever can be spared. A little of this, a little of that. Every little bit helps. We have a few Jewish friends in the British forces, and now maybe we can also have a few in the American forces."

Lieutenant Blum raised both his hands as if trying to hush a crowd. "Wait a minute . . . you're asking me to steal American equipment?"

Marek nodded, his eyes grave, his mouth caught halfway between a serious frown and a conspiratorial grin. Josef Meyerwitz stepped into the breech. "I wouldn't call it stealing." He placed a hand on Lieutenant Blum's shoulder. "Think of it as foreign aid to an ally, what you call lend-lease."

Cohen slumped further in his chair as Blum came abruptly to his feet. The lieutenant, his mouth a tight slit, buttoned his blouse, turned to Cohen. "Let's go."

"I think I'll stay a while."

"You're leaving with me right now. That's an order, Sergeant."

Cohen, stifling a blunt rejoinder, nodded and said, "Soon as I use the john, sir."

In the bathroom, he used soap to write on the mirror: "BACK

TOMOR. EVE." He returned to find Lieutenant Blum glaring emphatically at one and all.

Meyerwitz said, "It's Shabbat, but I'll drive you to your hotels, if you'd like."

"No, thank you." Blum's words were pronounced stiffly with equal emphasis on each.

Meyerwitz said, "There won't be many taxis tonight."

"We'll walk."

"Go right when you leave here, then left. It'll lead you to the Allenby Road."

There was no moon, few streetlights. They walked in silence until they were in sight of Cohen's hotel. Blum said, "It was a put-up job. They tried to take us for suckers."

"I don't think so, Lieutenant."

"All that horseshit about a Jewish duty to invite lonely strangers home for Friday dinner. Christ! And those fake photographs? They even had me conned for a minute. I mean, c'mon!"

"They weren't fake."

"What are you, an expert on photography?"

"No, but neither are you, Lieutenant."

"All that crap about murdering Jews in Europe. 'Killing factories,' they called them. I suppose you believe that, too."

Cohen hesitated for a moment. Finally, he said, "Yes."

"Okay, then how come it hasn't been in the newspapers?"

"What newspapers? Once in a while, I see the *Stars and Stripes*, and that's it."

"Well, I get the *Plain Dealer* in the mail about every week— the GI airmail edition—not a word about Jews being slaughtered by the Germans or anyone else."

"Good for you," said Cohen.

"They probably have some kind of deal to peddle GI stuff on the black market or something." Lieutenant Blum's voice was hoarse with suppressed anger. "They were softening us up and they had you hooked like a poor fish. Jewish army, my ass! I pulled you out of there to save your neck. You would have spent the rest of your life in jail—San Quentin. I mean, they wanted us to commit treason!"

"Not treason, grand larceny. We're not at war with Palestine."

"You some kind of shithouse lawyer, Cohen?"

Abe Cohen stopped in mid-stride. "Lieutenant, get off my back."

They walked on in silence. In front of Cohen's hotel, a single taxi occupied the cab rank. Lieutenant Blum got into the back seat, stuck his head out the window. "Just remember Sergeant, we Americans have to stick together."

Abe Cohen nodded, watching as the big La Salle sped down the deserted Allenby Road until its taillights disappeared. Then, in a quiet voice to himself, he said, "I think I like being a Jew."

THE MISSION

AUGUST 1, 1943

Forty-five minutes southwest of the target, at 16,000 feet and 170 miles an hour, Sally's Wagon banked to the south. An eighty-eight-millimeter antiaircraft shell detonated just yards over the right inboard engine. A billow of smoke from the engine was lit internally by a bright, flickering orange. Cohen, standing just behind pilot and copilot, moved back into the bomb bay to turn off the fuel selector valve. Captain Maguire shut the engine down, feathered the prop to keep it from windmilling. Lieutenant Deutsch's actions were equally automatic as he closed the cowl flaps on number-three engine, checked that the booster pump was off, then set the selector valve on the engine fire-extinguisher panel, just to his right. He pulled the CO_2 release handle just as a second flak burst rocked the aircraft.

"I'm hit . . . Jesus, I'm hit!"

The interphone came alive with a confusion of buzzing voices. Deutsch was trimming the aircraft, adjusting throttle settings to compensate for the missing engine. Maguire was attempting to throw the flak gunners off with an evasive course. A scent of panic was in the air—virulent, contagious. Pilot and copilot were too busy now to cope with it.

Cohen flicked on his throat mike. "Who's hit?" There was immediate silence. He waited five seconds for a reply. "All right up front?"

Lieutenant Taylor's North Carolina drawl was unmistakable. "Bombardier and navigator okay."

"Junior?"

"No complaints, Abe."

"Waist?"

"Both okay."

Sergeant Cohen looked over his shoulder to see the top turret traversing. Only Yardbird Smith in the tail was unaccounted for. He tapped Captain Maguire on the shoulder, gestured toward the rear, and was rewarded with a quick nod. Disconnecting oxygen, heated suit, and interphone, he grabbed a walk-around oxygen bottle, plugged in, and made his way aft.

The aircraft's skin in the bomb bay had been punctured by flak. Cohen could make out three holes big enough to pass one's arm through. A single bomb was hung up on the top station of the left, rear rack. Cohen hesitated long enough to establish a priority between the bomb and a wounded crewman who might be bleeding to death. The bomb, he decided, was an immediate threat to all of them. He checked the shackle. One actuator arm was bent, jammed.

He plugged into a convenient interphone jack. "Engineer to pilot, we got a bomb hung up."

"Pilot to bombardier . . . get rid of it, Beel."

Lieutenant Beel's voice was strained. "The damned doors won't open!"

"Forget it," said Cohen. "Drop it through the doors."

"Wilco . . ." There were a few moments of silence, then, "The circuit's out."

Cohen said, "Salvo the goddamned thing manually, Lieutenant."

"Lord's name in vain," said Junior from the ball.

There was a pause, then a short curse. "The salvo lever's jammed. Everything's screwed up."

"We took some hits in the bomb bay," said Cohen.

Maguire said, "It's your baby, Sergeant."

Cohen grabbed a heavy screwdriver from the toolbox he kept in the waist. The bomb was about four feet in length and two and a half in diameter. Roughly half its weight consisted of RDX, a new and more powerful explosive then the TNT it had recently replaced. The olive-drab steel casing accounted for the rest of its weight. It was tipped with a nose fuse sporting a tiny propeller. An arming switch in the bombardier's compartment controlled small shackle hooks to which arming wires were attached. In the armed position, the hooks were set to retain the wires. When a shackle opened, releasing its hold on the two bomb lugs, the bomb would drop free, but the arming wire would pull out of a hole in the small fuse propeller, allowing the wind to turn it. After about a dozen revolutions, when the bomb was well clear of the airplane, it would spin off, freeing the firing pin to strike a small mercury fulminate primer on impact.

Cohen wrapped an arm around the bomb rack stringer and unhooked the arming wire from the shackle, rendering the bomb safe. It would be no help to the war effort to kill Rumanian peasants and their equally innocent livestock. On the Rome mission they had been careless. After the abort, Beel, without thinking, had left the arming switch in the "on" position. They dumped sixteen heavy bombs through the clouds on the way home and were told later that they had wiped out a small town in the south of Italy.

Cohen inserted the screwdriver into an opening in the shackle to pry up the locking sear. There was a snap as the bomb dropped away, a crash as it fell onto the left rear bomb bay door. There was a rending screech, a blast of wind as the flimsy sheet metal gave way. Both bomb and door were gone. Rid of the load, the airplane gave a little upward hop as a turbulent blast of frigid air almost cost Cohen his footing. The catwalk was a ten-inch-wide strip of corrugated aluminum supporting him sixteen thousand feet above what looked to be a giant relief map of the Rumanian countryside. He grinned to himself, remembering how he and Sally had consecrated the narrow catwalk. According to the laws of luck, he would be safe on it.

He stared down through the eight-foot gap created by the missing door, at the glinting threads of a twin railway line leading into the hazy southwest where the neat green-and-brown oblongs of farm country gave way to the even more complex geometry of an industrial area. It explained the presence of heavy antiaircraft guns evidenced by angry black puffs of smoke drifting rearward a few hundred feet below. The flak gunners had, for the moment, lost the range.

Aft of the bomb bay, Cohen grabbed a medical kit from the bulkhead. He stepped around the well in which the belly turret was slowly revolving. Junior Darling, suspended beneath the aircraft in his tight little ball, was searching the lower quadrant for enemy fighters. Further back, the two waist gunners were leaning on their guns, peering out their large windows like tourists on a train. Sergeant Woike glanced over his shoulder to point with his thumb toward the tail. Neither man could help with wounded. It was Captain Maguire's order that while over enemy territory no gunner was to leave his post unless specifically ordered to do so, not even for a quick piss into the relief tube. It fell to Cohen to treat the wounded and, when required, fill in for disabled gunners. If anything happened to him it became Lieutenant Beel's job. The squadron medical officer had given all flight engineers and bombardiers two-day courses in first aid.

The noise level in the waist was much higher than on the insulated and relatively luxurious flight deck. It was something Cohen could never get used to, a constant metallic pandemonium. Each of a hundred thousand parts banged, clattered, screeched a discordant symphony; all of it played against the deep, unceasing bass chord of the engines and the roar of the slipstream along aluminum skin no thicker than cardboard. Junior Darling had once compared flight in a heavy bomber to spending a day locked in a barrel of loose nuts and bolts during a hurricane.

The tail turret was turned to starboard. Cohen had to crank it around manually to get at the little door.

Sergeant Smith was slumped forward, his body supported by the turret control column, his head resting against the eight-inch-thick slab of "bullet-proof" glass. Cohen switched off the hydraulic power, disconnected oxygen and interphone. He wrestled the unconscious gunner out of the turret, dragged him forward to prop him up against an armor bulkhead just aft of the waist gunners' position. He reconnected the wounded man to a more convenient oxygen nipple.

Blood was seeping through a rip in the leather of Smith's flight pants. His face was blue. He was wheezing, the rubber bladder of his oxygen mask just barely inflating. The wound would have to wait. Cohen removed the tail gunner's mask to replace it with his own.

Sergeant Woike, at one of the waist guns, started rearward to help. Cohen waved him back. The wounded man was beginning to breath normally, the rubber bladder inflating and deflating with regularity. He checked Smith's original mask. A mass of frozen vomit was blocking the demand valve.

Cohen removed his gloves. With fingers stiffening rapidly in the low temperature, he dug most of the stuff out. Then, feeling light-headed, he switched again with the unconscious gunner.

Using the knife from his survival kit, he enlarged the rip in Yardbird Smith's sheepskin-lined leather flight pants and the layers of fabric beneath it. Smith's leg was a mess. A shard of gray metal protruded about a quarter-inch from an ugly mass of tortured flesh. Fortunately, the hot shell fragment had partially cauterized the wound, resulting in a minimum of bleeding. There would be no need for a tourniquet.

The tail gunner, with a drawn-out moan, slid into consciousness. He stared upward, his eyes wide in pained confusion. Cohen said, "Good morning, asshole."

"My leg. Christ it hurts. Help me, Abe!"

Cohen poured an entire packet of sulfa powder on the wound. They had to shout to be heard over the aircraft's noise level.

"Oh Christ. It smarts something fierce."

"Take it easy." Cohen was tempted to yank out the metal shard, as a dentist would pull a tooth.

"You're a *good* Jew, Cohen. My daddy always said you guys were the chosen people." Smith groaned, closed his eyes, clenching the lids in pain. "Fucking leg's killing me."

Cohen retrieved a premeasured morphine hypo from the kit. "You're lucky your balls weren't shot off, Yardbird."

"Oh shit. Did you check 'em?"

Cohen, grasping both of Smith's wrists in one hand, turned him on his side. "Yeah, they're okay, Yardbird."

"You're not kidding me?"

"If they weren't both still there, I'd shoot you right between the eyes. Put you out of your misery."

"You're a good buddy, Abe."

"You're fucking-A I am." With a deft motion, Cohen slit open the seat of his patient's flying pants, cutting through the leather and sheepskin lining, then the olive drab coveralls, blue nylon heated suit, OD cotton boxer shorts. "Special blend of arsenic, snake venom, and strychnine," he said, holding up the syringe to squirt a little out. "It's fast, won't take more than fifteen, twenty minutes, and you won't feel much pain."

"You always were a funny guy, Abe."

"Bye-bye, Yardbird." Cohen jabbed home into Smith's plump buttock. Yardbird responded with an incoherent string of curses.

Using the knife sheath as a splint, Cohen immobilized the knee, then wrapped it in about a yard of bandage.

Yardbird said, "How bad is it?"

"I'll kid you not, Yardbird. It's pretty bad." Cohen plugged in Smith's heated suit. He seemed to remember that warmth helped to prevent shock. Or was it the other way around? "But you won't lose the leg. You'll just have a little trouble doing the jig, or whatever the fuck you hillbillies do."

"You mean it's a ticket home?"

"Yeah, but what in hell you want to go home for?" Cohen repacked the medical kit, stood up. "I mean, you never ate so good and you're making more money than you ever made in your life."

The morphine seemed to be taking effect quickly. Dribble, a side effect of the drug, seeped from under Yardbird's oxygen mask, ran down his cheek to freeze on the sheepskin collar of his flying jacket. His words were slurred. "Yeah, but it's a little hairy, these fucking Krauts shoot a lot straighter then the goddamned revenuers."

Cohen took a moment to glance out the waist window. Chloe was just off their right wing, throttled back, holding formation and providing escort to the handicapped Sally.

Sally, despite the missing engine, was still slowly gaining altitude. Maguire was taking her up into more familiar territory and the security of overcast. About twenty-five miles to the south the gray wall of a front offered concealment, a possible haven from fighters and flak.

Cohen made his way aft. It was risky to leave the tail turret unmanned. He discarded the walk-around oxygen bottle. Cursing the bulky encumbrance of heavy flying clothes, back chute, flak jacket, and Mae West, he squirmed into the turret.

He connected his umbilicals to the aircraft system. There was a trio of jagged holes, each the size of a half-dollar, in the turret floor. Yardbird Smith's GI helmet and liner were under the seat, where he had placed them in an obvious attempt to protect his gonads. Yardbird, it was clear, valued his balls more than he did his brain. Cohen retrieved it, placed it on his head, fastened the chin strap.

About a third of the view through the heavy turret glass was blurred by an amber smudge on its outer surface. It was frozen urine from the waist relief tube. The tube, just forward of the waist gun positions, was topped with a funnel and led out to the exterior. In an unwelcome example of capillary action, the urine would quite often flow along the bottom of the airplane toward the tail, where a slipstream vortex blew the stuff up onto the turret glass. At altitude, it quickly froze, obscuring the gunner's view.

Countless squadron armament chiefs and engineering officers had submitted standard "Unreliable Reports" to the Consolidated Aircraft Corporation to correct the design malfunction. To no avail. Viewing enemy fighters through frozen urine had become a traditional aspect of the B-24 personality.

Cohen switched on. The hydraulic accumulator whined. He grasped the turret-control handle, twisted it quickly to the left while tilting it upward. The turret swung around, rotating smoothly and rapidly as the guns elevated. He adjusted the reticle brightness on the optical gunsight. Pleased to find that the flak burst that had wounded Sergeant Smith had left the turret intact, he flicked his throat mike switch to bring the pilot up to date.

Encapsulated aft of the twin rudders, Cohen could see nothing of his own airplane. Isolated, he flew backward through empty skies. The Danube was a gleaming snake fifteen thousand feet below. They were over Yugoslavia now. A hundred and fifty miles to the east a black smudge on the horizon marked the burning refineries of Ploesti.

He reached into the small stowage box, removed an old-fashioned, long-necked oil can. Through the left gun port, he raised the gun cover to squirt kerosene onto the bolt mechanism. He repeated the procedure on the right gun, then stowed the can and hit the charging switches a few times. The squadron armament shop would, as usual, piss and moan about the resultant rust and pitting. But the rear guns, more than any others on the airplane, were, for some reason, prone to freezing up. Kerosene was an effective, if primitive, deicer.

He sat back against the door, making himself as comfortable as possible in the cramped quarters. With the turret facing directly rearward, oriented to the line of flight, none of the aircraft structure was visible. It was as if the small capsule was independently airborne—a tiny projectile hurtling him backward through the hostile sky.

Cohen tracked the turret slowly back and forth, surveying his quadrant of sky. At the traversing limits, the bottom half of each of the twin oval rudders loomed into view, the horizontal stabilizer formed a kind of half-roof; comforting reassurances that, indeed, the tail turret was actually attached to an airplane.

The earth below was lost in a buff-colored haze. Fluffy contrails—condensation from the three functioning engines—flowed past him on either side, trailing miles of elongated, white clouds.

He raised his mask long enough for a quick drink. His canteen had imparted a metallic taste to the rum. He took a momentary pleasure from a shudder that racked his body. "Antifreeze." He muttered the word aloud, barely hearing it over the din. Gulping another drink, he raised the mask over his face, breathed deeply. Pure oxygen was a stimulating chaser. He sang into his mask, thinking of Sally and inventing graphic lyrics to a few choruses of "Melancholy Baby."

CHAPTER 15

JULY 1943

Master Sergeant Arthur Spielman, armament chief of
the 413th Squadron, ground five and a quarter inches
of perfectly good Havana cigar under his heel and shuffled, once
more, through the pictures. "What's this all about? Who are
they?"

Cohen told him.

Sergeant Spielman looked up, his eyes filled with angry tears.
"Fucking bastards!"

Cohen said, "Maybe I shouldn't have shown them to you."
Even as he muttered the words, he realized their banality.

"Why not?" said Spielman. "They're Jews. They're our people.
If my grandfather hadn't brought his family to America one of
those women could have been my mother."

Cohen felt a rush of guilt. He glanced quickly around the armament tent, seeking something on which to settle his eyes.

Sergeant Spielman was quiet. Finally, he said, "When I was a
kid in Philly, I used to have to fight my way to school every day.
They called me a Christ-killer. Yelled at me to go back to Palestine where I belonged. My grandfather told me about the po-
groms in Russia—the Cossacks, all that. My mother would say,
'The Goyim hate us. Don't do anything that'll draw their attention. Mind your own business. Don't fight, walk away. Don't
make trouble.' And now the Krauts are making Jews dig their
own graves." He held up one of the photographs, tapped it with
his free hand. "I mean, look, when they finish digging, they put

their shovels down and stand there not making trouble, just like their mothers told them."

Once again, Sergeant Spielman went silent. Cohen glanced around the tent. There were two workbenches backed with a large series of shelves containing toolboxes, turret spare parts, bomb shackles, gun barrels and other assorted armament paraphernalia. A trio of makeshift racks held about twenty or thirty fifty-caliber Browning machine guns. Everything was wrapped in parachute silk to keep the sand out. On three sides large crates were piled to the top of the tent flies.

There was little spare room. Cohen perched himself on one of the workbenches to await the armament chief's emergence from introspection.

Finally, Spielman said, "I feel like I got to do something." He was quiet again, this time for only a few seconds. Then, in a voice pitched an octave lower, "Fuck this noise, Cohen, I'm going on flying status."

"The hell you say. They won't let you. You're a good armament chief. There ain't too many around."

"I got a couple of connections."

"You mean you want to be a hero," said Cohen.

"You should talk . . ."

"You're too fat."

"So, I'll lose weight."

"I got something better you can do."

"What?"

Cohen told him.

Spielman spoke this time with no hesitation. "Okay."

"Okay, what?"

"Okay, for Christ's sake, let's do it!"

"You know," said Cohen. "We get caught, it could mean twenty—thirty years."

"What gives with you? First you talk me into it, now you try to talk me out."

"I just want you to know what you might be letting yourself in for."

"My parents were Zionists. I grew up with it."

"What about Lieutenant whatsisname, your armament officer?"

"O'Connell?" said Spielman. "No problem. He just runs interference and signs papers. That's what officers are for."

"And inventory, that kind of thing . . . ?"

"Listen, nothing lasts in this sand. The stuff grinds everything down. Crew chiefs change engines every sixty hours instead of two-fifty like everywhere else. As far as armament is concerned, the fifties chew themselves up, the turrets wear out, bomb racks jam. We even get sand in the tail turret hydraulic fluid. So, you get a crack-up on the runway, or a ship comes back shot up so they have to scrap it, or send it to the service squadron, every armament man in this group runs out to it. First come, first served, and my guys are faster then any of them. I don't know about the other three squadrons in this group, but cannibalism is what keeps this one flying. It's like eating your young. Half the stuff in this tent is from wrecked airplanes, spare parts, guns, the works. But, the point is: nobody has the time to keep track."

"Sounds like we got it made,"

"Right, Abe. You get it set up, I con a truck from the motor pool, and we load up. That's it, old buddy. Piece of cake."

THE MISSION
AUGUST 1, 1943

"Three bogeys . . . ten o'clock, low." Junior placed equal emphasis on each word, like a train conductor announcing the stations. "About twelve thousand and climbing fast."

"*I see them. They're One-nineties.*"

Cohen scanned the empty sky to the rear. The Focke-Wulfs were lining up for a frontal attack. From his position in the tail he wouldn't see them till after they passed overhead into his sector of the sky. But there could be others.

"*Bandits coming up on twelve o'clock, low. They've headed south in a climbing turn to get out in front of us.*"

"*Crank this baby up and let's get the fuck out of here.*"

"*Jesus! What the hell they got against us?*"

"*D'Amato, cut the chatter! Taylor, where are we?*"

"*Just crossed the Bulgarian border.*"

"*Any flak around here?*"

"*Probably at a place called Pleven, an industrial area, about thirty miles west. But don't worry, you're not going to pass anywhere near it.*"

"*Give me a heading, Taylor.*"

"*For what . . . ?*"

"*Pleven, for Christ's sake!*"

"*That's crazy! My map shows a whole bunch of red hatch marks— heavy flak, maybe even radar-directed One-oh-fives!*"

"*Now!*"

"*Okay-okay. West-southwest—Course two-three-seven . . . but . . .*"

The big Liberator banked too sharply into its dead engine. Cohen held his breath, feeling the airframe quiver in a prestall warning. Captain Maguire was in a hurry to reach flak country. A sky full of the stuff would discourage the fighters. Maguire, assumed Cohen, was a gambler who figured the odds were better with the fire then with the frying pan.

"Keep your eye on them, Junior . . ."

"They're climbing fast . . . turning . . ."

Maguire was holding Sally's Wagon on a thin edge, feeling her through the seat of his pants. He maintained the steeply banked turn, the dead engine supplying nothing but drag. It was delicate. Any more and they'd spin out. The aircraft, like an old car on a washboard road, was shuddering on the edge of a stall. Cohen hung on, sweating it out as the left wing fought for lift. It seemed forever before it came up.

"Two bandits . . . turning in, about two o'clock level."

"Where the hell's the third?"

"Down here. He's sneaky . . . all by himself. Climbing . . . about one o'clock, sliding back."

"Don't lose the bastard."

"Roger wilco. Have no fear, Junior Darling's here."

Though he couldn't see the enemy fighters, Cohen figured that Maguire's right turn had precluded a head-on approach. The sneaky sonsabitches had split up. Two of them would attack level or possibly high, while the third would come in on a simultaneous climbing approach to divide the defenses and inflict belly wounds—a one-two punch. He estimated that the high Focke Wulfs would press their attacks starting from about three o'clock, pass behind them left to right, and then, if there was still anything left to shoot at, come around for a second pass. He rotated the turret in order to be ready for them.

"Top turret to pilot . . . drop the left wing just a hair."

"Coming in . . . two—three o'clock level . . ."

Cohen sat, tensed forward, his eyes scanning empty sky, his earphones alive with gunner's chatter. A single fifty in the waist was the first to fire. Simultaneously there was a dull thud that shook the aircraft to its bones, a cannon shell bursting somewhere inside. It was the downbeat for a mad timpani. Sally's Wagon trembled from the brute percussion of its own guns. Enemy machine-gun strikes stitched the length of the fuselage sounding like the paradiddle of heavy hail on a tin roof.

In seconds, their pursuit curves caused the German fighters to slide back into Cohen's bailiwick. For only an instant their noses, sporting bright red propeller hubs, were pointed at him. He managed a short burst at the inside Focke-Wulf and was close enough to see some hits on the wing surface. Then his target and its wingmate banked right and pulled up into a shallow climb. Cohen managed a few more hits as the range increased. Finally he ceased fire. To continue shooting would result in nothing more than a waste of precious ammunition. The deflection problems, magnified by the increasing range, were too complex to solve in the split seconds allotted him.

Only seconds had passed since the two fighters had begun their run-in. The relative position of the third was made clear when an exultant Junior broke through the interphone clamor. "I got him! He's smoking."

The third Focke-Wulf materialized instantaneously two or three hundred feet in front of Cohen. It had made a low pass starting from about two o'clock low, taking hits from Junior's guns, and was now in an almost vertical climb trailing black smoke. Cohen watched as it reached its nadir to fall off on one wing. A black figure detached itself as the stricken fighter seemed to hesitate for an instant in a motionless stall. Licks of flame blossomed at the wing root, grew quickly into full flowering. In seconds, the Focke-Wulf was a corkscrewing ball of fire, shedding parts of itself on the way down.

Its pilot fell through the thin air, arms and legs akimbo, a solitary figure in the now empty sky. Cohen was surprised to see the emergence of a parachute. It was a stupid mistake. A few thousand feet of free-fall would have dropped the German quickly out of range of the defending guns and into more breathable air. He was a fool to trust the American gunners to honor an unwritten code. Fuck him.

Cohen rotated the turret, lining up the optical-sight reticle. The target was hanging almost motionless at a range of less than two hundred yards, close enough for Cohen to depend on tracer. He fired a quick burst. The enemy pilot was aware of his peril, waving his arms as if to indicate that it was all a mistake. Then for a moment it seemed to Cohen as if he were climbing the shroud lines in a vain attempt to collapse the chute. A longer burst while traversing a few degrees azimuth saw the figure freeze, arms by its side as if it had been called to attention.

"Cohen, you bastard!" It was Charlie Crenshaw, the radio operator, calling from the top turret. "You do it to them, they'll do it to us!"

"Well then, don't ever bail out, shithead." War was war. There was nothing complicated about it; kill or be killed. The ceremonial morality insisting that a parachute was a kind of sanctuary was, to Cohen, a sucker's game. The enemy, parachute or no parachute, was a sonofabitch who was dedicated to seeking out and killing Abe Cohen, personally. In a day or two, had his life been spared, the Nazi bastard would be shooting at him from another cockpit.

"Fucking murderer!" Crenshaw's voice registered near hysteria. "You ever bail out, you won't have to worry about the Krauts, I'll personally blow your ass off!"

"Fuck off, Crenshaw," said D'Amato. "You couldn't hit a barn door at twenty feet."

"Cut the chatter," said Maguire. "We got two One-nineties out there and God knows what else."

Cohen searched out the parachute. It had diminished to a white speck a few miles back and a few thousand feet lower. He had killed a man. It was different than killing an airplane. Charlie Crenshaw was right. He was a murderer. The act had been premeditated—first-degree murder. In real life, in a civilian court, a plea of self-defense would be useless, the victim at the time was unarmed. He checked his canteen. It was empty. Of course, in a civilian court, a good lawyer would get him off with a plea of temporary insanity. He bottomed out in a sudden depression. The whole fucking war was temporary insanity. Then, for a moment, he thought of Meyerwitz's 8x10 glossies and realized that if the enemy pilot had been Italian or Rumanian or even Japanese he probably would have let him live.

He tracked the turret back and forth, searching the sky. A full minute had gone by since the last enemy pass.

There was something hidden in the contrails. A dark shape was submerged in the white billows—little more than a shadow. Cohen flicked on his throat mike. "Tail to pilot. Bandit at six o'clock level, it's trying to hide in our contrails, out of range, about two thousand yards."

"Any ideas what it is, Cohen?"

"It's making two contrails of its own—twin engines—I'll bet on an ME-110." The Messerschmitt 110 was a destroyer. It lacked the agility of a true fighter but was a stable gun platform packing a monstrous punch: six heavy machine guns, two twenty-millimeter cannon, and whatever else they could hang on her. Cohen studied it. It was playing cat and mouse, peeking out of the white fluff every now and then. It was taking its time, easing up on them, closing slowly, like a tiger slithering forward on its belly in the high grass. Soon, still safely out of range of Cohen's guns, it would let loose with its cannon.

Cohen squinted into the contrail. He could just make out the wingtip projecting out of one side of the fluff. He was certain now it was an ME-110. "The bastard still thinks we haven't seen him, Captain. He's creeping up to get into cannon range."

"Can you try a burst?"

"He's still too far for me to use these diddly-shit fifties, and if I give the show away he might fire off his rockets, if he has any. If you throttled back you might be able to get me into range fast, before he realizes it. I only need a couple seconds."

"Hang on."

The tone of their three functioning engines grew deeper. They assumed a slight nose-up attitude as the aircraft vibrations segued to a lower frequency. Cohen was aware of an abrupt but gentle inertial tug as the flaps were lowered to supply compensating lift for the reduced airspeed.

He concentrated on the obscure target, half-hidden in the bil-lowing contrail. With luck, the enemy pilot would remain un-aware of the quick change in relative speed long enough to bring him into range of the bomber's defenses. Ten seconds or even less might be enough. Cohen began a countdown from fifteen, then lined up the projected reticle in the optical sight, waiting for the target's protruding wings to fill the circle.

The ME-110 was hanging there, enabling Cohen to align the turret's azimuth almost precisely along the axis of his own aircraft. At a more reasonable range it would have been a tail gunner's dream, a no-deflection shot: the only situation in which an aerial gunner could find himself on an equal footing with an attacking fighter. There was no necessity to compensate for angle of attack or relative speed. It was comparable to firing at a stationary target on the rifle range where one only needed to allow for range.

At the count of eight, the target, though getting closer, still hadn't filled his reticle. The remaining seven seconds felt like seven minutes. At any time the Kraut pilot was sure to return from lunch. They were now well within the range of his twin twenty-millimeter Orlikons, though still a little too far for American fifties. Cohen wondered what the guy was waiting for. He tensed his muscles in expectation of a hail of explosive shells.

Finally, it was now or never and to hell with the range. He checked azimuth again, then depressed the firing button while tilting up the control grip. Marksmanship, at this distance, would get him nowhere; there were too many variables: barrel dispersion, faulty boresighting, improper headspace. The best bet was to sling a lot of lead, spray the general area, and hope for the best. The pair of Browning heavy machine guns, less than a foot on either side of him, where deafening. At nine rounds a second, each of them spewed out a stream of half-inch-diameter bullets, every other round either an incendiary or a tracer, the rest steel-jacketed, armor-piercing projectiles, discharged at huge muzzle velocity. Three seconds later, at about forty-five degrees elevation, he reversed the procedure, this time firing while slowly depressing the guns. It was a long six-second burst, covering all the bases.

Two missiles streaked by about fifty feet beneath them. Junior announced them as Cohen observed two more coming in. This time they were high and to the starboard. One of them seemed to curve away, like a pitched ball.

Cohen fired another burst, this one short. The ME-110 banked sharply out of the contrail. It was trailing the white smoke of burning glycol from its starboard engine coolant tank. Then, suddenly, in a flash of brilliant orange, the airplane was gone, leaving behind only a small, jagged black cloud to memorialize the midair cremation of its three crew members.

Cohen spoke calmly. "Tail to pilot. I got the bastard."

Listening to the engines rev up, he checked his canteen again. It was still empty. But he had done his bit. It was time for the war to end. He felt like laughing but couldn't think of anything funny. Maybe he'd take out a GI life insurance policy. A good investment, it was bound to pay off. He tried to think of a beneficiary . . . nobody, except possibly Junior Darling. Junior would buy a farm in Oklahoma and live happily ever after. He forced a laugh, then thought about Natalie Marek. As a beneficiary, she and her brother would probably use the ten thousand to buy guns for their Jewish army.

"Two bandits, eleven o'clock high . . . coming in!"

It had been minutes since the previous Folke Wolfe attacks. Cohen judged that the leader was addicted to high frontal approaches and had taken the time to get into position. Once again the interphone was alive with reports. They were attacking almost head-on from a high angle and would pass behind the bomber before diving away. He centered the turret, elevating his guns so as to be in good position to track them when they slid around.

CHAPTER 16

JULY 1943

Leutnant Hermann Stumacher was on the beach, awaiting the dawn and his morning swim. He heard the engines a full five minutes before he could make out the two pairs of blackout lights. He raced inland about two hundred feet to the nearest palm. There was little else by way of natural cover. He made it just in time to observe the two vehicles pull up and park about fifty feet away. One was a fifteen-hundred-weight buff-colored British desert lorry, the other a two-and-a-half-ton olive-drab American Studebaker truck. Four men emerged, two Americans, two Brits. They shook hands, lit cigarettes, introduced themselves. Leutnant Stumacher knelt behind the boll at the base of his tree and pondered the peculiarity of the situation.

Actually, though two of them wore British uniforms, it was obvious from their accents that neither was actually British. Leutnant Stumacher, though no expert in linguistics, was sure that one of them was speaking English in a German accent. Stumacher applied his imagination. They were, he conjectured, two groups of fellow Axis spies, meeting in a safely isolated place for some kind of clandestine activity, perhaps to exchange information. For just a moment, he felt like popping up to introduce himself—Robinson Crusoe, he thought.

One of the Americans said, "I kind of thought Uri Marek would be here."

"I'm sorry," said one of the Tommies. "We're from a regular transport company. It's much safer that way."

The slim American was about to say something but seemed to

change his mind. The heavy American, speaking briskly, broke in. "We've got eleven fifty-caliber machine guns packed in cosmoline. Heavy firepower. Only problem is, they're aircraft guns, so you'll have to come up with some kind of tripods or mount them on jeeps or something."

"Perfect. No problem. Believe me, we'll make excellent use of them."

"There are twenty extra barrels and some other parts. We also brought eight thousand rounds of ammunition; about two thirds armor-piercing; the rest, tracer. Your people will have to load it into belts, there's a crate of links. It only comes to a little over one-minute firing time for each gun. But if I know how to contact you, I may have more, maybe twenty, thirty thousand rounds in a couple weeks. There's a guy in ordnance I got to speak to."

For ten minutes, the puzzled German officer watched from behind his tree as they transferred the load from one vehicle to another. It was obvious that the four men were involved in a black market in arms.

Finally they finished. The slim American said, "Do you guys know Uri's sister, Natalie?"

"Of course."

"I mean, will you be seeing her soon?"

The one with the German accent said, "In a few days. As a matter of fact, this shipment goes to her kibbutz." He grinned. "Don't worry, I'll give her your regards."

"Thanks, and mention that I'll be dropping in on her, one of these days."

There was more handshaking, gestures of camaraderie. The slim American produced a canteen, passed it around. The fat American raised it in a toast. "Next year in Jerusalem."

"Lachaim."

THE MISSION

AUGUST 1, 1943

Her guns were firing again. Then, suddenly, Sally's
Wagon staggered. There was a heavy thump of exploding cannon shells, the rattle of bullets piercing the thin skin.

A pair of Folke Wulfs hurtled into view, diving at about thirty degrees, at an airspeed touching four hundred miles an hour. They crossed Cohen's sights at short range as he twisted the control grip downward and right to track them. Nothing happened. The turret remained locked in place. Cursing aloud, he pressed the trigger, hoping for a miracle. The short burst was way off the mark.

The enemy, having lost two of their own, flew on to the north. Cohen reasoned for just a moment that they had broken off the attack due to low fuel supply or lack of ammunition. Then a half-dozen bursts of flak off to their left constituted a better explanation. Cohen reasoned that Captain Maguire's gamble of minutes ago, the turn toward the Bulgarian industrial town of Pleven, had paid off. Of the two evils, flak was the lesser. Crippled, shot-up, and with no tail guns, the odds were dead against their surviving another fighter attack. The German pilots obviously had no stomach for a third pass that would have them flying through their own antiaircraft barrage. The interphone reverberated with frantic, incoherent voices. There seemed little sense in attempting to add his to the confusion. Someone was screaming.

Once again, he tried to activate the turret. It refused to budge. Keeping his voice calm, he spoke into the throat mike. "Tail to pilot, the turret's out." He repeated it twice in order to be heard over the clamor.

"Christ . . . okay, get your ass up here."

He cranked the turret around by hand, then disconnected his umbilicals, reached up for the door latch cord. Tumbling backward off his seat, he rolled awkwardly out of the turret onto the deck.

The hydraulic accumulator that supplied power to the tail turret motors had been shot up. Mounted on the fuselage wall, just forward of the turret, its working parts had been eviscerated by a twenty-millimeter explosive shell. The aberrant drip of pink hydraulic fluid formed a pool beneath it. Two vertical slabs of armor, aft of the waist windows, had protected the gunners from shell fragments. Cohen wondered briefly what had protected him.

He plugged into a walk-around oxygen bottle and started forward, working his way between the two waist gunners. The deck was littered with hundreds of fifty-caliber shell cases, making footing in the soft leather sheepskin-lined flying boots somewhat precarious. Daylight gleamed through a profusion of bullet holes in the upper part of the fuselage. Like an orchestra of mad flutists, they whistled and hummed discordantly. Sally's Wagon had taken a beating, and there was still a long way to go.

Out the window he could see a pattern of flak bursts. At the moment the black blossoms were about three hundred yards off and a thousand feet low. The enemy gunners were obviously new at their job. Then Cohen realized that except for the flak bursts— clusters of deadly little black clouds—the sky was empty. Chloe was not in place on their right. He glanced questioningly at Woike. The waist gunner made a thumbs-down gesture, then motioned toward the northeast. Cohen stepped up to the window. A few miles back a Liberator was corkscrewing toward the ground. Beyond it, at about seven or eight thousand feet, the white umbrellas of ten scattered parachutes floated in the empty sky.

Sally's Wagon was now a straggler, crippled, alone, deep inside enemy territory. Without the mutual protection of the massed guns of a friendly formation she was a prime target for marauding enemy fighters. One look at the feathered engine would confirm her as cold meat.

Cohen turned away, clambered up onto the half deck to retrieve the last bottle of rum from behind the transmitter. He helped himself to a quick slug, transferred the contents to his canteen, then made his way back to the waist.

Yardbird Smith, propped up against the armor bulkhead, stared at him glumly. Cohen offered him the canteen. Yardbird removed his mask to reveal an antithetic grin. He took a long pull, stopping only to breathe before helping himself to another. Cohen retrieved the canteen, handed it to Woike, who glared at Yardbird while making a show of wiping the mouthpiece with his gloved hand. Next was D'Amato, who shook his head, pointed to his own canteen hanging on the gun mount.

Cohen nodded, turned to go. D'Amato tapped him on the shoulder, pointed to his headset. Cohen unplugged D'Amato's interphone line to plug in his own. "Cohen here. . . ."

"Where in hell you been, Sergeant? I've got no elevator control." Maguire's voice was calm, pitched low; conversational despite the fact that without elevators he could point the nose neither up nor down. "Fix it."

Elevator, rudder, and trim control cables ran along a track on the side of the fuselage. Cohen tugged one at a time. The third one he tried was loose, the slack end forward. He entered the bomb bay, switched on the work lights. A single cable hung loose, dangling from one of the small pulleys mounted on the fuselage. A large gash in the aircraft skin just beneath it indicated the entrance wound.

He went forward onto the flight deck, tapped Captain Maguire on the shoulder. He lowered his mask and said, "The cable's busted." He glanced through the windshield. The antiaircraft gunners were correcting their azimuth, the bursts were getting closer. It was big stuff, 88s and 105s.

"Fix it, Cohen." Maguire eyes were glazed, sunken. He looked as if he hadn't slept for a week.

"I'll need help. Can I have Lieutenant Beel?"

"He's dead."

"Shit."

"A couple cannon shells in the nose compartment. That last fighter attack hurt us."

"Lieutenant Taylor too?"

"Crenshaw says he's lost a lot of blood. He's down there with him now."

Cohen felt a fullness in his ears. They were losing altitude. He glanced at the instruments. The altimeter was unwinding. "Why we going down, sir?"

"So Taylor can breathe. Crenshaw says his hose was torn up." With his right hand, Captain Maguire adjusted the throttles with the unconscious precision of a violinist tuning his instrument. "Get your ass in gear, Cohen. Take Sergeant D'Amato from the waist and make it fast."

"Okay, Captain. Tell D'Amato I'll be in the bomb bay and he should bring a knife and pliers and a pair of wire-cutting dykes from the tool kit. And keep the stick neutral till I'm finished."

"Cohen . . ."

"Yeah?"

"I was wrong."

"About what, Captain?"

"You—Jews, you know . . ."

"Fuck you, Captain."

"That's the second time you've said that, Cohen. It's getting to be a bad habit."

CHAPTER 17

JULY 1943

There will be pain, not when I'm doing it—I use a local anesthesia—but afterward."

"For how long?"

"A week, maybe more. Are you a drinker?"

"Yeah."

"Good."

"How do babies stand it?"

"I don't remember." The moil laughed. "Actually, it doesn't seem to bother them, but adults are another story.'

"Have you done many adults?"

"Once in a while. As a matter of fact I did one a few days ago, an English captain. I guess that makes me 'Moil to His Majesty's Forces.' He was marrying a Jewish girl, a Canadian nurse. He brought her with him. Frankly, for this lady, I personally wouldn't cut off even a fingernail . . . forgive me, I like to make jokes."

"Will I be able to leave right afterward?"

"Yes, but you'll have to take it easy for a while, keep it from rubbing against your clothes, change the dressing. And don't worry, there won't be any infection, but God forbid there is, don't come back to Alexandria, go to your medical officer. Unless you're very rich, there's no penicillin in Alexandria."

"Okay." Cohen lit a cigarette and willed his nerves to calm.

"I don't mean to be too personal, Sergeant, but tell me, why are you doing this?"

"I want to be a Jew."

"It takes much more than this to be a Jew."

"I know."

"Is there a woman involved?"

"No."

"Are you sure?

"No."

"The Christians use missionaries. With the Jews, it's almost always a woman." The moil handed Cohen a double shot of scotch. "But, not to worry, it's like having a new personality. She'll love you for it. And may I add that you're a fortunate man to be so well endowed."

"Thanks." Sergeant Cohen sipped the scotch. He stood, staring straight ahead, hobbled by the trousers around his ankles. The moil, wearing a white skullcap and a white medical gown, sat before him on a chromium stool. Cohen was at first disconcerted, then amused by the lack of dignity in a procedure he had assumed would be more ritualized.

"Hold still."

It was over in a matter of seconds. He felt nothing.

The moil bandaged him up, handed him a jar. "Apply this salve to the dressing and change it twice a day."

"What about showers?"

"You want to keep it dry for about five days—a week maybe." He patted Cohen on the back. "Good luck, Sergeant. And don't forget, until it heals completely, no erections."

THE MISSION

AUGUST 1, 1943

On the bomb bay catwalk, Cohen removed his parachute, pulled the rip cord to open it. Using D'Amato's knife, he cut out about six feet of shroud line, then dropped the ruined chute through the open bomb door.

Manna from heaven. He was a god, dispensing thirty yards of pure white, virgin silk from which a lucky and perhaps deserving Rumanian beauty would make her wedding trousseau. Women. He'd never be able to step foot on the bomb bay catwalk again without thinking of Sally. He thought about her momentarily, then flashed a picture, not of a naked Sally, but of a fully clothed Natalie. He shrugged it off, wishing he were somewhere else.

The air temperature was rising with their loss in altitude, but it was still close to freezing. He removed his gloves, then stretched out on his back at right angles across the narrow catwalk while the two-hundred-pound D'Amato squatted astride his hips. With his upper torso hanging in space over the missing bomb door, the broken cable was just within arm's reach. The air had gotten bumpy. There was nothing below him but Yugoslavia. It was going to be awkward.

Cohen's plan was to loop the ends of the cable, then, using five lengths of parachute cord, connect the two ends through the loops. The gap would be less than eight inches. He judged that five strands of nylon would hold with a minimum of stretching.

There was a loud crunching that sounded to Cohen like an automobile collision. Sally's Wagon shuddered, then bounced, almost throwing both of them off the narrow catwalk. Sally was taking flak hits. D'Amato wrapped one arm around the bomb rack. With his free hand he grasped Cohen's collar in an effort to supply some support.

The strain on Cohen's arms and back was excruciating. He stopped his work in order to restore the feeling in his hands by warming them for a half-minute within the soft sheepskin confines of his armpits.

Once again the aircraft jolted. D'Amato grinned in an unsuccessful attempt to hide his nervousness. "Don't worry, Abe, you can always flap your arms on the way down."

"I'll take you with me, fuckhead." The pliers stuck to his hand, ripping off a chunk of skin.

"We get out of this, Cohen, I'll buy you a drink in Alex; maybe even a broad. Three broads, and they'll smell like Lux soap and speak American. You name it, old buddy."

"How come you're so friendly all of a sudden?"

"You're a miserable bastard, but you're the best damned flight engineer in the squadron—in the whole fucking Air Corps."

"I get paid well. War Department pays me a fortune to do this shit."

"And you got a lot of guts."

"It has nothing to do with guts." Cohen tied the last knot with fingers devoid of feeling. "If this fucker goes down I ain't going to be any deader than you."

"Don't bet on it. I've got a parachute."

Cohen sat on the edge of the catwalk, his feet dangling. He arched his aching back until he felt it snap.

D'Amato placed a hand on his shoulder. "You okay, Abe?"

Cohen nodded, blew on his hands. His fingers were bleeding from cuts inflicted by the jagged cable strands. He put his gloves back on.

D'Amato said, "And it also takes a hell of a lot of guts to screw the boss's wife and then have her painted naked as a jaybird on the nose of her husband's airplane."

"You bastard!"

"I mean, we're talking about real guts, Abe, big-league stuff. You're a hero. The French hand out medals for that kind of stuff."

"Where in hell you hear about it?"

"Can't say, old buddy."

"Fibich, that prick!"

"Don't be so sensitive. What you did is real history, like discovering America or climbing Mount Everest or something."

"I'll kill the bastard! I'll blow his fucking brains out and yours too if you tell anybody about this!"

"Mum's the word, Abe. Scout's honor."

D'Amato headed back to the waist. Cohen stood, stretched once more. Somewhat unsteadily, he made his way forward to the cockpit hatch. He opened it to be greeted by a cold wind that almost blew him back into the bomb bay. The flight deck carpeting was a blood-soaked sponge underfoot. He hesitated in confusion, attempting to digest the phenomenon. Shards of "shatterproof" glass from the left-hand windshield littered the deck. A blizzard of white insulation particles filled the air. A blood-stained Charlie Crenshaw leaned motionless against his radio table, eyes locked on his own trembling hands. The liaison transmitter looked as if it had been hit with an ax. Cohen pushed Crenshaw aside. There was blood everywhere. At first glance it seemed as if the right seat were empty. It took a moment to register the fact that its occupant had no head.

Cohen stood motionless for a moment, struggling to accept the evidence of his eyes. With hands grasping the wheel, a headless Lieutenant Deutsch seemed to be flying the airplane. The copilot's jacket collar remained folded properly around what remained of his neck. It was a neat job of work, as if performed by an experienced French executioner. Cohen felt a pang of regret for having emptied his canteen.

Captain Maguire was slumped forward in the left seat. At first, he seemed only to have been wounded in the shoulder. His flight jacket was ripped. The pilot's right hand was still grasping the throttle levers. With some difficulty, Cohen pried it loose. The fingers, inside the glove, were like tubes of hard, unyielding rubber. He felt for a pulse, found it. It was then Cohen saw that a portion of the pilot's face had been shot away. Part of his jaw, along with most of the flesh of his cheek and his right eye was gone. Cohen could make out shattered molars, the pulpy remnants of Maguire's tongue, the ragged shard of a jawbone.

Fighting a sudden nausea, Cohen closed his eyes, swallowed, breathed deeply. It was his guess that a single shell had entered through Maguire's windshield to explode in the cockpit between pilot and copilot. The instrument panel, like everything else, was dripping blood. A few instruments were shattered. Using his glove, he wiped the glass of the airspeed indicator, altimeter, and flight indicator. They were slightly nose-up in a shallow climb. Airspeed was 145 indicated and dropping. At this rate, Sally's Wagon would soon be on the edge of a fatal stall.

As gently as he could, Cohen removed Deutsch's hands from the wheel. He pushed the three usable throttles forward, waited till the airspeed reached 200. He picked up a few feet, than leveled out. After a few moments of juggling back and forth between control column and throttle, he had Sally's Wagon cruising reasonably straight and level, holding 9,850 feet at 160 knots. He punched in the automatic flight control. Glancing out the side windows he noted with relief that they were out of the flak.

Mickey Maguire was conscious. His one good eye stared upward, blinking rapidly, Cohen said, "You in pain, Captain?" The response was an almost imperceptible nod.

Cohen fetched the flight-deck medical kit from the bomb bay bulkhead. He administered the shot in Maguire's leg, then, with his head just inches from Maguire's, he said, "You're going to be okay, Captain. We're going to get you back." Maguire good eye flitted back and forth between both of Cohen's. Cohen said, "Those pictures—you know—I don't have them, never even saw them." It was all he could think of to say.

The pilot slipped back into unconsciousness. Cohen got out of his flight jacket, draped it gently over Maguire in order to protect his shattered face from the hurricane blowing through the demolished windshield section. There was nothing else he could do.

Leaning forward, he pulled Deutsch's mike and headset leads from the copilot's interphone jack and was about to plug in his own when his eye, guided by the disconnected cord, came to rest on what had been missing.

Deutsch's severed head was jammed between the rudder pedals. A soft, jaunty garrison cap was clamped in place by a pair of earphones. The eyes were wide open, unblinking; staring upward into Cohen's. The oxygen mask had been wrenched part-way off to reveal a grimacing mouth set crookedly in a pale, unpainted, wax museum face. The expression was indecipherable. It was as if Second Lieutenant Jordan Deutsch had been caught in the middle of an emotional transition.

Cohen plugged in, trying not to look downward into the open neck cavity of the copilot's torso. Sergeant Crenshaw's mutterings filled his headset. ". . . the blood was gushing out like there was a pump."

Cohen clicked on his throat mike. "Take it easy, Crenshaw."

"It just wouldn't stop, I didn't know there was that much blood in a person."

"Just relax, Charlie, everything's okay. Get back in your turret."

"I can't."

"What the fuck's going on?" It was D'Amato's voice.

"Get up here and bring Woike."

"Who in the hell do you think you are, pal?" D'Amato was shouting. "You been promoted to lieutenant or something?"

"Captain." He fought to retain his patience. "You and Woike get your asses up here, fast."

Sergeant Woike said, "Who's flying this here-now airplane?"

"Nobody."

"I'm going out the fucking window!"

It occurred to Cohen that they had heard Crenshaw on the interphone. D'Amato's bluster was a product of fear. In quieter tones, Cohen said, "We got a few problems. I really need both you guys up here."

There was silence for a moment, then D'Amato said, "On our way."

"And if you got any booze in your canteen, bring it." Through the copilot's intact windshield Cohen could make out a line of deep blue on the horizon—the Adriatic. He said, "Junior, you okay?"

"Okay, Abe. But you don't sound so good."

"It's a little rough. Right now you're our only eyes and our only guns. You wearing your chute?"

"Roger dodger you old codger." Then as if an afterthought, the belly gunner said, "Who's flying the airplane, Abe?"

"The AFC. And listen, if I give you the word, get out. Okay?"

"Okay, good buddy."

"And remember Junior, feet first, and keep your head back."

There was little room for a seat or back pack parachute in the ball, even for someone as small as Junior Darling. Instead, he wore a compact chest chute of a type that had strangled a number of his peers in shroud lines.

There was no need now for oxygen. Cohen switched off the system, then checked the compass heading. It was 248 degrees SW. He stood for a minute, realizing that he had taken over and wondering why.

D'Amato and Woike came through the flight deck hatch. D'Amato took one look around, unscrewed the top of his canteen, took a deep swig. Woike vomited on the deck.

Cohen motioned D'Amato forward, raised the jacket off Maguire's face. They had to shout in order to be heard over the wind noise. "We've got to get him out of that seat, D'Amato. Stretched out on the deck where we can deal with him."

"Jesus, you mean he's alive?" He handed Cohen the canteen.

"Yes."

"If he knew, he wouldn't want to be, poor bastard."

"You can ask him about it later."

"Where's Deutsch's head?"

"Jamming the rudder pedals."

D'Amato grimaced. "What's the matter with Crenshaw? What's he doing out of his turret?"

"He's a little psyched out."

"What do you mean, a little?" said Woike. "I heard him on the interphone."

Cohen said, "Lieutenant Beel's dead."

"Poor bastard," said Woike. "I owed him ten bucks."

"Christ . . ."

"Lieutenant Taylor's down there too," said Cohen. "I don't know what kind of shape he's in. Crenshaw went down to take care of him, then chickened out. We got to get him up here if he's still alive."

"I'll go," said Woike.

D'Amato said, "Let's all get the hell out of here, Cohen. You can use Deutsch's chute, he don't need it."

"We can't bale out and leave Maguire and Taylor."

"Why not?"

"Don't fuck with me D'Amato, you know why not."

"You're Section Eight material, Cohen! We got no pilot. We got an engine out, no nose guns, no tail turret, no top turret gunner, no navigator, and the fucking AFC gyros will probably tumble any second like they usually do and Christ knows what else and your heart's bleeding for some chickenshit officer who's been riding your ass and who's probably going to die anyway! The biggest favor you could do for Maguire is shoot him. As for Taylor, he's a nice guy, but tough shit. I don't see why we have to die with him. And we're sure as hell all going to die, unless we get the fuck out of here! You want to ride this thing down and be some kind of hero—go ahead. But I'm leaving, baby. A fucking prison camp ain't so bad. Nobody shoots at you and if it's Italian you get to eat a lot of pasta."

"Look, Frank, I wish I was somewhere else, anywhere. But I'm here."

"Bullshit. You could be somewhere else a couple minutes after you pull the rip cord." D'Amato was silent for a moment. "Okay . . . okay . . . we can hook Taylor's chute up with a static line and shove him out . . . all right?" He put his hand on Cohen's arm. "You're a nice guy, Abe. I'd hate to see you dead."

"D'Amato, do me one favor. A little housekeeping before you go."

"You're really staying?"

"Yeah."

"You're nuts."

"Okay, I'm nuts. But I'm going to get this airplane home."

"Why?"

Cohen stared down at the deck, searching for words.

D'Amato repeated the question. "Why?"

"I don't know why . . ."

"What're you trying to prove, for Christ sake?"

Cohen hesitated. "Something . . . I don't know." He grabbed D'Amato's arm. "Just give me fifteen minutes . . . ten."

Woike's voice on the interphone was strident. "Hey, Lieutenant Taylor's in bad shape. I need some help down here."

"On my way." D'Amato turned toward the hatch.

Cohen placed a hand on his shoulder. "Thanks, Frank."

D'Amato hesitated, as if reconsidering. "What about Turkey?" said D'Amato. "We could sit out the whole war."

"I thought about it, but according to the compass, Maguire set a western course off the target. "It wouldn't pay to turn east. All we'd gain now is a couple hundred miles, but we'd probably pick up a lot of fighters over Greece and Bulgaria."

"Okay." D'Amato seemed to shake himself. "Ten minutes and then it's bye-bye and that goes for Woike, too." D'Amato stared at Cohen, a wide grin on his face. "And don't try to bullshit me, when the time comes you'll change your fucking mind. I'll bet everything I got on it."

When he had gone, Cohen got on his hands and knees to reach blindly across the console to the rudder pedals. He fumbled about searching for a handhold. Finally, with an ear in each hand, he worked the copilot's head free of the pedals. He stood, taking a moment to straighten its hat, remove its oxygen mask, brush some dirt from its cheek. He had trouble associating the thing with Lieutenant Deutsch. At best it seemed little more than a distorted likeness, a sculpted parody of the original.

He was at a loss as to where to put it. A sense of weakness spread to his groin, his spine, his wrists. He slowed his breathing, allowed his muscles to go limp, attempted to swallow the lump forming in his throat. He glanced around. Crenshaw was seated now, slumped over the radio desk.

Cohen placed Deutsch's head on the desk. Taking charge of himself, he grabbed the radio man by his flight-jacket lapels, pulled his headset off. Speaking into the naked ear as if it were a microphone, he said, "Crenshaw, there might be bandits buzzing around up there right now."

"I can't help it." Crenshaw closed his eyes tightly and began to shake.

Deutsch's head fell over onto its side, rolled to the edge of the desk. It was an action that released Cohen's tightly repressed feelings, coalesced them into a flash of rage, "Son of a bitch! You want to go psycho, shit in your pants, or whatever the fuck it is you're doing, you do it on the ground!" Cohen grasped him even tighter, choking him.

Crenshaw struggled to break free. "Leave me alone."

With no warning Cohen slapped him, forehand, then back hand. "Get into the top turret."

"I can't."

Cohen ripped Crenshaw's oxygen mask off, clutched his cheeks with his free hand, and squeezed, forcing the radio operator's lips into a grotesque, pouting kiss. "Open your fucking eyes!"

The lids fluttered open. A pair of bulging eyeballs fixed themselves, unblinking, on the center of Cohen's forehead. Cohen released him.

Crenshaw's face was wet with tears. "Don't hit me, Abe."

Fighting his temper, Cohen stepped back. He breathed deeply then picked up Lieutenant Deutsch's head, thrust it into Crenshaw's midsection. In a tight, knife-edged voice, he said, "This is yours, fuckhead, your responsibility. You take care of it till we get home. Anything happens to it, I'll kill you." Cohen looked directly into his eyes. In measured cadence with equal emphasis on each word, he said, "You move from here, even to take a leak, and Sergeant D'Amato and I will pull your chute off and drop you overboard. That's a fucking promise, Crenshaw. It's a long way down. You think about it."

Cohen checked the instruments. Sally's Wagon was straight and level at 9,600 feet.

D'Amato and Woike appeared carrying an unconscious Lieutenant Taylor. D'Amato also had Beel's parachute. They leaned the wounded navigator against the bulkhead.

"He was conscious and talking," said Woike, struggling to keep Taylor upright. "It was murder getting him around the nose wheel. He passed out when we lifted him, poor bastard."

Lieutenant Clyde Taylor was unconscious, breathing erratically. He had suffered a belly wound. The front of his flight jacket was in bloody tatters, The heavy zipper was jammed. They split the jacket open. It took minutes to cut away the blue cotton heated suit, more minutes to get Taylor's pants down, his shirt tucked up. They were greeted by about six inches of intestines protruding from a wound that encompassed a third of his lower abdomen.

"Crenshaw," said Cohen. "He didn't do anything, just left him there."

Cohen dusted the wound with sulfa powder, then, winding a bandage around his hand, pushed the ropy coil of intestines back into Taylor's abdominal cavity. He felt a hard metallic edge—the jagged piece of shrapnel that had created the wound. He debated removing it, pulling it out like a rotting tooth, removing the source of the problem and thus curing the patient.

Woike said, "He going to make it?"

"Beats me." Cohen withdrew his hand. "I'm not a doctor."

"You're not a pilot, either," said D'Amato.

Using a wide bandage, Cohen, with D'Amato's help, wrapped yards of it around Taylor's midsection. They tied it off, then laid the young navigator down under the top turret. Cohen slipped Beel's parachute under Taylor's head. Woike removed his flight jacket to use as a blanket.

Buffeted by the raw wind blowing through the open windshield section, Cohen and D'Amato wrestled Maguire out of the pilot's seat. The laid him on the deck next to Taylor. D'Amato folded his flying jacket into a pillow, slipped it gently under Maguire's head. The right side of his face resembled a graphic cut-away from an anatomy textbook. Cohen dusted the wound with three packets of sulfa, then applied a half-dozen large gauze pads. There was nothing else he could do. It was a lousy war. He felt suddenly very tired.

He tried taking Maguire's place in the left seat but found that he couldn't keep his eyes open against the force of the wind howling through the shattered windshield section. He said, "Either of you guys have goggles?"

"What's Lieutenant Taylor need goggles for?"

"He doesn't, asshole. I do."

"I wear them at the waist window," said Woike.

"Get them. And while you're at it, go down into the nose and get me Taylor's mission map from the navigator's desk."

Cohen helped himself from D'Amato's canteen. It was Egyptian rum, astringent and overly sweet, but well over one-hundred proof. Maybe, he thought, D'Amato was right and he was crazy. Bailing out would be easy. He could point Sally's nose due west, toward Italy. They'd be there in less than an hour. When he was out of prison camp, he could live there happily ever after. Maybe by then Lucky and the FBI would have given up on him. He could use the dead Beel's chute and could get off the hook by attaching static lines to Taylor and Maguire's rip cords. The rest of the crew could fend for themselves. He would be out of the war for the duration. He stared ahead at a limitless sky. It was all bullshit. He knew he was committed. Why?

If the shit hit the fan, who would be dead, Abe Cohen or Danny Esposito? He thought of Natalie. She didn't even know Danny Esposito. Cohen would be dead, Esposito was already dead. Natalie.

He up-ended the canteen to swallow another mouthful, almost choking in the process, then he turned to stare at Jordan Deutsch's head on the radio table. Its mouth was askew, grotesquely off-center in a face that seemed made of pale cheese or modeling wax—an unfinished caricature. Death had not been kind.

D'Amato said, "Real life stinks."

Tech Sergeant Cohen grunted, tasting sour bile. He recalled Lieutenant Deutsch's wedding in Florida. His fiancée, a beautiful girl who looked like Merle Oberon, had come down from Boston. The crew had attended and Maguire had been best man. Cohen said, "Deutsch's class-As were tailor made."

"He was sharp."

"First time I ever saw a Windsor knot. Took me a week to learn to tie one. You can get laid from a Windsor knot and a little Aqua-Velva."

"Listen, Abe," D'Amato grasped Cohen's arm. "You may be nuts, but I've got a lot of respect for you. You ever landed a B-24 on three engines?"

"Hell no."

"Four engines?"

"I'm a flight engineer. I've never landed anything."

"You know there are three of us against one. We could get a chute on you and toss you out."

"I can't swim, Frank."

"What do you mean, swim?"

Cohen grinned. "If you look out, you'll see the Adriatic. It's going to be water all the way home."

"You conned me, you bastard! We're supposed to be over Albania by now, like we came . . ."

"Right. But Maguire set up this course, maybe thought there'd be less chance of fighters, this way. Me, I'm not sure. But you go out now, you'll get all wet. Glub-glub."

"You're crazy! What the hell you doing this for?"

"Patriotism."

"You're full of crap . . . I'm going out."

"How are you at the doggie paddle, D'Amato?" Cohen slapped him on the shoulder.

"Bullshit. We float in our Mae Wests."

"If you don't drown, or get eaten by sharks, you'll float for a year, two years, till you're nothing but bones. There's not much traffic in the Adriatic. No fishing boats for the duration because of the mines." It was a guess, but what the hell did D'Amato know?

"Listen," said the gunner, "you want to kill yourself, that's okay. But what in the hell you want from us, for Christ's sake!"

"I may need gunners in case fighters show up."

"Shit! My life depends on a crazy Yid, a total nut case . . . and there ain't no fucking sharks!"

"Sure, that's what they tell you, old buddy. But one way or another it's sink or swim, and you'll probably sink. Anyway, I'm liable to need some gunners, at least for a while, then we can talk."

"Talk about what? And what in the hell makes you think you can fly an airplane?"

"I'm a flight engineer, D'Amato, a good one. And I was a crew chief for two months at MacDill. I could take this thing apart and put it back together, blindfolded. And I've stood right here between Deutsch and Maguire for a couple hundred hours, watching everything: landings, takeoffs, bad weather, bomb runs, that engine fire we had coming into Havana, the works."

D'Amato looked at him sourly as Sergeant Woike handed Cohen the goggles. Cohen put them on. He said, "D'Amato, how about taking the top turret—we'd stand a better chance."

"Fuck you, Cohen. I'm a waist gunner. I like being near a big window, just in case."

"What about you, Woike?"

"We're a team, you know, Abe, like Laurel and Hardy."

With no further words, the two airmen turned to make their way back to their waist guns.

Sally's Wagon was over water. For once, the automatic flight control was functioning as it was supposed to. They were just under 9,500 feet and at a compass heading of 245 degrees SW.

He made a quarter-inch circle on the map. As near as he could guess, it encompassed their position, roughly seventy-five miles southwest of the Yugoslavian coast. It would have them over southern Italy near Bari and the whole Italian air force unless he turned soon. The best way to avoid fighters was to stay at sea. He would stay on the current heading for, at most, about another ten minutes before turning south. Cohen slid into the left seat, put on the goggles as protection against the incessant hurricane blowing through the open windshield. He raised his collar. A slug from D'Amato's canteen also helped.

He monitored instruments, adjusted the throttles in order to hold altitude. Five minutes after occupying the pilot's seat, he found that number one had begun running hot.

He clicked on his throat mike. "Junior, take a look at the left outboard engine."

There was a pause while Junior rotated his turret. "She's throwing oil, Abe."

"How much oil?"

"Not much."

Engines that run hot and throw oil suffer a fatal disease. It was only a matter of time before number one seized up or caught fire. Feathering it was inevitable. His choice was to keep it going till the last moment or shut it down sooner in order to conserve what power remained for an emergency. A B-24 could be flown on two engines—barely. Anyway, that's what the hotshots said. He would soon have the experience.

He decided against shutting it down until after he made his turn to the south. The turning maneuver would constitute his first real piloting experience and he felt it best to have at hand all the power he could get.

He crossed himself, took a deep breath, and switched off the AFC. Sally's Wagon was now his airplane. In an instant he found himself in a shallow dive. The controls were neutralized, so he suspected the trouble lay in some slack in the emergency repair he made on the elevator cable. He cranked in some trim. Finally, in reasonably level flight, he noted a tendency to skew to the right because of the feathered engine. He attempted more rudder trim but found it was already at its maximum. A slight pressure on the rudder pedal corrected the situation.

The altimeter read 9,150 feet. Airspeed had crept up to 180. He pulled the wheel back slightly in the hope of trading off a bit of airspeed for altitude. He was feeling his way, monitoring the instruments to determine whether his choices were correct.

Ten minutes later, with all going well, he began a slow, shallow turn to the left. It seemed to take minutes, during which he fought a tendency, brought about by increasing self-confidence, to sharpen the bank, get it over with. He played it safe, came out of it straight and level at an altitude of 8,800 feet. He had a lot to learn. The turn had cost him altitude. According to the map, his compass bearing of 170 degrees was about right.

His experience at map reading was minimal, but he reasoned that if he were headed too far east, the Albanian coast would come up on his right and he could adjust. There was less chance of fighter attacks if he stayed over water, the farther out the better. Perhaps the enemy wouldn't bother scrambling fighters for a lone aircraft out at sea . . . perhaps. The plan was to fly down the center of the Adriatic, threading the needle through the Straits of Otranto. After that he would be free and clear over the Mediterranean.

Slowly, he throttled back the left outboard engine, increasing power on the two healthy power plants and correcting trim as he did so. Finally, when he felt he had everything in balance, he shut it down completely, feathering the prop to keep it from windmilling. Despite his fear, he took pleasure in getting it right. He was learning fast.

Steeling himself against growing trepidation, Cohen watched his instruments. Where before three engines had been doing the work of four, now there were only two, one on each wing. He would have to sustain flight just over the stalling speed in order to keep from straining the little he had left. He knew that at high throttle settings, sustained over hours, heat and vibration could trigger even the slightest engine weaknesses into disastrous malfunctions. Worn piston rings, hairline camshaft cracks, chafed oil lines, or any one of a thousand other imperfect moving parts could give way. The result might be comparable to that of a heart patient deciding to run rather than walk the last hundred yards home.

Altitude was important. With only two engines he could not

recoup any he lost. An attempt to do so could result in a deadly stall.

He concentrated on throttle settings, fuel mixture, and propeller pitch in an attempt to find the most economical settings capable of sustaining altitude. The experimentation cost him some more height, but he was learning how to fly. He leveled off at 7,500 feet, settled down to 140 miles per hour, indicated.

A half-hour later, the altimeter read 6,650 feet, a critical loss. He faced a dilemma. The engines were already running hotter than he would have liked, but a quick calculation told him that at her current rate of descent Sally would be in the water somewhere in the middle of the Mediterranean. He had no choice. He went onto full auto-rich, 2300 rpms and 34 inches manifold pressure, increasing his indicated airspeed to 160.

He felt that their salvation might lie with their sick left outboard engine. If there was an hour's life to be squeezed out of it, he figured that they could make it into one of the many strips along the Egyptian or Libyan coast. It was an ace in the hole, their only one. But it wouldn't pay to play it prematurely. He decided to wait till their altitude was reduced to about four thousand feet before starting it up.

He put Sally's Wagon on AFC and left his seat to check the wounded. He administered another shot to Maguire, then turned to Taylor. The young navigator's eyes were opened. He spoke in soft, sibilant tones. "How you doing, Sergeant?"

"Okay, Lieutenant." Cohen took a piece of gauze from the nearby first-aid kit to wipe the perspiration off Taylor's forehead. "You feeling any pain?"

"I'm fine." Taylor grinned a crooked grin, but his eyes betrayed him. "Where was I hit?"

Cohen hesitated, searching in vain for words that would make it easier. He said, "In the gut, but it's not bad."

"Jesus . . ."

"I patched you up pretty good."

"I don't think I want to die, Abe."

"You'll be okay."

Taylor's eyes darted to the right. He gestured in that direction with his thumb. "Who's that?"

"Captain Maguire."

"He alive?"

"A head wound," said Cohen, once again swabbing Taylor's forehead. "It knocked him for a loop, but he should be up and around soon."

"Deutsch doing okay?"

"Fine. I'm flying as copilot."

"Terrific, Abe. Maybe we'll put you in for a field commission when we get back." Taylor spoke haltingly, his words jumbled as if he had a mouth full of potatoes. "What's the course?"

"Southwest. We're coming up on the Straits of Otranto."

"How come we didn't head for Turkey? We'd be there by now. Could have checked into the Grand Hotel in Ankara and had a party. How come?"

Cohen said, "To hell with Turkey. You don't want no Wog doctor poking around."

"I guess you're right." Taylor grinned. A trickle of blood ran from the corner of his mouth. "You know, I went to college, played basketball, studied law."

"Well, I'm going to need a lawyer pretty soon." Cohen wiped the blood from Taylor's chin.

"You'll be my first case."

"I hope I can afford your fee, Clyde."

Taylor hadn't heard him. The navigator's eyes were closed, his breathing labored. Cohen administered a shot of morphine. It was the only thing he could do.

Back in the left seat, he noted the auto-pilot was deviating to the left. He adjusted the AFC turn control.

Junior announced land on their right. A half-minute went by before Cohen could see it: a buff-colored streak on the horizon. He checked the map, concluding that it was the heel of the Italian boot. He had been bearing a little too far west. He turned east a few degrees, marked his position and time on the map. Getting through the middle of the straits separating Italy from Albania would be a narrow squeak. If D'Amato and Woike saw land below them, they'd hit the silk. He needed them now, more than ever. If they were going to get fighters it would be here. He prayed he could get through on tiptoe.

Someone tapped him on the shoulder. He turned to find

D'Amato standing behind him. "I'm going up into the top turret."

Cohen nodded. "Nice view from up there." He watched as D'Amato squirmed up into the turret. A half-minute later it was traversing.

Italy became a smudge on their right. They were free of the Adriatic. Cohen made a slow turn to the west to avoid Corfu. He came out of it on a heading due south, the shortest distance to a landfall on the African coast, a long way over the horizon. The altimeter was reading 4,800 feet. The sea was a sparkling cobalt stretching on forever. He wondered if the fuel would hold out, then decided not to think about it.

A half-hour later, they were clear of the Ionian Sea and over the Mediterranean, just about out of enemy fighter range. He said, "Junior, you can get out of that fucker now and stretch your legs."

"Praise Jesus."

CHAPTER 18

JULY 1943

The terrace at Shepheard's Hotel in Cairo, reflecting the British preoccupation with social class as applied to the military, was strictly officers' country; an outpost of the Empire for dusty Eighth Army lieutenants, Royal Australian Air Force flight officers, and others fresh from the desert war—*in from the blue.*

Upholding a tradition dating back to the First War, they sprawled quietly, still encrusted with desert grit, their khaki uniforms stained with the high-tide marks of sweat; winding down at little tables with iced gin and quinine in the soft light of the Egyptian sunset. The drink was an invention of Shepheard's legendary bartender, providing both relaxing libation and a bitter malaria protection in one go.

Slumped in an oversized wicker chair nestled between two potted palms, Abe Cohen tried not to concentrate on "A Nightingale Sang in Berkeley Square," as played by a small, befezzed orchestra on untuned instruments. As a guest in the hotel, he was accorded the privilege of the terrace and bar, despite his "other-ranks" status.

Natalie Marek arrived exactly on time, appearing at the entrance to the terrace as if by magic. She stood, surveying the crowd, searching for him. He sat back, partially obscured by palm fronds. It was the first time he had seen her in uniform. He sipped his bourbon-and-soda, taking delight in observing her undetected and wondering at his feelings for her.

In the past his needs had been easily filled; his ego stroked, his hunger satisfied by a variety of women. It had always seemed a sport, bound by well-established rules in which both parties played for the sheer love of a game that in his experience neither side ever lost. But this was different. She was different. The game this time, if it was a game, seemed much more serious, even threatening. The sight of her, the mere thought of her, shook him to his bones, at the same time creating a void that he knew only she could fill. It was a kind of delicious anguish he had never before experienced. It troubled him, but he cherished the agony. Abe Cohen, for the first time in his life, was in love.

He stood. She saw him, raised a hand in greeting, smiled. He surveyed her, head to toe, as she approached.

Seated across from him, she ordered a cassis, leaned back in her chair, and sighed. "Ah . . . it's so good to just relax."

He said, "You had a tough day, Corporal?"

"Please call me Natalie, and it's been a very hectic day."

"You'd never know it," he said. "You look so crisp and fresh."

She smiled. "You make me sound like a salad."

He laughed. "I guess I kind of have a way with words, don't I? I mean, anybody can see you're not a salad. You're the main course. Or should I quit while I'm ahead?"

She reached across the table to pat his hand. "How long is your leave, Sergeant?"

"Three whole days, and please call me Abe. I landed at Heliopolis an hour ago, rushed right to a phone, and called you."

"Abe."

"Natalie."

"You called just in time," she said. "Five more minutes, I would have been out of the office."

"It would have been a major disaster." He meant it.

"Yes," she said, staring at him with wide eyes, over the top of her glass.

He had trouble breathing.

She said, "When there's nothing urgent going on we usually don't work on the Christian sabbath. I have the whole day tomorrow. Have you been to the pyramids?"

"No, and I think I'm in love with you." He put his drink down, stared at it for a moment before summoning the courage to look up at her. He was surprised at what he had said, but there seemed to be an urgency over which he had little control. To hell with it.

She fumbled for a cigarette, waited for him to light it. He said it again, just to hear the words. "I think I'm in love with you."

She said, "What a charming way to greet a lady."

"I guess I had to tell you. You know, put it on the table, clear the decks, whatever . . ."

"You don't even know me. We've only been together twice before in a room full of other people."

Grabbing hold of himself, he grinned. "That's why I'm not sure. It might be indigestion, and there were a couple days there, I didn't take my Atabrine, so it could also be sandfly fever or malaria. I mean, I don't know, I've never been checked out in this kind of thing . . . love."

She spoke quietly. "I don't think I can help you." She put out her cigarette, twisting it into the ashtray. "I too have been suffering from a little indigestion."

They were both quiet. Cohen felt light-headed. He left it to her to restart the conversation. They spoke of the weather, the Sicilian invasion, her brother Uri being called back to active service.

Finally he said, "We could have dinner here in the hotel. It's probably as good as anywhere else in Cairo, and they have a dance floor."

She nodded.

He said, "But what about your indigestion?"

"It doesn't seem to effect my appetite. And you?"

"I'm starving."

"Where are you staying?"

"Here. I booked a room."

"It must be expensive."

"Yes, but it's a real treat. Reminds me of home. I mean, they have sheets and mattresses and the only bar in the Middle East that stocks American whiskey . . . Old Granddad."

"Are you rich?"

"No. I'm just a good poker player."

"Mazel tov."

"One little problem," he said. "I've got to take a shower and get out of these sweaty clothes. I'll be quick . . . honest. You can wait for me here or in the lobby."

She looked around. "I think I'd rather wait in your room, if you don't mind. There don't seem to be any unescorted women out here."

The elevator was a plush, gilded carriage riding in an open shaft encircled by a winding staircase. Between the second and third floors he took her in his arms.

The kiss, at first, was tentative. For the first time in his adult life Cohen was unsure. Then her arms tightened around him.

A few minutes later, in the shower, he made the water as hot as he could stand, filling the marble cubicle with steam. He squeezed his bandaged penis into a condom to keep it dry. He soaped himself down, lathered his face.

Unable to open his eyes, he felt the draft as the shower door opened. She said, "I've decided to join you, that is, if there's room for two." Her voice was pitched low, the words spoken hesitantly.

He wiped the soap out of his eyes, turned to see her. She was standing there, a naked angel, shrouded in steam. For an instant he thought his heart had stopped. It was suddenly too hot.

She was looking down. "The bandage . . . my God! You were wounded!"

"No." He attempted to cover himself with his hands.

"You have some kind of infection?" She stepped back.

"No, nothing like that." He turned off the hot water, turned up the cold. The shock seemed a momentary reprieve, but only momentary. He felt trapped.

She said, "Abe . . . what?"

She seemed truly concerned. He thought of the kiss in the elevator. He said, "You see . . . I'm not really Jewish."

She began to speak, but there were no words. She closed her eyes for a moment, then opened them to stare into his. "You mean, you were circumcised?"

"Yes."

"Why?"

"I wanted to be a Jew."

"But you are."

"No . . ."

She took a step forward. "I don't understand."
"It's a very long story." He placed his hand on her shoulder.
"Oh, Abe . . ."
"I love you, Natalie."

THE MISSION

AUGUST 1, 1943

The airspeed indicator hopped a full ten miles an hour as Junior's turret retracted up into the belly. It was a welcome bonus created by reduced drag.

D'Amato came down out of the turret. The gunner stared at Cohen with obvious distaste. "Your face looks like raw hamburger."

Cohen, pressed two fingers to his cheek. There was no feeling. "The fucking wind." Once again he punched in the AFC.

They wrestled Lieutenant Deutsch's headless body out of the seat, laid it on the deck. Cohen took his place in the copilot's seat. Breathing a sigh of relief at the calm air, he took off the goggles and bummed a cigarette from D'Amato. He switched off the AFC. The nose was up slightly, bleeding off airspeed. He corrected, fought off a desire to increase throttle settings. It was time to take another action. Holding the throat mike tightly against this neck, he said, "Let's toss all the ammunition overboard, tail turret, waist, and ball, every round, all of it." He wondered just how much it would take to stop Sally's inevitable descent. "After that, get rid of the waist guns and all the oxygen bottles and everything else you can think of."

"You kidding?"

"No, we're going to make this baby a few thousand pounds lighter."

D'Amato said, "Giving orders again, you chickenshit bastard?"

"Yeah, Frank. I'm the ranking son of a bitch on what's left of this airplane."

"By one lousy stripe. . . ."

"Right. And you can go up in the nose and get rid of the guns, the ammunition, the bombsight and anything else that's not nailed down."

A little later they dumped it all through the open bomb door, including the two heavy steel armor slabs from the waist. Finally, Cohen said, "And don't forget Lieutenant Deutsch."

"That's sacrilege," said Junior. "He deserves a decent Christian burial."

"They can bury his head. His body weighs at least a hundred and sixty pounds. And Lieutenant Beel weighs even more. He goes too."

Sergeant D'Amato and Sergeant Woike rolled the bodies off the bomb bay catwalk. Junior read the Twenty-third Psalm from a Bible he kept stashed in his turret.

Later, D'Amato, standing behind Cohen, said, "If we dump Smith, we can get rid of another two hundred pounds, give or take."

"Why not? It would be worth it and with time off for good behavior, we'd be out in thirty or forty years."

"And what about him?" D'Amato, an evil grin lighting his face, pointed to Sergeant Crenshaw. "The bastard is about one sixty-five in useless weight."

The two of them stared at Crenshaw. He seemed not to have moved in over two hours. He was muttering to himself, his eyes focused on the deck. D'Amato offered him the canteen, saying, "Maybe a shot of this will make you feel better, Crenshaw."

Wide-eyed, his mouth hanging open, Sergeant Crenshaw stared at D'Amato for a moment, then turned away.

D'Amato said, "Never trust a man who doesn't drink." He handed his canteen to Cohen, slapped his back, and squirmed up into the top turret.

During the next hour they lost only seven hundred feet. Cohen was pleased with himself. He had Junior and Woike tend Captain Maguire. It was time for another morphine shot.

Twenty minutes later, Cohen, feeling a presence, turned to see Crenshaw standing there, fidgeting as if he had been waiting a very long time for a bus.

"I'm feeling better now." Crenshaw looked washed out, colorless. "What can I do?"

"I told you to take care of Deutsch's head."

"It's okay, I secured it. It's in the bombsight bag."

"You said I was a murderer, remember? You were going to shoot my ass off if I ever bailed out, right?"

"I didn't mean it, Abe."

"Bullshit."

"I figure I can help with something."

"Okay, welcome back to the world of the living. What should the frequency be on the command set?"

"Eighty-seven-point-three, like for the tower and everything. It's got a red mark."

"Set it."

Crenshaw leaned in over the throttle console, glanced up at the dial.

"It's already set."

"Check it, I want to know if the damned thing is working."

Crenshaw flicked the switch, plugged in his headset, switched over from interphone to radio and listened. Cohen's earphones responded with heavy static. Crenshaw reached up, twisted some knobs, cranked the tuner to another frequency. There was no change. He switched off, removed his headset. "Kaput. The antenna's probably gone."

"Shit."

"Nothing we can do," said Crenshaw. "I guess it was flak."

Cohen sighed. He had been counting on the command set. The tower at any number of fields along the coast could have talked him in. He said, "What about the RDF?"

Crenshaw checked it. An Arabic radio station came in dimly. Cohen rotated the loop until it was loud and clear. The radio beacon indicator pointed southeast, probably Alexandria or Cairo. They dialed around, searching in vain for something farther west. Finally, Cohen switched it off. Perhaps a little later he might have some luck.

He said, "Okay, now beat it. I don't want you standing behind me."

"C'mon man, what in the hell you got against me?"

Cohen twisted in his seat, locking eyes with him. "You left the top turret unmanned."

"I couldn't help it. I mean everybody fucks up once in a while."

"Not when it threatens my life. If we got fighters they would've had a party. We'd all be dead, especially me. I don't like that. And you left Taylor in the nose with a belly wound. You just up and left him to die."

"You going to say anything?"

"You're fucking-A."

"Give me a break, Abe . . ."

"Beat it."

Junior's voice was flat, toneless in Cohen's headset. "Lieutenant Taylor's not breathing and there's no pulse."

Cohen glanced over his shoulder to find the little ball gunner bending over the navigator. "You sure?"

"Nothing. God rest his soul, Abe."

Cohen felt hollow, suddenly useless. He tightened his grip on the wheel. "What about Maguire?"

"Okay I think, but he's breathing kind of funny."

"Raise his head a little and give him another shot. With any luck he'll be in a hospital in a couple hours."

Junior Darling read the Lord's prayer over the interphone. Cohen shut him up after the third line.

Sally's Wagon droned on, losing about ten feet in altitude each minute; an improvement, but still critical. Cohen felt a sudden anxiety. The moment of truth—landing—was still to come. He checked the hydraulic pressure gauge, found it adequate. When the time came, he would have flaps and landing gear. All he would need was enough guts not to panic.

"Hey! There's a parachute!" It was Sergeant Woike calling from the waist. "What the hell's going on?"

"D'Amato," said Cohen, his voice matter-of-fact. "You see any more airplanes up there?"

"You'd be the first to know, hotshot."

"Junior, you okay?"

"Roger dodger."

Cohen twisted in his seat. Crenshaw was not at the radio desk. He said, "Scratch one radio operator."

"How the fuck he get out?"

"Probably through the bomb bay."

They were silent for a minute. Then Junior said, "He's in the water, I see him."

"Dumb bastard . . ."

Woike said, "What do you suppose he weighed?"

For the next half-hour, no one spoke. Indicated airspeed was a steady 155. They were down to 4,700 feet. There was something gleaming on the horizon. "D'Amato, you see something from up there—straight ahead?"

"No . . . yes . . . a ship . . . more than one."

Cohen thought to turn on the command set, then remembered the antenna was gone. As they approached he counted seven ships, headed due west.

"A convoy," said Junior, peering over Cohen's shoulder. "Two destroyers and five—six freighters."

"Oil tankers," said D'Amato.

"Okay, but whose?"

"Beats the shit out of me."

Cohen said, "Woike, break out the flare pistol and a couple of red flares."

"Roger wilco."

Cohen began a slow turn to the left, just enough to increase the range if it were the enemy. He studied the ships carefully. There was still no way to ascertain their nationality, but he felt a growing conviction that they were British. Except for Crete, which he assumed was supplied from Greece, there were no enemy bases this far east and thus no reason for an Axis convoy.

They drew parallel with the ships a few miles off. Junior shot off a red flare. It arched upward, then fell toward the sea, a bright, flickering red star trailing smoke. Within a minute, as Cohen circled, they were answered by a green flare from the ship. He tightened the turn as much as he dared, edging in closer.

"Hey hotshot, they ain't shooting at us."

"They're British, D'Amato."

Woike called out, "Hot damn!"

Cohen neutralized the controls, putting Sally's Wagon on a straight and level course. He punched in the AFC. D'Amato was out of the top turret, watching him as he squirmed about in the seat, unzipped his heated suit. He said, "I guess I'll be seeing you."

"Don't be an asshole. Come with us." D'Amato squatted between the seats. "Maguire's not going to make it and even if he does, he'd only have half a face. You'd be doing him a favor."

Cohen, for just a moment, was tempted. He said, "No, I can't, Frank. I came this far, I got to go the distance." He retrieved control from the autopilot, continued circling.

"No one would say anything."

"Yeah I know, but that's not the point. I guess I shouldn't have committed myself."

Junior came on the interphone. "Hey, Abe, Woike just went out the belly hatch."

"His chute open?"

"Yes."

"Okay, you're next, Junior."

"Roger dodger, you old codger."

D'Amato said, "You're crazy, Cohen. What in the hell makes you think you're so important? You're a fucking sergeant just like the rest of us. You're not a pilot. You've never even flown an airplane and it's not your fucking job to fly this one! There's nothing in the Articles of War about tech sergeant engineers flying airplanes. It's not your fault if Maguire dies. Tough shit, everybody dies. There's a war on."

Cohen said, "I think Junior understands."

"Junior's a religious fanatic, is that what you are?"

Cohen twisted in his seat to look at him. "You'd better get your ass in gear, Frank. This is the second time around and it's costing me fuel and altitude. Tell them that I'm going to hold course due south and that they should call the RAF or someone for an escort. It would help if they switched on a radio beacon. The radio direction finder is working. And tell them to search for Crenshaw. The dumb bastard may still be floating."

"You're out of your skull, Cohen." D'Amato stood. "You're going to kill yourself."

"Maybe. But first I'm going to get this baby home."

"Maguire's been riding your ass since we formed the crew back in Florida. He hates Jews. I mean, it beats the shit out of me why you should give a good flying fuck whether he lives or dies. Why?"

"He's a good pilot, the best."

"That's not an answer."

"It's the only one I've got."

"You crazy bastard . . ."

"Drop Yardbird out the belly hatch. He's in good enough shape to pull a rip cord. With luck, maybe he'll drown. Then close the hatch, it probably creates drag. Go out the bomb bay, not the waist window, you're liable to hit the tail."

"You're giving fucking orders again."

"Get the hell out of here, but leave me your cigarettes, no sense getting them wet."

"Good luck, Abe." Staff Sergeant D'Amato stuffed his Camels into Cohen's breast pocket, then went through the hatch into the bomb bay.

Cohen turned to stare down at the sea. There was a tiny figure floating on the water, the orange dot of his Mae West fluorescing against the deep blue water of the Med. One of the destroyers had lowered a boat and was turning.

Cohen completed his final circle to get back on course. He could see two white canopies floating lazily downward. There was one man missing. He searched the sea. Who? To hell with it, he had his own problems.

CHAPTER 19

JULY 1943

I 'll try not to take up too much of your time, Colonel Greeves. I understand you're very busy at the moment." The man's credentials identified him as Harold F. Gordon, Special Agent, FBI. He removed an extra thick cork pith helmet that had probably been recently purchased in Cario. Without being asked, he helped himself to a chair at one end of the desk. Colonel Greeves took an immediate dislike to the man.

He was dressed in a well-tailored khaki uniform minus all insignia. His appearance, thought the colonel, was totally uncharacteristic of the G-men, usually exemplified by the likes of Edward G. Robinson, who wore dark, chalk-striped double-breasted suits and wide-brimmed gray fedoras while nestling Thompson forty-five-caliber submachine guns equipped with impractical but sporty-looking drum magazines.

The group commander had no idea of the reason for an FBI visit, but he did have a strong notion that it would prove necessary for him to dominate it. It was hot in the Quonset hut. He reached out, flicked off the fan. A little sweat would do Special Agent Gordon some good.

The visitor snapped open his briefcase, thumbed through a sheaf of papers, handed one across the desk. The colonel let it lie there, lit a cigarette, established eye contact. "Just tell me what this is all about, Mr.Gordon."

"I'm here to pick up one of your men." Gordon read aloud from a small notebook. "Technical Sergeant Abraham Cohen, U.S. Army Serial Number 13027217." He looked up to find the colonel's intense eyes awaiting his. He said. "The paper in front of you is a provost-marshal order to place the man in my custody."

"What do you intend to do with him?"

"Place him under arrest and escort him to Tunis to await first available air transportation stateside."

"And the charges?"

"Enlisting in the United States Army under an assumed name."

"That's it?"

"He enlisted while under a criminal indictment."

"Indictment for what?"

"I'm not free to tell you, Colonel."

"Was he out on bail at the time?"

"Sorry, sir. I can't comment on that either."

"You're asking me to give up the best flight engineer in this group, Mr. Gordon." The colonel came to his feet, circled the desk. The back of Gordon's bush jacket was soaked through with perspiration.

"Don't make it hard for me, Colonel. We're both under orders."

"My orders are to fight the war."

"If you'll just turn over Tech Sergeant Cohen, I'll be on my way."

"What's his real name?"

"I can't divulge that either."

"Okay, here's one you'll have to answer. How'd you get on this base?"

"In a C-47. It's parked out there waiting for me and my prisoner."

"This is a closed base, Mr. Gordon." Colonel Greeves buzzed his first sergeant.

"Yes, I understand," said Gordon. "I was told about Tidal Wave and that things might be a little sensitive."

The colonel slid open his desk drawer, removed a GI Colt forty-five-caliber pistol, pointed it toward the ceiling, casually checked the magazine, removed the safety, and cocked the piece. Out of the corner of his eye, he confirmed First Sergeant Seidell's presence in the open doorway.

With his elbow on the desk, the group commander lowered

the muzzle till it pointed directly at the visitor's head. "Please get to your feet, Mr. Gordon."

The FBI man, a startled look on his face, said, "What the hell's this all about?"

The colonel jerked the pistol upward. Agent Gorden stood, tight-lipped.

The colonel said, "Sergeant, search this civilian for weapons."

First Sergeant Seidell patted the man down, removed a snubnosed revolver from a shoulder holster. He stepped back, transferring the piece to his left hand.

Colonel Greeves said, "Mr. Gordon is to be placed under guard—locked and loaded, Sergeant—in the outer office until the officer of the day gets here. Use two of the clerks. If he attempts to leave the premises, or to use the telephone, or engage you in conversation, shoot him. Understood?"

"Yes, sir." The first sergeant grinned.

"And find Sergeant Abraham Cohen. He's in the Four-Fifteenth Squadron. Get him here, right away."

Colonel Greeves called the guardhouse. The officer of the day was Captain Krause, a navigator from the 413th Squadron. The group commander informed him that an armed civilian had landed at the base and had made his way into group headquarters. The prisoner was to be arrested and placed in isolation until further orders.

THE MISSION

Except for the desperately wounded Maguire, Cohen was alone. He brought the aircraft out of its shallow bank, leveled off, switched on the left outboard engine, unfeathered the prop, and let it windmill to a start. He spent a minute synching it up with the other two and then trimmed the ship as best he could. The increase in power was immediately evident. At 3,800 feet, the airspeed indicator was reading 200 mph. He kept his eye on it and pointed the nose up slightly. The indicator crept slowly downward. When it had dropped to 175, he leveled out. The altimeter read 4,250 feet. He had picked up over four hundred feet—probably enough. Prudence dictated he throttle back. He set up a cruising speed of 165 indicated, then patted his empty pocket for a lighter.

Someone tapped him on the shoulder. Startled, he turned to find Junior grinning at him.

"Boy, you can sure fly this thing."

"I make it up as I go along. What the fuck you doing here?"

"Changed my mind. Okay? I don't weigh much."

"You sure, Junior? I can make one more turn."

"I'm sure, old buddy. Chest chutes make me nervous. Anyway, I figured maybe you could use some help."

Once again, Cohen pretended to listen attentively as Junior Darling spoke about Doris, his young bride waiting on the farm back in Oklahoma. The tiny snapshot he usually showed Cohen was of a skinny, nondescript, teenage girl grinning into the camera. She was wearing an ankle-length print dress and holding what appeared to be schoolbooks. She seemed more like a kid sister than a wife.

Sally's Wagon droned on for another forty-five minutes. Number one engine was running hot again. Cohen decided to keep it going until the needle dropped below the red line on which it was sitting, then throttled it back slightly to eke out as much as he could.

Junior said, "I'll bet they give you a medal, the DFC or something."

"To hell with that noise. If I wreck this thing they'll probably bring me up on a statement of charges. What's a B-24 cost?"

"I don't know. Maybe fifty, a hundred, two hundred thousand dollars, maybe even more."

Cohen laughed. He said, "They hit me every payday, I should have the damned airplane paid off in thirty years."

"No, they wouldn't do that. You're a hero—above and beyond the call of duty—like Sergeant York and Colin Kelly and those other guys."

Cohen breathed deeply, sat erect to stare out the windshield at the single deep-blue expanse of sky and sea. He heard himself say, "You got to stop believing in Santa Claus. Everybody's out for numero uno, including me."

"I don't believe you." Junior looked as if he were about to salute. "If it was true, you wouldn't have volunteered to be on a combat crew. You're risking your life for your country."

"Yes, well, that was a mistake in judgment, old buddy. I got my own war to worry about."

The little ball gunner's voice was pitched higher than usual. "I still don't believe you, Abe."

"You're a pain in the ass, Junior. You should have gone out the belly hatch with Woike and Yardbird."

The altimeter was indicating a little under four thousand feet. He estimated enough fuel for about two hours' flying time. There were two hours of daylight left. Sally's Wagon was holding a course due south at an indicated airspeed of 155 mph. On the map, he figured his position as being roughly 100 to 150 miles north of the African coast. Cohen did some mental arithmetic. At her current speed and altitude, Sally's Wagon should be over land in less than an hour at a height of about three thousand feet.

THE LAST LIBERATOR / 249

With just a little luck, there would be enough fuel and enough remaining daylight to search out an airfield; if not, he'd do a crash landing on the beach. He remembered that the B-24 was one of the few aircraft requiring wheels down in a crash landing. Once again he switched on the radio direction finder. This time he found a steady tone that seemed right. The British navy had come through and gotten word to Benghazi. The radio beacon had obviously been set up for him. He twisted the loop knob, first left, then right, causing the shielded loop antenna to turn in its aerodynamic housing atop the airplane. When the signal in his headset was at its loudest, he took note of the radio compass indication, then turned the airplane in that direction. It was only a matter of a few degrees. The signal got weaker, then stronger again, as he aligned the loop along the axis of flight. Now it was just a matter of keeping the aircraft headed in the direction of the strongest signal strength until he found himself directly over the transmitter—home—or very close to it. He removed his headset and instead used the tuning meter as a course indicator.

Cohen checked his instruments again, then stared out at sea and sky searching for the dark, thin line that would indicate land on the horizon. The Med was sparkling in the late afternoon sunlight all the way to the horizon. A million little whitecaps were dancing in the wind. A shock of anxiety passed through his body. Head wind! It was a factor he had left out of the equation. Cohen knew that the prevailing winds over the Mediterranean blew northward. Therefore, the whitecaps indicated a head wind. But how much was it slowing him up? Indicated airspeed was one thing, ground speed another. He was at a loss, incapable of calculating wind strength or of using a driftmeter. He might very well run out of fuel before he reached the coast.

To add to his problems, number one was finally over the red line. If he ran it any longer he would probably have to contend with an engine fire. He had gotten all he was going to get out of it. With now-practiced motions, he shut it down, adjusted trim. He set both remaining engines on auto-rich at 2300 rpm and 34 inches of manifold pressure.

He looked to his right. Junior was sleeping in the radio operator's seat. He reached out and shook him.

"Roger dodger," said Junior. "Where are we?"

"Still over the Med, old buddy. Wake up, I want you to check Maguire's pulse."

Junior Darling worked his way out of his seat. A minute later he said, "Captain Maguire's still alive, Abe. Thank the Lord."

"Amen," said Cohen.

CHAPTER 20

JULY 1943

The sign on the door read:

COMMANDING OFFICER
Col. Edward Tecumseh Greeves

Sergeant Cohen stepped through, advanced three paces toward the desk, and saluted. Colonel Greeves acknowledged his presence with a nod but did not order him at-ease. Instead, he said, "You're in real trouble, Sergeant."

Cohen replied, "Sir?" He wondered if Spielman had talked. It was hard to believe. Maybe Lieutenant Blum, the sterling American patriot, had told all about their little adventure in Tel Aviv, arousing suspicions enough to set up some kind of surveillance.

"Sergeant, we've all got a rough mission to fly tomorrow. I've got plenty to do between now and then, so let's not waste time. In other words, I don't want a lot of denials that are going to lead nowhere. Understood?"

"Yes, sir." Cohen breathed deeply, tensed his muscles to prepare himself for the ordeal. There was no getting around the fact that they had him nailed, and his only game now was to somehow protect Uri and Natalie and their little band of Jewish merry men and of course, Spielman, if he was, indeed, innocent of ratting.

"One other thing," said the colonel. "The only reason you're here in this office and not on the way to the States to stand trial is because I think you're a credit to the uniform. It doesn't matter what the hell you did in civilian life—I mean within reason. The point is, you're one hell of an airman." Colonel Greeves paused to clip the end of a long, thick Havana cigar with a silver tool. "It's also clear to me now, why you refused the medal . . . at ease."

Cohen assumed the stance, legs apart, hands clasped behind his back, attempting to sort through a turmoil of confusion.

"What's your real name, Sergeant?"

The question came as a shock. Cohen's initial reaction was to bull it through. In clipped tones, he said, "Abraham Cohen, Technical Sergeant, U.S. Army Serial Number 13027217."

The colonel laughed. "You snaky bastard. You're really something, Cohen, or whatever the hell your name is. Jesus!" He lit his cigar, taking his time. "And you can dispense with the wiseguy prisoner-of-war crap. Let me put it this way. About an hour ago, an FBI agent walked into this group headquarters—into my office—and informed me that he had come here to place you under arrest and transport you back to the States, probably in chains, if he's smart."

"FBI?"

"Genuine. At the moment, he's in the guardhouse under arrest for unauthorized entry into a restricted military area. Until Tidal Wave hits the target tomorrow, nobody goes in or out of this air base—on foot, on wheels, or on wings—without specific orders from Headquarters, Ninth Air Force. Agent Gordon, in his ignorance, walked into a hornet's nest. Now, what's your real name?"

"Danny Esposito . . . thanks, Colonel."

"Okay. Now tell me about that indictment."

"It was for breaking the Sullivan Law."

"What's that?"

"Carrying an unlicensed firearm."

"And you jumped bail? Left the state?"

"No, sir. The indictment was dropped when I turned state's evidence."

"Against who?"

"Lucky Luciano."

"The gangster?"

"Yes, sir."

"And they dropped the charges?"

"Yes, sir."

"Then why'd you change your name? What in hell are you hiding from?"

"Luciano. He wants me dead—revenge—and it looks like he's found me."

"He didn't find you, Sergeant, the FBI found you."

"You checked that guy's credentials?"

"Yes, I called the judge advocate's office in Cairo. Mr. Gordon is the real thing, and as for you, you're down as a wanted criminal."

"Well, sir, I figure that explains the wanted poster in the post office. Anyway, my country's double-crossed me. I guess maybe the Mafia's running the U.S.A. now."

"What happened to Luciano?"

"He got thirty years."

"What was your connection to him?"

"I drove his limo. I was his chauffeur and sort of bodyguard."

"And you testified against him in order to stay out of jail?"

The question, thought Cohen, was a low blow, impossible to answer with a simple yes or no. He took a few seconds to formulate a rationalization, then changed his mind. With his eyes boring into those of Colonel Greeves, he said, "Yes."

"Did you ever kill anybody with that illegal gun?"

"No, Colonel, I never even fired it. The only people I ever killed were with the guns mounted in a B-24 gun turret, and I got a legal permit for those."

"Why the name Cohen?"

"Well, if you change your name in order to disappear, you might as well pick one that's unlikely. I figured they'd still be looking for an Italian."

The colonel stood, clasping the cigar between his teeth. His head came within six inches of the tin ceiling. "Okay, Sergeant. You've got two choices. I can have Gordon released this afternoon and you can surrender to him and fly back to the States for whatever fate awaits you, or I can continue to hold him in the guardhouse until after takeoff for Ploesti tomorrow morning—maybe even longer. But either way he's got you eventually."

"I'll fly the mission, Colonel."

"Why?"

"It's my crew, sir. I don't think they'd be too happy with a replacement flight engineer, I mean, not on this mission."

Puffing clouds of blue smoke like some internally fired oversized mechanical man, the colonel paced to one end of the room. "There's always the inspector general." He paused for a moment in concentration. "Okay. I can't think of anything else right now, but after the mission, I'll speak to General Brereton. Maybe we can do something—stir up some kind of trouble; maybe even all the way up to Hap Arnold."

"Thanks."

"I see now why you refused the medal. You felt the publicity might nail you."

"Yes. I'm sorry I gave you a hard time, sir."

Colonel Greeves seemed deep in thought. Finally, he looked up into Cohen's eyes, a grin lighting his face. "Maybe that FBI bastard could be shot trying to escape."

"Thanks, but they'd send another one."

"I know. But I'll do everything I can."

"Colonel, you flying the mission tomorrow?"

"Yes. I'll be leading the group and your element." They exchanged a long glance. Colonel Greeves said, "Dismissed."

Cohen replaced his cap, came to attention, saluted and executed an about-face.

"One more question . . ."

"Sir?"

"Given your choice, which name would you choose now?"

"Abraham Cohen."

"Okay, good luck, Sergeant Cohen."

"You too, sir."

THE MISSION

AUGUST 1, 1943

Sally's Wagon lost the sun before she gained the coast. Junior said, "It's like a Technicolor movie, Abe. I mean, isn't it?"

"What is?"

"The sunset."

"You're crazy." Cohen allowed himself to laugh. "Nuttier than a fruitcake." They were down to just over three thousand feet. He said, "We're in a lot of trouble, Junior."

"I know."

"I'll spell it out for you. I didn't realize it, but there's a strong headwind. I don't know how to figure it. I mean, I'm not a navigator. Point is, it's slowed us up and I really don't know how far we are from the coast. We've got two engines. I've been running them at about sixty-five percent power. More than that and they'd gobble up twice as much fuel. As it is, we might still run out before we get to the coast. In five minutes it's going to be darker than the inside of your hat—no moon tonight, Junior—so we won't be able to see the coast even if it's there. You want to hear more?"

"No."

"Shut up and listen." Cohen raised the canteen to his lips. It was empty. "The RDF is homed on a radio beacon I hope is Benghazi. Once we're over the town it's a cinch to find our field. A right turn will take us there and the runway lights will still be on for stragglers like us. The problem is that the town of Benghazi is blacked out. We won't know it in the dark. I mean, if we can't see it how in hell are we going to know we're on top of it? We can just keep on going and the radio compass won't know the difference. It reads off the back of the loop exactly the same as the front. You know you're on track but you don't know whether you're coming or going. We can end up bailing out in the middle of the desert. "Ready for more bad news?"

"No thanks, Abe."

"Good. I'll be glad to tell you. I've saved the worst till last, old buddy. As you can see, we're down to three thousand feet. Somehow, these two engines are keeping us in the air, but just barely. Maybe a real pilot could do better. But in fifteen or twenty minutes, we're probably going to be down to two thousand feet or so. It'll be time to bail out. I don't want to chance it any lower. I think maybe you should pray that we're not over water, but please, Junior, not too loud."

"Roger dodger. And what about Captain Maguire?"

"I got that figured. We'll rig a static line to his chute and dump him, just before we go out. In the meantime, we'll need the flare pistol and a couple of flares, and there's a few cans of peaches in the waist. And find something to use for Maguire's static line. The peaches will supply food and drink if we land in the desert, or—God forbid—the water. You'll carry the flare pistol. When you're down, shoot one off, so I can locate you. Then stay where you are, so I can walk or paddle to you. Our Mae Wests will keep us afloat."

Cohen turned on the instrument lights. Sally had lost another two hundred feet. He stared ahead into the gathering darkness for a sign of the coast.

As a last effort to decrease their rate of descent, Cohen, hoping that his action would supply more lift than drag, lowered flaps eight degrees. He guessed that at that conservative setting the Fowler flaps increased the chord of the wing without dropping down into drag territory. With luck, it might stretch things out for an extra fifteen minutes or so. By now, sky and water, under a thick overcast, had blended into total blackness.

Junior returned with the flare pistol, four cans of peaches, and about eight yards of electrical wire he had cut from the intercom system in the waist. He said, "How we going to open the peaches?"

"You got a penknife?"

"No."

"Then if you can't find a rock, bash the cans open with the flare pistol." Cohen then asked Junior to wrestle a chute onto Maguire. He put Sally onto AFC. At the radio desk, with Junior's back to him, he removed Deutsch's head from the bombsight bag. He looped his own dogtags around the copilot's left ear, then placed the head back in the bag. Cohen was now officially dead, providing someone found the wrecked airplane. He turned and lent Junior a hand with the chute.

He gave Maguire one last shot of morphine, just in case he regained consciousness. Then he and Junior manhandled the unconscious pilot out onto the bomb bay catwalk. They wedged him between the two rear bomb racks, then rigged one end of the wire to his rip cord and the other to a bomb-rack stringer. It would be a simple matter, when the time came, to roll Maguire out the open bomb door and then follow him.

Twenty minutes later, the altimeter had dropped to 2,000 feet. It was time to leave.

CHAPTER 21

AUGUST 1-2, 1943

L eutnant Hermann Stumacher was jolted awake by the sound of aircraft engines directly overhead. He poked his head out the tent to observe the glowing exhaust in order to determine the aircraft's course. If west, it would be returning to the 287th, if east, it belonged to the 98th. He would report the final number of returned aircraft on his morning transmission.

He watched for a while to determine its course and was surprised to note it was headed almost due south. As far as he knew, there were no airfields to the south for a thousand miles. He looked out over the sea for signs of others. A solid overcast blocked the light of the stars. There was nothing to break the continuity of total blackness. It was blackness that seemed not merely a phenomenon caused by the lack of light but rather a palpable mass unto itself.

They had been counting returning B-24s in the late afternoon and early evening. They sent the prelimenary report at seven P.M. The numbers were appalling. Almost half the aircraft that had taken off in the morning had not returned. And now, here was a twin-engined airplane coming in from the sea and headed south; unless, of course, it was a B-24 with two engines out, a more likely possibility.

He was about to move back to the makeshift tent when out of the corner of his eye he became aware of a vague presence suspended over the invisible sea. Sensed, rather than perceived, it seemed a visual aberration, more a discontinuity in the solid blackness then a tangible object. With some effort, over a period of seconds, he forced it to resolve into a gray smudge that promptly disappeared when he looked directly at it.

Lance Corporal Strink, now awake, beside him, whispered, "Parachute . . ."

For a minute or so, the two men searched the blackness. Finally, Stumacher, speaking in a husky whisper, said, "Get the pistol."

He sat up outside the tent, tuning his ears to the night sounds: the rhythmic choruses of the surf, the gentle rattling of palm fronds in the breeze, the liquid breathing of their sleeping camels. There was nothing else.

Strink returned with the Luger. Stumacher took it off safety, checked to make sure there was a cartridge in the chamber. He hoped he didn't have to use it. It would be best for all concerned if the parachutist drowned, or just walked off without seeing them. The shooting war was over for him.

A loud *pop* shattered the silence. From the beach, a ball of light arched into the sky, illuminating its own tail of white smoke. At its apogee, it burst into a brilliant red sun.

The darkness sprang into life, illuminated in bright red. A figure stood on the beach holding a flare pistol, still pointed skyward. A short figure, dripping water, he was dressed as an American airman. Twenty feet behind him, glowing in the ruby light, his parachute billowed in the tranquil surf.

He saw them. "Hey!" He waved, took a step forward. "Hey, you guys . . ."

Leutnant Stumacher took careful aim, squeezed the trigger. The figure collapsed on the wet sand, just as the flare winked out.

"You bastard!" Strink's voice was choked, then strident. "You killed him! He was unarmed . . . no danger to us! Why?"

"Calm yourself, Strink. He was a *great* danger to us. The Americans don't know we exist. That would have changed. Remember, we're spies, Strink, they catch us they shoot us—hang us. Or are you suggesting we should have taken the fellow prisoner? Built a stockade to keep him in? Geneva Convention and all that." Stumacher paused. "Get the lantern."

They made their way down to the beach by the light of the spirit lamp. The American was alive, stretched out on his back, clutching his stomach. In slow cadence, he was groaning and repeating the words "Oh, Jesus." As they got closer, he grew silent, looking up at them. His entire mid-section was bathed in blood—a belly wound. Leutnant Stumacher dropped the Luger onto the sand and turned away.

Strink picked it up, stood over the wounded airman. He was a kid. Strink pointed the Luger down at his head. Their eyes met. The American said, "The Lord is my shepherd, I shall not want. He maketh me to . . ."

Strink, though he didn't speak English, understood. He waited for the prayer to end, then shot the American between the eyes.

Leutnant Stumacher awoke shortly after dawn to find Lance Corporal Strink gone. One of their two camels was also missing. The radio transceiver was on the ground, gutted, its tubes shattered.

Stumacher grabbed their small entrenching tool and made his way to the beach. The dead American had two cans of peaches stuffed into his coverall pockets. There was also a small compass, a tattered pocket Bible, and a Waltham pocketwatch. Stumacher laid aside the peaches, left the rest with the victim.

He dragged the body fifty feet inland, where he dug a shallow grave. It was good exercise; he could forgo his morning swim. He wrapped the body in the parachute.

Finally, he squatted on the sand, opened one of the cans with his jackknife, then looked up to see a figure standing less than ten feet from him: an American sergeant who seemed to have materialized out of nowhere.

The previous night, Cohen had heard shots as he made his way toward Junior's flare. In the first light of dawn, hidden behind a palm, he watched as a man in Arab garb smashed the tubes in what looked to be a radio transceiver and then rode off on a camel. At the time, there was nothing Cohen could do to stop him.

Shortly afterward, a second Arab, wearing a striped kaftan, emerged, yawning and stretching, from a small makeshift tent. He watched as the man made his way down to the beach to drag the body of Junior Darling about fifty feet inland, where he proceeded to dig a shallow grave.

With the gravedigger's back to him, Cohen came from behind the tree to make his way to the tent. The Luger was inside in plain sight.

The man in the kaftan was squatting on the sand eating peaches from Junior's can, singing to himself in German—"Lili Marlene." Cohen came around in front of him, motioned him to his feet. Smiling stiffly, the man in the kaftan said something in German. Cohen stared, unblinking, into his eyes until the smile disappeared. He glanced down to see Junior's body in the shallow grave.

The man said, "C'est la guerre." Then, in Teutonically flavored English, he said, "Or as you would put it, 'It's the war.' " He shrugged, apologetically.

Cohen gestured for him to remove his kaftan. When the man was naked, Cohen emptied the Luger into his chest.

He threw the pistol into the sea, removed his clothes, then walked into the surf, where he allowed the gentle swells to wash over him. There was a sound of distant aircraft engines. Four of them were starting up, gasping and farting as they eased themselves into a smooth chorus.

Cohen removed Junior's dog tags and filled in the grave. He constructed a cross from a few palm branches and some rope from the tent. At the head of the grave, using the German entrenching tool, he pounded the cross into the sand then hung Junior's dog tags from it. He stood for a moment, trying in vain to think of a prayer. Quietly, he said, "So long, old buddy . . ."

Cohen dressed himself in the dead German's kaftan and headdress. The engines grew louder now, all four thundering in concert. There was no mistaking the characteristic roar of a quartet of big Pratt & Whitney engines: a B-24 was taking off.

He dragged the body of the German into the shade at the base of one of the palms. A moment later, a desert-pink Liberator, at about five hundred feet, swung in over the sea. She carried the black triangle of the 413th Squadron, 287th Bomb Group, on her tailfin.

The airplane passed almost directly overhead. He watched as she circled for another pass, this time a little higher and further inland.

It was clear to Cohen that the 287th had heard Sally pass low overhead the previous night and might have even spotted Junior's flare. Now, in the first light of morning, they were searching for the wreck.

He had figured it close. In the blackness, they had exited the doomed airplane at almost the perfect moment, bailing out less than five miles from the air base. Maguire, too, must be be somewhere within a square mile, more than likely in the sea, as they had dropped him out about fifteen seconds before their own departure. Cohen wondered how far Sally's Wagon had flown on her own.

He found a sack of rations: bully beef, powdered eggs, American C-rations, German canned sausages. There was a five-gallon jerry can of water, a good sheath knife, a roll of Egyptian-made toilet paper, and a six-inch thick stack of British one-pound notes. He untethered the remaining camel. In the first hundred yards, he was thrown twice. It took a little getting used to.

The Coast Road was about a mile to the southeast. He thought about Junior Darling and wondered if by some miracle Maguire could have possibly survived. He reeled the names off, visualizing each of them in turn: Beel, Deutsch, Taylor. He had done his best. And there were others: Orange, Haney, Musielski. He wondered how long it would be before the faces became blurred, indistinct, gone completely.

Then he stopped thinking about any of it. The 287th was just to the west. He turned east, staying on the shoulder. Home was a thousand miles down the road. Next year in Jerusalem . . .

EPILOGUE

1989

I t was the fiftieth anniversary of the first test flight of the Liberator bomber. There was a small grandstand from which a small crowd watched the only remaining airworthy B-24D buzz the field, escorted by two shiny Confederate Air Force P-51s.

She landed to the stirring strains of the Air Force anthem: "The Wild Blue Yonder." A little heavy bomber from an old war. She was pristine, newly restored, her dents ironed out, her paint freshly applied, her fuselage unmarred by mud splatters, oil stains, or the black effluvium of engine exhaust. The airplane when new had cost fifty thousand dollars; the restoration had cost two million.

The naked lady sat, as she always had, in her champagne glass, fizzed up with newly painted bubbles; a major example of twentieth-century American art. Colonel Avram Conan (Ret.) patted her affectionately on one of her plump nether cheeks. It was by way of a proprietary pat.

"It's only a painted replica, Abe. You've experienced the good-goods—the real thing." The voice was at his right ear; musical, slightly husky, sexy. He could feel her breath on the back of his neck. He turned to find an old woman standing there. She was clothed in a basic black dress with little straps, the kind one doesn't see very often these days. She clutched a beaded purse and was holding a glass of pink vodka-laden punch.

She was, he thought momentarily, an apparition, a trick of the light: an old woman projected onto the body of one a third her age. She smiled at him, displaying perfect teeth, her eyes gleaming through the spiked cage of false eyelashes. "Hi ya, Abe."

He said, "Sally . . ."

"It's been a very long time."

Her eyebrows were penciled a full half-inch above where they were supposed to be. There was no sign of the originals. Her makeup was a trifle excessive, but applied with a degree of expertise that had easily obscured a decade of her years. He wondered just how much actual value was represented by a mere decade's savings at her age. No matter, it was a restoration job, like the airplane, and also like the airplane, there was still a lot going on under the fresh paint.

"What are you doing here?" she said. "You're supposed to be dead."

"This isn't me."

She read aloud from his name tag. "Avram Conan . . . Colonel . . . retired . . . IAF . . ." She looked up at him. "You've come up in the world. What's IAF?"

"The Israeli Air Force. I read about this in the New York papers and thought I'd come to catch one last look at Sally. Never dreamed I'd see you in the flesh."

"Oh, Abe . . ."

"What are you doing here?"

"Well, you know. I'm the loving widow of a war hero, the original pilot of this thing. That makes me an honored guest. They were nice enough to fly me down from LA for the festivities."

"It's been a long time."

"Yes. And, 'after-the-war' seems to be going on forever." She turned toward the airplane. "What do you think of her?"

"She's much smaller than I remember, and they mixed the paint a little too pink."

"She's ancient."

He said, "We're all ancient."

"Yes. When I say 'the war,' people think I'm speaking about something else."

They were both silent for a moment as a small group gathered to take pictures of the nose art.

She said, "Were you married?"

"Natalie," he said. "She died two years ago."

"I'm sorry."

"It was the other side of the rainbow." He stared at the girl in the champagne glass. "And you?"

"My life consisted of a few husbands, a few gold records, and a lot of songs that no one sings anymore."

He said, "Little Miss Bonnie Astor."

She said, "Little Miss Round Heels."

He thought, "Melancholy baby." Aloud, he said, "It's still your wagon."

AUTHOR'S NOTE

Tidal Wave, the low-level bombing mission on the Ploesti oil fields on August 1, 1943, ranks, in terms of courage and daring, with any battle in the history of warfare. Carried out by 1,627 American airmen and one British volunteer flying in 164 B-24D Liberator bombers of the United States Army Air Force, it was the most heavily decorated single action in U.S. military history. The awards included five Congressional Medals of Honor, 56 Distinguished Service Crosses, 41 Silver Stars, one Silver Star Oak Leaf Cluster, 1,368 Distinguished Flying Crosses, 156 DFC Oak Leaf Clusters, one Soldier's Medal, one Distinguished Service Medal, 4 Legion of Merit decorations, 5 Presidential Unit Citations. The mission itself rated a battle star.

Tidal Wave destroyed 40 percent of the refining capacity of the Ploesti oil fields. It was not enough. Through a massive use of slave labor and the utilization of reserve facilities, within four months Ploesti was once again producing its share. (Its production capacity was eventually reduced to zero by an extensive series of massive, more conventional high-altitude attacks.)

The cost was high in both men and aircraft. Of the 1,627 men who flew to Ploesti that August morning, one third were casualties: 310 dead, 128 wounded, over 100 taken prisoner. Forty-one B-24s were lost over the target, 8 were interned in Turkey, 14 were lost to other causes; 178 Liberators took off for the target, 164 got there. Of those that made it back to Benghazi, only 30 remained airworthy.

Though *Sally's Wagon* is a work of fiction, I have endeavored, to the best of my ability, to retain historical accuracy about the mission and the functioning of the U.S. Army Air Force.

General Ent, Colonel "Killer" Kane, Colonel K. K Compton, Captain Pitcairn, and a few other pivotal figures actually existed. Though little is known about them, there were actually two German spies operating in the Benghazi area, much as depicted in my story. All other characters and events are products of imagination.

In August 1943, the B-24D Liberator was the only aircraft in the Allied arsenal capable of carrying bombs to Ploesti, Rumania. The round trip from Benghazi, Libya, was 2,700 miles, half of which was over enemy territory. At the time, it was the longest nonstop mass flight in history. The target was the most heavily defended in Europe.

Five heavy bomb groups participated: the 376th (Liberandos), the 98th (Pyramiders), the 44th (Eight Balls), the 389th (Sky Scorpions), and the 93rd (Traveling Circus). To these I have added a fictional group, the 287th. In order to do this and at the same time remain historically accurate about the numbers participating, I was forced to shortchange the 44th. My sincere apologies to any of its veterans who might read this. The 44th Bombardment Group (H), from its inception at MacDill Field in 1941, was a credit to the U.S. Army Air Corps and later to the Army Air Force. It proved itself in hundreds of missions out of England and the Middle East, most of them without the aid and comfort of "little friends," (fighter escort). It fought the good fight and took far more than its share of casualties.

The B-24 Liberator bomber, designed and initially built by the Consolidated Aircraft Corporation, went from drawing board to prototype in one year. Unlike its more glamorous sister, the B-17 Flying Fortress, the B-24 flew in every theater of war. It was utilized, with great success, by both the U.S. Army and Navy air forces and sported the colors of almost every Allied nation.

The Liberator was produced in greater numbers than any aircraft in history. Over eighteen thousand were manufactured between 1940 and 1945. Of those, only nine remain, just a few flyable. Of the particular mark, the model B-24D, that flew to Ploesti on August 1, 1943, there is but one: a desert-pink Liberator from the 376th Bombardment Group. Her name is Strawberry Bitch. She sits forlornly grounded on the tarmac at the Air Force Museum at Wright Patterson Field, Ohio. They paint her every few years.

Jerry Yulsman
New York City
August 1990